MIND
AND·THE
BODY
POLITIC

MIND

AND·THE

BODY

POLITIC

ELISABETH YOUNG·BRUEHL

Routledge

New York   London

Published in 1989 by

Routledge
An imprint of Routledge, Chapman and Hall, Inc.
29 West 35 Street
New York, NY 10001

Published in Great Britain by

Routledge
11 New Fetter Lane
London EC4P 4EE

Library of Congress Cataloging in Publication Data

Young-Bruehl, Elisabeth.
   Mind and the body politic / Elisabeth Young-Bruehl.
      p.   cm.
   Includes index.
      Contents: Hannah Arendt's story-telling — From the pariah's point of view—Reading Hannah Arendt's The life of the mind—King Solomon was very wise—so what's his story? — Cosmopolitan history — What are we doing when we think? — What Thucydides saw — Innovation and political imagination — The writing of biography — Psychoanalysis and biography — The education of women as philosophers—Anna Freud for feminists.
      ISBN 0-415-90117-0.   ISBN 0-415-90118-9 (pbk.)
      I. Title.
   AC8.Y64 1989   88-26466
   081—dc19

British Library Cataloguing in Publication Data

Young—Breuhl, Elisabeth
   Mind and the body politic
   1. Judgment—Philosophical perspectives
   I. Title
   121'.68

   ISBN 0-415-90117-0
   ISBN 0-415-90118-9   Pbk

For Jerome Kohn
anima in amicus una

Contents

Preface

The twelve lectures and essays collected here stretch over a decade and, in my writing life, span two biographies: the earlier ones were produced while I was starting on *Hannah Arendt: For Love of the World* (1982), and the later ones were written while I was finishing *Anna Freud: A Biography* (1988). Somewhere in about the chronological middle of the collection, I left the domain of political philosophy, where Hannah Arendt had been my teacher, my mentor, my ideal, and set out toward a theory and a practice for which she had no patience whatsoever: psychoanalysis. For several transitional years I was impressed by how different my *ancien régime* and my new intellectual world were, but now I am only amused by how superficial were the distinctions I drew between them.

Themes recur in these pieces, for I approached the same concepts and phenomena again and again, from different angles, for different purposes. The early essays grew out of an effort to imagine what the last third of Hannah Arendt's *The Life of the Mind*—called "Judging"—might have been like had she lived to complete it. My interest in judgment as a mental activity and as a topic of philosophical reflection converged with my interest in showing people judging in various historical and political contexts—the biographical impulse. The later essays depend on the idea that individuals—including individuals as writers of biographies and subjects of biographies—can be examples, presenting the nature of judgment rather than reflecting on it theoretically.

But the later essays also begin explicitly to connect this evolving concern with judgment to psychoanalytic theory. Since those connections are not highlighted in the essays and lectures, I have added a retrospective postscript that makes them clearer.

1

Hannah Arendt's Storytelling

Hannah Arendt loved to tell stories. She told her cherished stories again and again, with a charming disregard for mere facts (*se non è vero, è bene trovato*) and unfailing regard for the life of the story. She was also a collector, a connoisseur of quotations and what Vico called "golden sayings." Her stories and her sayings were the threads with which she wove her conversations and her works. She knew that she lived in "dark times," times in which a long tradition had unraveled and scattered in a vast mental diaspora to the ends of human memory. But she viewed this rupture as a sign that the threads, the thought fragments, were to be gathered, freely and in such a way as to protect freedom and be made into something new, dynamic, and illuminating. She was heiress to an aphoristic technique: the *capita mortua* of the broken tradition were assembled with this technique, reincarnated, full-bodied and vital. "Insofar as the past has been transmitted as tradition, it possesses authority; insofar as authority presents itself historically, it becomes tradition." But when the past is not transmitted as tradition, it can be freely appropriated; and when such free appropriation presents itself historically, it becomes the occasion for dialogue. Hannah Arendt used the image of Penelope's weaving to describe thinking; what is thought is rethought, ceaselessly, spurred by internal and external dialogue. And she knew very well the difference between this process and writing. For writing she had tools of *assemblage*—large silver scissors and quantities of Scotch tape.

Many of Hannah Arendt's stories are what has been called, since Callimachus wrote his *Aetia*, etiological tales. When she told, for example, how Walter Benjamin (another collector of quotations) was tripped up by his *bucklicht Männlein* (his little hunchback) whenever he came into the vicinity of success, she was in the Ovidian mode of how the mulberry's berries got to be red. She told tales about how people appear and move about in the world, easily or uneasily, about their words and their deeds. She did not tell the Story of Philosophy; she told the stories of the philosophers. She knew that in Greece of the Golden Age "mankind first discovered the human condition on earth, so that from then on the mere chronological sequence of events would become a story and the stories worked into a history, a significant object of reflection and understanding."[1] She reworked the stories, without reliance on the chronological sequence of events, into a collection of significant objects of reflection and understanding—a collage, a mobile. She told how Thales fell into a well while star-gazing, to the amusement of a Thracian peasant girl, and this story became the story of the dangers of unworldliness. And, rather than condemning the Thracian girl, as Hegel did, Hannah Arendt admired her common sense. But she also told how Thales the astronomer predicted a good year for olives and bought up all the olive presses to rent out at a profit, and this story became the story of the possibility of relating star-gazing and shrewdness, of the far reaches of common sense. Telling these stories, she brought the philosophers out of their chronological residences and into what Karl Jaspers called "the common room" of present conversation and communication. And even while she did this, she kept her fine sense of the mysteries of empathy; she once claimed, very insistently, that only G. K. Chesterton had ever really understood St. Thomas Aquinas—as one fat man to another.

She told stories of the philosophers, but she never reduced their thoughts or their works to matters of individual psychology. When she wrote a *laudatio* for Karl Jaspers, she looked to Cicero for guidance: "in eulogies . . . the sole consideration is the greatness and dignity of the [persons] concerned."[2] She praised Jaspers not as an individual but as a person who appeared in public with and through his works—manifesting thus his *humanitas*. Her public praise of Jaspers, who was both her teacher and her friend, illuminated his relation to public life. This praise is also appropriate for Hannah Arendt herself:

> Jaspers' affirmation of the public realm is unique because it comes from a philosopher and because it springs from the fundamental conviction underlying his whole activity as a philosopher: that both philosophy and politics concern everyone. This is what they have in common; this is the reason they belong in the public realm where the human person and his ability to prove himself are what count.[3]

The conviction that philosophy and politics concern all people was one that Jaspers and Hannah Arendt shared; it is the key to understanding her activity as a philosopher as well as his. It is also the key to understanding how she drew a distinction between what concerns everyone and what is private, individual.

Always critical of romantic subjectivism and its attendant confusion of introspection and thinking, she states her reasons clearly in her early work, *Rahel Varnhagen:*

> introspection accomplishes two feats: it annihilates the actual existing situation by dissolving it in mood, and at the same time it lends everything subjective an aura of objectivity, publicity, extreme interest. In mood the boundary between what is intimate and what is public becomes blurred; intimacies are made public, and public matters can be experienced and expressed only in the realm of the intimate—ultimately, in gossip.[4]

When Hannah Arendt told stories, she did not gossip in this sense; she told of people in the world, not of the worlds in people. Thus she used the objective and objectified categories of times when the public and the private were distinct; she spoke of Fama and Fortuna; she spoke of *déformation professionelle* where others would not have feared to rush in with psychological analyses. When she spoke of the "banality of evil" rather than of Adolf Eichmann's perversity or sadism, she spoke as one who cared more for clarity and what concerns everyone than for vengeance.

The quality of her mercy was its relation to the person in the world. "To judge and to forgive are but two sides of the same coin . . . while justice demands that all be equal, mercy insists on inequality, implying that every man is, or should be, more than whatever he did or achieved."[5] Those who commit crimes must be brought before the law; but there are other courts as well, and other judges. Brecht's case was tried in the poet's court: "a poet's real sins are avenged by the gods of poetry," whereas "mere intellectuals or literati are not punished for their sins by loss of talent."[6] Heidegger's *Gelassenheit,* his worldless releasement into thinking's serenity, blinded him in the very tyranny that is deadly to thought, that can destroy the thinking space.

The mercy that acknowledges inequality, that allows that a person can be, should be, more than his or her works and deeds, is the public face of a humaneness that, if turned only inward, is sentimentality. For this introversion Hannah Arendt had no sympathy and very little mercy. She admired the virtue of not feeling sorry for yourself as much as any other virtue. She realized

> how deadly ridiculous it would be to measure the flood of events by the yardstick of individual aspirations—to meet, for instance, the international catastrophe of unemployment with a desire to make a career and with reflections on one's own success or failure, or to confront the catastrophe of the war with the ideal of a well-rounded personality, or

to go into exile, as so many . . . did, with complaints about lost fame or a broken-up life.[7]

She was a harsh critic of those who wrote only of "psychological deformation, social torture, personal frustration and general disillusion," who were not even worthy of the title "nihilists." These writers "did not cut deep enough—they were too much concerned with themselves—to see the real issues; they remembered everything and forgot what mattered."[8]

The breakdown of tradition that Hannah Arendt viewed in political terms as the decline and fall of the nation-state and in social terms as the rise of mass society she experienced in spiritual terms as the spread of nihilism. Fully aware of the political and social dangers of nihilism, she was also aware that nihilism can have as its correlate—though it is very rare—free thought, the "beaten pathways of thought" having been swept away, dynamited.

Neither of her great teachers, Heidegger nor Jaspers, had a Philosophy, a system, a beaten path. For both thinking was a motion. Heidegger left traces of his movement—what he called *Wegmarken*, pathmarks— and Jaspers left systematizations, thought-schemata, always insisting that these were not systems or formulae. Hannah Arendt described Heidegger's seminars in words that well describe her own:

> What was experienced was that thinking as pure activity—and this means impelled neither by the thirst for knowledge nor by the drive for cognition—can become a passion which not so much rules and oppresses all other capacities and gifts as it orders them and prevails through them. We are so accustomed to the old opposition of reason versus passion, spirit versus life, that the idea of a *passionate* thinking, in which thinking and aliveness become one, takes us somewhat aback.[9]

Thinking can be a silent dialogue between self and self; it can be—as it was for Jaspers—a present dialogue, communication; it can also be an "anticipated dialogue with others"—as she described Lessing's thought, adding that "this is the reason why it is essentially polemical."[10] These forms of dialogic thinking need "no pillars and props, no standards and traditions to move freely without crutches over unfamiliar terrain."[11] But Hannah Arendt was well aware that such dynamic thinking is not easy to practice "with the world":

> For long ago it became apparent that the pillars of the truths have also been the pillars of the political order, and that the world (in contrast to the people who inhabit it and move freely about in it) needs such pillars in order to guarantee continuity and permanence, without which it

cannot offer mortal men the relatively secure, relatively imperishable home they need.[12]

It was Hannah Arendt's deep sense of responsibility as a thinker for the world's needs and for thinking "with the world" that made it possible for her to cut so deeply, to remember everything, and not to forget what matters.

The virtue of not feeling sorry for yourself and the capacity not to forget what matters manifested themselves in Hannah Arendt's life and thought in two interconnected qualities: reticence and self-confidence. Her reticence was similar to that which she claimed was a necessity for poets; a poet, she said, is "someone who must say the unsayable, who must not remain silent on occasions when all are silent, and who must therefore be careful not to talk too much about things all talk about."[13] And for her this reticence particularly concerned "the realm of the intimate." Her self-confidence was very similar to that which she recognized in Auden: it was a self-confidence "which does not need admiration and the good opinion of others and can withstand self-criticism and self-examination without falling into the trap of self-doubt. This has nothing to do with arrogance, but is easily mistaken for it."[14] Such self-confidence depends on a refusal to indulge comparisons of oneself with others.

Perhaps she recognized these qualities of her own in poets because they are qualities related to respect for language. Auden and Brecht were able to leave their hearers and readers "magically convinced that everyday speech is latently poetic"; she was able to leave her hearers and readers magically convinced that everyday speech is latently philosophic. Her conviction that philosophy and politics concern everyone was tied to her understanding that both have their lives in the language everyone speaks. When we say "philosophy" and "politics," we are speaking Greek. In language "the past is contained inextricably, thwarting all attempts to get rid of it once and for all."[15] It was Hannah Arendt's peculiar gift to be able to open up our words and find in them the surviving threads of our tradition.

Her sensitivity to language was one facet of a capacity—it is perhaps not inappropriate, even though she would have smiled a wordly smile at the word, to call it an innocence—to appreciate the sheer appearance of things, "the wonder of appearance." During her last summer, in Switzerland, she told all her visitors the story of the neighbor's cat—how the cat had mourned the loss of her kittens for three days, crying and wandering about the yard, and then had resumed her routine. When Hannah Arendt told the story to me, as dinner was being prepared, she ended it by quoting the *Iliad* in Greek with a strange, profound simplicity that did justice at once to her own life, to Priam's, and to the cat's:

νῦν δὲ μνησώμεθα δόρπου.
καὶ γάρ τ' ἠύκομος Νιόβη ἐμνήσατο σίτου,
τῇ περ δώδεκα παῖδες ἐνὶ μεγάροισιν ὄλοντο,
ἓξ μὲν θυγατέρες, ἓξ δ' υἱέες ἡβώοντες.

Now let us think of supper.
For even fair-haired Niobe thought of eating;
She whose twelve children died in her halls,
Her six daughters and her six vibrant sons.

2

From the Pariah's Point of View

On attache aussi bein toute la philosophie morale a une vie
populaire et privée qu'a une vie de plus riche étoffe: chaque
homme porte la forme entière de l'humaine condition.
—Montaigne

Hannah Arendt finished her doctoral dissertation, *St. Augustine's Concept of Love*, in 1929. Soon afterwards she began her biography of a late-eighteenth-century Berlin salon hostess, *Rahel Varnhagen: The Life of a Jewess*. But she did not complete this manuscript until 1938, when she was living in Paris, and she did not publish it until 1958, when she was living in New York. *Rahel Varnhagen* was the book of her exile, and its theme, Rahel's development into "a self-conscious pariah," was the theme of Arendt's exile years.

Even after her work was well known and her years of displacement and poverty were well past, Hannah Arendt continued to think of herself as a pariah. In 1959 she was honored with a visiting professorship to Princeton University and prepared there the lectures that became her fourth American book, *On Revolution*. But the comfortable surroundings and the genteel society of Princeton made her uneasy and restless. She wrote to her old friend Kurt Blumenfeld, the president of the German Zionist Organization during her youth and one of her favorite Berlin café companions, that the gentility of Princeton was "nicht fur meiner Mutters Tochter. Ich schreibe über Revolution, nämlich über Revolution überhaupt. Das hier! Est is eigentlich von einer makabren Komik (not for my mother's daughter. I am writing about revolution, namely, about revolution in general. That here! It's really something of a macabre comedy)."[1]

Regardless of her circumstances, Hannah Arendt worked with a furious energy, a startling intensity—an intensity she converted, with startling abruptness, into listening energy at the behest of "history." She could have said after every crisis she lived through—and there were many—what she said in a letter to Mary McCarthy after the 1973 October War in the Middle East: "I have some trouble to get back to work chiefly, of course, because of this unexpected outbreak of 'history.' "[2] The pariah's task, in Arendt's understanding, was to be alert to the unexpected, to look at how things and events appear without preconceptions about history's course or pattern, to avoid sacrificing the outsider's perspective for the parvenu's comforts. The personal ideal of pariahdom Arendt framed in her youth was transformed in her later years into a political idea: she was able to generalize on the basis of her experience about the conditions of political action and the nature of good judgment.

Hannah Arendt's mother's daughter learned her first lessons in social and political independence while she was growing up in Konigsberg, East Prussia. Her grandparents on both sides of the family were comfortably middle-class synagogue-goers. The Cohns, her maternal grandparents, were Russians by birth, refugees from Russian anti-Semitism, who made a good living in Konigsberg importing tea. Both the Arendts were from established Konigsberg families. Max Arendt, Hannah Arendt's grandfather, was a wealthy and prominent man, a member of the Konigsberg Jewish community council and a leader of the city's branch of the Centralverein deutscher Staatsburger Jüdischen Glaubens. Both he and his wife, who made a career of philanthropy, were assimilated Jews, Jews who sought a reconciliation in their lives between the claims of *Judentum* and the claims of *Deutschtum*. Both of Hannah Arendt's parents had left behind their claims of *Judentum,* and both were, unlike their parents, politically concerned. They joined the reformist branch of the Social Democratic Party and ardently read Eduard Bernstein's *Sozialistischen Monatsheft.* But Martha Cohn Arendt was also a great admirer of the revolutionary branch of the SPD, the group that became the Spartacists, and particularly of the woman who led the Spartacists, Rosa Luxemburg.

Martha Arendt was not troubled by her own Jewishness, and she hoped that her daughter would learn the lesson she had to teach: the fact of having been born a Jew is undeniable, and any attempt to deny it is undignified. Recalling the atmosphere in her childhood home, Arendt remarked:

> You see, all Jewish children encountered anti-Semitism. And the souls of many children were poisoned by it. The difference with us was that my mother always insisted that we never humble ourselves. That one must defend oneself! When my teachers made anti-Semitic remarks— usually they were not directed at me, but at my classmates, particularly at the eastern Jewesses—I was instructed to stand up immediately, to leave the class and go home. . . . My mother would write one of her many letters, and, with that, my involvement in the affair ended completely. . . . There existed house rules by which my dignity was, so to speak, protected, absolutely protected.[3]

Maintaining her dignity was Arendt's task from childhood. And there were many trials in the face of which to undertake the task. The Arendt's household, comfortable but not genteel, equipped with a fine library but decidedly provincial, was broken apart by a great grief when Hannah Arendt was five years old. Her father, Paul Arendt, was institutionalized with tertiary syphilis, and he died two years later, in 1913. A year after that, with the unexpected outbreak of World War I, Martha Arendt and her daughter fled to Berlin, fearing that the Russians, then advancing into East Prussia, would capture Konigsberg. During the war years, Martha Arendt and her daughter lived in financially strained circumstances, and Hannah Arendt suffered through a series of illnesses and absences from school that left her nervous and ill at ease in public. In 1920, when Martha Arendt remarried, they found domestic peace and financial security in the household of Martin Beerwald and his two teenage daughters. But financial trouble came again in the mid-1920s. Martin Beerwald's small manufacturing firm went bankrupt and was absorbed into one of the huge manufacturing concerns that became typical of Germany in the 1920s, when 2 percent of all businesses employed over 55 percent of all workers. During these years Arendt continued her university studies, aided by an uncle.

The years during which Arendt studied at Marburg, Freiburg, and Heidelberg, 1924 to 1929, were relatively peaceful politically. Arendt herself was not concerned with politics, and neither were the philosophers with whom she studied—Martin Heidegger, Edmund Husserl, and Karl Jaspers. Her doctoral dissertation, written under Jaspers'supervision, was not a politically aware work, though it did contain seeds of concepts that later became central to her political philosophy. The concept of "natality" is a particularly important example, and it is also the one concept in the dissertation that does not bear the stamp of Heidegger's seminars, where Arendt had cultivated her interest in St. Augustine. In the dissertation she questioned how it was possible to live in the world, to obey the commandment "love thy neighbor as thyself," while adhering to an unworldly or extraworldly Christian vision. In her biography of Rahel Varnhagen an equally difficult conflict posed a question even more personally pressing: how is it possible to live in the world, to love one's neighbors, if one's neighbors—and even you yourself—will not accept who you are? Arendt struggled with this question—which can become a political question, though in Rahel Varnhagen's life it was a social one—until she herself was brought to politics by an unexpected outbreak of history: the rise to power of Adolf Hitler.

The Varnhagen book had resulted from the prelude to this unexpected outbreak, the rising anti-Semitism in Germany in the late 1920s and the rising influence of the National Socialists. Arendt had met Kurt

Blumenfeld while she was studying in Heidelberg and had been astonished by this extraordinary man, if not converted to his cause, Zionism. When she moved with her first husband, Gunther Stern, to Berlin in 1931 to work on the Varnhagen biography with support from the Notgemeinschaft für deutscher Wissenschaft, she renewed her acquaintance with Blumenfeld and came to know his Zionist friends and associates. With these friends and in those times, she began to be aware of what it meant politically to be a Jew in Germany. But before 1933 her awareness was still largely tied to Rahel Varnhagen's social struggle with her Jewishness. Arendt's biography concentrates on how Rahel dealt with what she called on her deathbed "the thing which all my life has seemed to me the greatest shame, which was the misfortune and misery of my life—having been born a Jewess," and the biography questions how Varnhagen came to conclude that "this I should on no account now wish to have missed."

The Zionists Hannah Arendt encountered in Berlin wanted to maintain their dignity as Jews, but they considered the task of reconciling *Judentum* and *Deutschtum* both impossible and undesirable, and they looked forward to the day when Jews could be Jews with pride in Palestine. Hannah Arendt did not become a Zionist; she was a pariah even among pariahs. But she was grateful for the opportunity they presented her with in 1933—the opportunity to act. She accepted a political task: she went to the Prussian State Library, where she had been working on her Varnhagen book, to make excerpts from official anti-Semitic tracts, which the Zionists wanted to use as "horror propaganda" at the Eighteenth Zionist Congress scheduled for August 1933. The Zionists wanted to inform German Jews and all others of the true nature and extent of German anti-Semitism. At the same time Arendt made another gesture of resistance: she harbored in her apartment German Communists who were preparing to flee from Germany. Both tasks came to an end when Arendt was arrested by the Gestapo and imprisoned. Because of the helpfulness of one of her German guards and the efforts of her friends, she was released after eight days. She left Germany without papers soon afterwards and went to Prague, to Geneva, and then to Paris in the company of her mother.

The German refugees in Paris were culturally, linguistically, socially, and politically isolated from the French. They lived where they could— in hotels, rented rooms, or borrowed apartments—moving from place to place, struggling to secure identity papers. Many were caught in the vicious circle so well known to modern refugees: jobs were available only to those with identity papers, and identity papers were available only to those with jobs. Unlike many, Arendt was able to find jobs with Jewish organizations. When she left Germany, she had resolved to do practical work for the Jews and also to have nothing further to do with the intellectual milieu in which she had lived. She had been deeply shocked when close German friends—including Martin Heidegger—had been infected by the Nazis' propaganda, and she had concluded that intellectuals were more inclined to collaboration with the Nazi regime than most: "The problem, the personal problem, was not what our enemies might be doing, but what our friends were doing."[4] This conclusion became subject to revision in France, where Arendt's circle included intellectuals like Walter Benjamin, intellectual friends of long standing like her Königsberg schoolmate Anne Weil, who had studied philosophy with Ernest Cassirer in Hamburg, and Anne's husband Eric Weil, who later became one of the most important philosophers in France. But these intellectuals were Jews. With a very few exceptions the non-Jewish refugees with whom she became friends were not intellectuals. Chief among these was a Communist from Berlin, Heinrich Blücher, a man of working-class origins with almost no formal education, who later became Hannah Arendt's second husband. Later, in the United States, she was less skeptical about intellectuals, but her pariah standards remained the same. She could say in 1948 that "social non-conformism as such has been and always will be the mark of intellectuals. . . . Intellectually, non-conformism is almost the *sine qua non* of achievement."[5]

In the spring of 1940, as Hitler's army approached Paris, the "enemy aliens" in Paris were ordered to report for transport to the French-run internment camps in the south of France. Hannah Arendt reported to a sports palladium, the Velodrome d'Hiver, where she stayed for a week before being transported by rail to Gurs, a camp that had been built for refugees from the Spanish civil war. After the occupation of Paris there was a brief period of administrative confusion in Gurs, and the women interned there were presented with a dreadful choice: to escape from the camp with, as Arendt put it, "nothing but a toothbrush, or to stay and hope for the best. After a few days of chaos, everything became regular again and escape was almost impossible."[6] Many of those who chose what they thought was the safer alternative were shipped after three horrible years to Auschwitz, where they were killed. Arendt secured liberation papers and left the camp. She was more fortunate than most of the escapees, for she had a place to go—a house rented by non-Jewish friends near Montauban—and she was able to rejoin her husband, Heinrich Blücher, who had also escaped from a camp. After six months of living here and there in southern France, the Blüchers were able to secure visas for themselves and for Arendt's mother to go to the United States. They left France as quickly as possible; those who waited longer fared less well. Repeatedly during her last year in Europe Hannah Arendt learned a lesson she was never to forget: when a choice between uncertain freedom and the precarious security of unfreedom comes, when a "unique chance" for action presents itself, hesitation can be fatal.

During the war years in New York the Blüchers' acquaintances consisted largely of German Jewish refugees—that is, of people with whom German could be spoken. Arendt knew that she had to acquire English, and she endured a period with an American family in Massachusetts to that end, but she was in no rush to assimilate. In a caustic, ironic article, written in a style that presages the controversial style of her later *Eichmann in Jerusalem,* she sounds the theme that had given her strength since her childhood and that became one of the mainstays of her political theory: to reject the identity you are born with, the identity your natality bestows on you, is to reject the possibility of a dignified existence.

> Man is a social animal and life is not easy for him when social ties are cut off. Moral standards are much easier kept in the texture of a society. Very few individuals have the strength to conserve their own integrity if their social, political and legal status is completely confused. Lacking the courage to fight for a change of our social and legal status, we have decided instead, so many of us, to try a change of identity. And this curious behavior makes matters much worse. The confusion in which we live is partly our own work. . . . It is true that most of us depend entirely on social standards; we lose confidence in ourselves if society does not approve us; we are—and always were—ready to pay any price in order to be accepted by society. But it is equally true that the very few among us who have tried to get along without all these tricks and jokes of adjustment and assimilation have paid a much higher price than they could afford: they jeopardized the few chances even outlaws have in a topsy-turvy world.
>
> All vaunted Jewish qualities—the "Jewish heart," humanity, humor, disinterested intelligence—are pariah qualities. All Jewish shortcomings—tactlessness, political stupidity, inferiority complexes and money-grubbing—are characteristics of upstarts [or parvenus]. . . . [The pariahs] have one priceless advantage: history is no longer a closed book to them, and politics is no longer the privilege of Gentiles.[7]

During the war years Arendt was first and foremost a Jew; and she understood her tasks as a Jew to be: to speak to the European emigrant Jews about Jewish identity, to urge the creation of a Jewish army to fight against Hitler's army, and to call for the founding of a binational Arab-Jewish state in Palestine. She called on the Jews to resist Hitler militarily and to forego the temptation of forming a state that would make another group of people, the Palestinian Arabs, into refugees. All that she hoped for failed to materialize. In her opinion the population of Jewish parvenus increased; she saw no Jewish army, only isolated resistance groups and Jewish brigades of Allied armies; and she watched what she considered a reversion to nineteenth-century nationalism as the State of Israel was founded as a Jewish state. The book of history was not opened to the Jews as she hoped it would be.

After the war Hannah Arendt made an enormous effort to open the book of modern European history to the Jews and to all who would learn from their suffering, and she called the result of this effort *The Origins of Totalitarianism*. This book, like all of Arendt's work in the 1940s, was an act of resistance. "I felt as though I dealt with a crystallized structure which I had to break up into its constituent elements in order to destroy it. This image bothered me a great deal, for I thought it an impossible task to write history not in order to save and conserve and render fit for remembrance, but, on the contrary, to destroy."[8] Arendt's aim, as she describes it, is reflected in the passionate, relentless tone of the book, which bothered many critics at the time of its 1951 publication and many more later critics of the "revisionist" sort who felt that the book had contributed to the cold war brand of American anti-totalitarianism. And it is true that Arendt's book, along with *Totalitarian Dictatorship and Autocracy* by Carl Friedrich and Zbigniew Brzezinski, "went far toward shaping lay and academic understandings of totalitarianism in the 1950s."[9] The book provided fuel for the cold warriors, but it also provided a call to resistance for those who feared not just the excessive anti-Communist attitude of McCarthy but his tactics. Thus, for example, the founders of the National Committee for an Effective Congress, the spearhead of the 1953 anti-McCarthy lobby, saw in Arendt's analysis of Stalin's totalitarian regime an analysis of McCarthyism.

The feature of *The Origins of Totalitarianism* that particularly excited "revisionist" criticism in the 1960s—other than its tone—is its claim that the Nazi and the Soviet forms of totalitarian government were basically the same. Critics argued that Arendt had developed her "unitotalitarianism" thesis by analogically extending her analysis of the Nazi regime to the less well-known, less fully documented Soviet regime. More recent studies of Soviet history have revealed inadequacies in her treatment of Stalin's regime and particularly of that government's social and economic policies. But most of the revisionist critics have missed the specifically political dimension of Arendt's claim in the work: she is concerned with the similarity of the *form of government* in Nazi Germany and Bolshevik Russia; she does not claim that the forms had come into being in the same way, on the basis of the same ideologies or policies, in the two countries. One of Arendt's great contributions to political theory is her revival of the traditional discussions—from Plato to Montesquieu—of forms of government and her attempt to add to the traditional types a new, an unprecedented one—totalitarianism.

Shortly after the 1958 publication of *The Origins of Totalitarianism,* Arendt received a Guggenheim Foundation grant to support her next project: a study of the Marxist elements of totalitarianism. This book was to address the imbalance in *The Origins of Totalitarianism,* to fill out the analysis of Soviet totalitarianism, and also to take up the differences she perceived between the Nazi and the Soviet ideologies: the Nazis' racism was not, she felt, connected to the "Great Tradition" of European thought, but the Soviets' Marxism was—for Marx was still a part of this "Great Tradition." Arendt spent a year working on her Marxism study, but her research led her to reformulate her task. It became clear to her that throughout the "Great Tradition" of European thought there had been modes of conceiving the activities of what she called the *vita activa* that reflected a blindness to the political realm, to what is specifically political—action and speech. She found much more important and much more amenable to her creative spirit the possibility of writing a nondestructive history, of writing a book that would "render fit for remembrance" the capacities she had come to understand as the only ones on which people of the problematic modern age can place any hope—action and speech. Instead of the proposed study of the Marxist elements of totalitarianism, she wrote the essays contained in *Between Past and Future* and then *The Human Condition,* and she planned another book, "Introduction to Politics." This last was never written. Its program called for more than Hannah Arendt could produce—for the consideration of thinking, willing, and judging to which she turned her attention in the last years of her life and about which she began to write in an unfinished work called *The Life of the Mind.*

In the 1950s, despite the tumult of the McCarthy era, despite the continuation of the cold war and the ominous development of nuclear arsenals and space programs, and despite numerous unexpected outbreaks of history, Hannah Arendt's anguished need to destroy the "crystallized structure" of the past abated. And one unexpected outbreak of history gave her grounds to hope that her concern for peoples' political capacities would not prove a dreamer's concern. She added to the 1958 edition of *The Origins of Totalitarianism* an epilogue in which she discussed this unexpected outbreak, the Hungarian Revolution of 1956.

> There is in this chapter a certain hopefulness—surrounded, to be sure, with many qualifications—which is hard to reconcile with the assumption of [the last section of *The Origins of Totalitarianism*] that the *only* clear expression of the present age's problems up to date has been the horror of totalitarianism. . . . [The Hungarian Revolution] has brought forth once more a government which, it is true, was never really tried out, but which can hardly be called new because it has appeared with singular

regularity for more than a hundred years in all revolutions. I am speaking of the council-system, the Russian *soviets*, which were abolished in the initial stages of the October Revolution, and of the central European *Räte*, which first had to be liquidated in Germany and Austria before [those countries'] insecure party democracies could be established. . . . While not unaware of the role which the council system had played in all revolutions since 1848, I had no hope for its reemergence. . . . The Hungarian Revolution had taught me a lesson.[10]

What the Hungarian Revolution suggested to Hannah Arendt was that the problems of the age—the rise of mass societies, technological changes of unprecedented sorts, and the breakdown of the nation-state—could lead to two different sorts of forms of government: totalitarianism or the council system. She put all of her hope on the council system, which is to say that she put all of her hope on the human capacity to act, to begin something new, to open, as she put it, "a political space."

Readers of *The Human Condition*, Hannah Arendt's study of labor, work, and action, the modes of the *vita activa*, have been troubled by her notion of action. All hope rests with this capacity, and yet Arendt gives no specific modern examples of it and no specific program for action— indeed, she lifts action right out of the means-ends categories she finds appropriate only for work. Even more troubling, she removes action from the sphere of what she calls "the social" and also from the scope of moral judgments. To anyone whose primary concern is with socio-economic reordering or with religious or moral renewal, such removals may seem completely impractical and reactionary—"Burkean Toryism," as one reviewer put it—or dangerously relativistic. These two reactions, if taken seriously—as they should be—and taken in conjunction, will perhaps bring into relief the challenge of Arendt's thought.

To moralists passages in *The Human Condition* like the following are startling:

> Unlike human behavior—which the Greeks, like all civilized people, judged according to "moral standards," taking into account motives and intentions on the one hand and aims and consequences on the other— action can be judged only by the criterion of greatness because it is in its nature to break through the commonly accepted and reach into the extraordinary, where whatever is true in common and everyday life no longer applies because everything that exists is unique and *sui generis*.[11]

The procedure of moral judgment, subsumption of a particular case under a general rule, is inappropriate for action. Each action must be judged on its own, in its uniqueness, without reference to an external standard or measurement. As Arendt comments in a footnote to this passage, Aristotle said in the *Poetics* that dramatic action, which imitates actions in life, should be judged by its greatness, by its distinction from the commonplace, as beauty also is to be judged. Arendt thought that a deep tie exists between aesthetic judgment (or taste) and the judgment appropriate to action, and the third part of her unfinished work, *The Life of the Mind*, "Judging," was intended as an exploration of this deep tie.

We do not, unfortunately, have this exploration, but the sort of experiences that propelled Arendt to think in this direction, that led her to follow suggestions from Aristotle and from Kant's *Critique of Judgment*, are recorded in several essays. One of these, written after she attended the trial of Adolf Eichmann in Jerusalem, is called "Personal Responsibility under Dictatorship." In it she considers those Germans who were able to live in Hitler's Germany without collaborating or participating in public life, even though they could not rise in rebellion against the regime. The essay implicitly extends Arendt's early concept of pariahdom into a concept of good judgment.

> The non-participants, called irresponsible by the majority, were the only ones who were able to judge by themselves, and they were capable of doing so not because they [had] a better system of values or because the old standards of right and wrong were still firmly planted in their mind and conscience but, I would suggest, because their conscience did not function in [an] as it were automatic way—as though, we [have] a set of learned or innate rules which we then apply to the particular case as it arises.... Their criterion, I think, was a different one: they asked themselves to what extent they could still be able to live in peace with themselves after having committed certain deeds.... The presupposition for this kind of judging is not a highly developed intelligence or sophistication in moral matters, but merely the habit of living together explicitly with oneself, that is, of being engaged in that silent dialogue between me and myself since Socrates and Plato we usually call thinking.... The total moral collapse of respectable society during the Hitler regime may teach us that those who are reliable in such circumstances are not those who cherish values and hold fast to moral norms and standards.... Much more reliable will be the doubters and skeptics, not because skepticism is good or doubting wholesome, but because [these people] are used to [examining things and making up their own minds]. Best of all will be those who know that, whatever else happens, as long as we live we are condemned to live together with ourselves.[12]

Hannah Arendt's admiration for those who, rising above moral standards, can judge for themselves is everywhere apparent in *Eichmann in*

Jerusalem, which was published in the spring of 1963 and quickly became a *cause célèbre.* In this book she describes Adolf Eichmann as a banal man: his evil was banal, she claims, because it arose not from some unfathomable or psychopathological depths but from thoughtlessness, from the complete absence of the "habit of living together explicitly with oneself." To Hannah Arendt "banal" means "commonplace" (which, let it be noted, is not the same as "commonly occurring"—she did not think that Eichmann was Everyman), and "commonplace" is the opposite, for her, of greatness.

This banal man was a typical parvenu—in Arendt's terms the very opposite of a pariah. Eichmann initiated nothing new: he did what he was told to do by those whose approval he wanted, and he obeyed the law of the land in doing so. He behaved; he did not act. "He did not need to 'close his ears to the voice of conscience,' as the judgment had it, not because he had none, but because his conscience spoke with a 'respectable voice,' with the voice of respectable society around him."[13] By the prevailing "moral standards" of Hitler's Germany, he behaved well; by the moral and legal standards prevailing when and where he was tried he behaved abominably and deserved to be punished as a man who was responsible for his deeds.

Arendt's portrait of a nondemonic, thoughtless Eichmann outraged many, and her portrait of the leaders of the Jewish councils who collaborated with the Nazis after 1941 during the "Final Solution" outraged many more. She claimed that for those Jewish leaders and members of Jewish police forces who knew what was in store for the Jews they registered and rounded up:

> There was no possibility of resistance, yet there existed the possibility of *doing nothing.* And in order to do nothing one did not have to be a saint, one needed only to say: I am just a simple Jew, and I have no desire to play any other role. . . . These people still had a certain limited degree of freedom and of action. Just as the SS members, as we now know, had a limited choice of alternatives.[14]

Arendt never called for resistance when resistance was clearly impossible; she spoke of the possibility of nonparticipation and of not denying one's birth-given identity. And, addressing her contemporaries, she spoke against a tendency to treat such matters as though there "existed a law of human nature compelling everyone to lose his dignity in the face of disaster."[15]

Judgments that touch on matters so agonizing to remember—matters of life and death, of dignity and lack of dignity—are of the utmost

difficulty. Hannah Arendt's judgments on the matter of Jewish collaboration with the Nazis were not only difficult, many felt, but "heartless."
What makes her judgments seem "heartless" is the criterion—never made
explicit—by which they are made, namely, "greatness." She contrasts
what she took to be the heart's mode of relation to men—pity—with
solidarity, and she rejects pity in favor of solidarity:

> because it partakes of reason, and hence of generality, it is able to
> comprehend a multitude conceptually, not only the multitude of a class
> or a nation or a people, but eventually all mankind. . . . Compared with
> the sentiment of pity, it may appear cold and abstract, for it remains
> committed to 'ideas'—to greatness, or honor, or dignity—rather than to
> any 'love' of men. . . . Solidarity is a principle that can guide and inspire
> action.[16]

No respect would be paid to Arendt's hope for action or her attempt
to understand judgment if the questions they pose were not raised. One
can ask of oneself the extraordinary, but can one ask of another, in the
present tense or in reflection on the past, the extraordinary? One can
say, "Here I stand, I can do no other," but can one say, "Stand here,
you can do no other"? Can one person say, under any circumstances,
disastrous or not, what the extraordinary should be? Does this criterion,
"greatness," allow for any specification? Surely the deeds that allow one
thoughtful person to live explicitly together with himself or herself will
not always be the same as those that allow another to do the same.
Each person's reactions are, as she puts it, "ontologically rooted" in the
conditions of natality, but each person's birth-given identity is his or her
own. One may say, "I am just a simple Jew, and I have no desire to play
any other role," but each simple Jew is an individual.

On the very grounds on which Hannah Arendt challenged traditional
morality she is challengeable—that is, insofar as she judged, implicitly or
explicitly, as though greatness were a rule, a standard by which to measure particular cases. But, on the other hand, if her challenge is abstracted
from the realm of what individual Jewish leaders, facing dreadful dilem-
mas, did and did not do, it carries a message of political importance.

In the funeral oration that Thucydides attributed to Pericles, praising
those who had fallen in battle against the Spartans, the Athenian statesman charged his people:

> It is for you to try to be like them. Make up your minds that happiness
> depends on being free, and freedom depends on being courageous. . . .
> Any intelligent man would find a humiliation caused by his own slackness

more painful to bear than death, when death comes to him unexpectedly in battle, and in the confidence of his patriotism.

Judgments that do not appeal to a general rule can appeal only to deeds called "exemplary" by general agreement. What is presumed—and was presumed by Pericles—is a community, a solidarity of the like-minded. Confident in fellowship in the community, each will follow the community's exemplary figures to the best of his or her abilities. Calls to greatness made in a community context and particularly those made when the community is threatened as a community do not shock us—indeed, we call them "great." Arendt's criterion, greatness or dignity, was posed to a community—the community of mankind, a multitude greater than any class or nation or people. If there were general agreement among the members of this community about the criterion "greatness" (as she, perhaps naively, assumed), her hope for mankind rather than her lack of pity would have been recognized.

Hannah Arendt wrote *Eichmann in Jerusalem* when her hope for action and for the council system was at its apogee. She did not write as a belligerent, so to speak, trying, as she did in *The Origins of Totalitarianism,* to destroy the "crystallized structure" of totalitarianism. She strove for the impartiality she so much admired in Homer, Herodotus, and Thucydides. She strove to relate how the collapse of respectable society in Nazi Germany affected all who had tied their lives to it—persecutors and victims. She strove to tell what the best and the worst people are capable of when such a collapse has occurred, to face the facts without flinching or waxing sentimental. The ironic tone of her book is shocking, just as the ironic tone of Thucydides' book is after centuries still shocking. The books are not comparable in artistry, but Arendt did amass her information, weave her statistics, observations, opinions, stories, and witnesses' accounts together with a reckless fervor comparable to that which is palpable on every page of Thucydides' history. For many of those who lived through the events Arendt told her ironic speech was pure pain. But her book is a *ktema es aei,* a possession for all times; it tells the story of a "disturbance," as Thucydides said, "affecting all mankind"—though hers does so, as she constantly reiterated, because what she wrote about was a "crime *against humanity.*"

When generations other than hers, or perhaps even ours, have corrected the book's factual errors and gained the distance that comes not only as an effort of judgment but as a gift from time, the message of her book may be clearer. It is very difficult for us not to feel as Thucydides' weary successors felt about his history, namely, in the words of Dionysius of Halicarnassus, that "he wrote about a war which was neither glorious nor fortunate—one which, best of all, should never have happened, or [failing that] should have been ignored by posterity and consigned to silence and oblivion."[18]

Simone Weil said of Homer's *Iliad* that its true central character is Force—the Force that reduced Greeks and Trojans alike to less than their human stature. The true central character of *Eichmann in Jerusalem* is not Adolf Eichmann nor his victims but the Force of individual human thoughtlessness and lack of judgment, which totalitarian regimes, more quickly than any other sort, are able to mold and which is capable of "laying waste the earth."

Hannah Arendt's hope for action and for the council system was tied to an exemplary historical reality—the very city that Pericles addressed. In *The Human Condition* she argues that "One, if not the chief reason for the incredible development of gift and genius in Athens, as well as for the hardly less swift decline of the city-state, was precisely that from beginning to end its foremost aim was to make the extraordinary an ordinary occurrence of everyday life."[17] Arendt hoped that the council system would provide modern people with what the city-state had provided the Greeks—a space for action, an opportunity for the extraordinary. But she knew that the council systems that have existed, that have appeared in the course of revolutions, have been notoriously short-lived, and she also knew that they have arisen *spontaneously*. She knew these things, and she wrote *On Revolution* to ask how the legacy of revolutions, the council systems, could be preserved, how the "swift decline" that has characterized the council systems could be forestalled.

On Revolution offers a comparative study of revolutions particularly focused on the American Revolution as a political revolution, a revolution that culminated in a duly constituted republican form of government. Arendt tries to understand why the men of the French Revolution did not appeal to the American political achievement, but only to the prerevolutionary American social condition that Jefferson called "the lovely equality the poor enjoy with the rich." She suggests that concern with "the Social Question," the problem of poverty, diverted the French from the goal of founding political freedom—the very weight of the misery they confronted was overwhelming. What troubles her was that during the subsequent century "It was the French and not the American Revolution that set the world on fire"[19] And it was the problem of poverty and not the problem of forming a government that set European theoretical discussions on fire.

Arendt set her schematic contrast of social and political revolutions in the context of her concern with how little Americans themselves remember of the story of their republic's founding and with how uncomprehending American governments have been of revolutions, particularly in the post-World War II world; "Fear of revolution has been the hidden *lietmotif* of post-war American foreign policy." Her task is to retell the American story, to render it fit for remembrance, and to warn that "In the contest that divides the world today and in which so much is at stake, those will probably win who understand revolution. . . . And such understanding can neither be countered nor replaced with an expertness in counter-revolution."[20]

This cautionary context was not troubling to readers whose primary concern was for "social justice," and neither was Arendt's praise of the council system at the end of the book. But Arendt's distinction between social and political revolutions most certainly was. The book was greeted with amazement by most of its reviewers. The socialist Michael Harrington, for a typical example, could not understand how such a conservative and such a radical could coexist in one person, so he concluded that there must be "two Arendts."

Harrington's assessment points to the central political challenge of Arendt's thought. Since the French Revolution, Right and Left, reactionary and progressive, conservative and liberal, have been standard oppositions. Because she did not accept these oppositions, because she did not embrace one alternative and attack the other but insisted on her own way, her *Selbstdenken*, Arendt has bewildered adherents of both sides. As a thinker she was a pariah—and she never wanted to give up her pariahdom to become a parvenu. Her reaction to the supposedly opposite alternatives of socialism and capitalism is characteristic of her stance:

> All our experiences—as distinguished from theories and ideologies—tell us that the process of expropriation, which started with the rise of capitalism, does not stop with the expropriation of the means of production; only legal and political institutions that are independent of the economic forces and their automatism can control and check the inherently monstrous possibilities of this process. . . . What protects freedom is the division between governmental and economic power, or, to put it in Marxian language, the fact that the state and its constitution are not superstructures.[21]

Brecht's ironic imperative "first bread, then ethics" is recognizably of the genre we call *épater le bourgeois*. "First politics, then socio-economic matters"—which seems to be Hannah Arendt's imperative—is less easy to classify. Is it not heartless to place the "public happiness" of acting and speaking, or participating in politics, before the needs of the hungry, the economically and socially unenfranchised? Is not an opposition of the social and the political just as simplistic as the oppositions Arendt rejected?

But Hannah Arendt did not really call for "politics first, then socioeconomic matters," for she knew very well that only those who have been liberated from dignity-destroying worry about how to put food on their tables or clothe themselves are free to participate in politics. In her terms liberation *precedes* revolution, which is constitution-making, a people's action of constituting a government, of instituting a balance of powers. Her point is that "While it is true that freedom can come only to those whose needs have been fulfilled, it is equally true that it will escape those who are bent upon living for their desires."[22] She distinguishes between the slogan of liberation from poverty—"to each according to his needs"—and the slogan she thought she read above the door of failed revolutions—"to each according to his desires." Her distinction is surely right, for it is obvious that a limitless quest for abundance can lay waste the earth, destroy what Arendt called "the world," the sum of relatively permanent artifacts, and subserve the human capacities for action and speech to its exigencies. In short, Hannah Arendt did not want revolutionaries to become parvenus. But in her ardent concern for the political, for action and speech, for "public happiness," she left unanswered two crucial questions: what exactly are the *needs* of each, and *how* shall the injunction "to each according to his needs" be followed? What she hoped for was a solution to the problem of poverty "through technical means," through a "rational, non-ideological economic development." What this might be, she did not say. Her assumption was that technology can be "politically neutral"—a very problematic assumption. However, her hope is clear: she wanted a solution to the problem of poverty that did not, does not, dictate a form of government.

One of the grave weaknesses of *On Revolution* is that the two questions the work implicitly poses—what are people's basic economic needs, and how shall these be met?—are neither explicitly raised nor answered. Its strength is that it highlights how basic the need to appear in public (to discuss, to debate, to act) is to people; it gives the examples of human speech and action that *The Human Condition* lacks. And it presents to those who think of conservation and revolution as opposites a powerful image of revolutionary conservatism, of the American Founders' concern for a new political science, one utilizing the traditional discussions of forms of government, with which to forge, in John Adams' phrase, "institutions that last for many generations." Hannah Arendt's mother's daughter addressed our worn-out political categories in the manner of Hannah Arendt's mother's idol—Rosa Luxemburg—who was a pariah among the socialists and Marxists of her time because she called for people's councils and for the founding of a republic.

What emerges from Arendt's reflections on thinking and judging and on action is an analogy that is—to borrow the title of one of her books—"between past and future." Since Plato proposed that the ideal city-state should be a human writ large, there have been in the "Great Tradition" many analogies in which model communities have been used to picture the human future or summon up the long-forgotten human past, but Arendt's analogy is not tied to a hierarchical ideal or eternal standard. It must vary from historical moment to historical moment and include antihierarchical principles. The checks and balances existing within an individual, who "lives together explicitly with himself" and can thus judge independently, are rooted in natality, as the human capacity for action, for freedom. Of the plurality within each of us—the me and myself—and the autonomy of the human faculties we can constitute a free self. The checks and balances existing within a community, which allow people to live freely with each other, are rooted in its natality, as is the community's capacity for action, for freedom. A free republic can be constituted of a plurality of autonomous individuals. When individuals forget or deny their original uniquenesses, their newness by virtue of being born, they foreclose the possibility of independent judgment and action—of greatness. When the people of a community forget or deny the community's origins, the impulse for freedom that brought the people together in action, they foreclose the possibility of further action—of greatness. Pindar's maxim holds both for people as individuals and for free communities: "Become what you are."

3

Reading Hannah Arendt's
The Life of the Mind

In 1958 Hannah Arendt announced that her task in *The Human Condition* was nothing less than "to think what we are doing."[1] Some fifteen years later, in the first volume of *The Life of the Mind,* she asked what we are "doing" when we think. Specifically, she wanted to know whether thinking people—as opposed to unthinking people like Adolf Eichmann—are "doing" something that prevents them from evildoing. But she framed her exploration very generally in Kantian terms: what is the *necessary condition* for evildoing? If thoughtlessness is the necessary condition for evildoing, is it possible that what we are "doing" when we think is what prevents us from evildoing?

Arendt states the possibility tentatively, claiming only that thinking is "among the conditions that make men abstain from evildoing."[2] Her tentativeness is important because, as her reflections unfold, she suggests that it is not thinking *per se* that makes people abstain from evildoing; thinking neither gives rise to, prevents, nor determines actions. But Arendt does hold that a person's ability to say "this is right" or "this is wrong" in the world presupposes that he or she has stopped to think, felt "the wind of thought." One of thinking's "byproducts" or "side-effects" is judging—but this means that thinking *is,* in some sense that needs exploring, the necessary condition for judging.

The last third of Arendt's *The Life of the Mind,* called "Judging," was left unfinished at her death in 1975. In this essay I am going to try to reconstruct "Judging" from the fragments Arendt left and from a careful, slow reading of the two completed volumes, "Thinking" and "Willing." *The Life of the Mind* has a clear philosophical style and process, and these— once noted—can point the way to "Judging."

1

In the opening pages of the "Thinking" volume Arendt takes Socrates as her model of a thinker. From existing portraits she extracted three similes: Socrates as a gadfly arousing people to thinking; he was a midwife delivering people of their unexamined preconceptions; he was an electric ray paralyzing people, stopping them in their worldly tracts (1;172ff). Socrates was the model of a thinker in search not of truth but of meaning; but Socrates was what Plato called a "noble nature," a man inspired with an *eros* for wisdom, and Arendt was looking for what in the thinking activity itself, not in any special qualities of a thinker's nature, might condition against evildoing. The abstract quality of Arendt's work comes from her quest for the nature of thinking rather than the nature of a thinking person. Her effort is resolutely impersonal because thinking is "an ever-present faculty of everybody" (1:191).

Thinking is, for Arendt, "dialectical." This "frozen concept" she resolves into its original meaning: "the soundless dialogue [*dialegisthai* as "talking through words"] between me and myself" (1:185). The actualization of our internal plurality has the effect of liberating us not only from conventional "truths" but from conventional rules of conduct. The last is, of course, crucial when conventions of conduct, to take one example, make murder the "norm." What a thinking person will not do is live with a murderer, live with an internal "myself" who is a murderer. From the point of view of the "thinking ego," it is better to suffer wrong than do wrong and live with the wrongdoer.

Thoughtlessness, it follows, is the absence of internal dialogue. The thoughtless person who does evil is different, in Arendt's terms, from the person who is wicked. A wicked person must overcome his or her thinking partner, silence all objections; the thoughtless person, who "does not know that silent intercourse," hears no objections or has somehow ceased to hear objections (1:190–191). When objections do not come from outside, in conditions where "everybody is swept away unthinkingly by what everybody else says and believes in," a thinking person, who may otherwise be inconspicuous, is conspicuous as a nonparticipant or resister (1:192).

Arendt had reached these conclusions by the time she wrote "Thinking and Moral Considerations" in 1971.[3] What she adds to them in *The Life of the Mind* is a long discussion that prepares the reader to seek the meaning of her reflections. The preparation discussion builds a *via negativa*: Arendt argues that the "thinking ego" is not the soul, not the self others perceive in the world, not the commonsense reasoning of everyday life, not science's reasoning. Thinking, unlike the passions of the soul, does not appear in the world or concern itself with appearances. Sensation and intellectual cognition are in Arendt's view intentional—that is, absorbed with and by the intended object—and thus without the "recoil" motion characteristic of thinking; they may produce "results" but they do not go on the endless self-referential quest for meaning that is characteristic of thinking. This dense *via negativa* discussion is designed to reveal the autonomy of the thinking faculty.[4]

When she reaches this station on her way, Arendt stops to give a preview of the characteristics common on the three mental faculties (1:69ff.). Thinking, willing, and judging are all autonomous, both in the sense that they follow only the rules inherent in their activities and in the sense that they are not all derived from some single source. As in Arendt's political theory, freedom and plurality always go hand in hand; to make any of the faculties the slave of any other or to make them all subjects of a sovereign One would be to deny their freedom. Each faculty, further-more, is self-motivating or spontaneous, and each "recoils upon itself"; each faculty is intra-active. And for this intra-activity to arise, each faculty must to some extent and in its own particular way withdraw from the world of appearances, from external determinations.

In the existing manuscript Arendt sketched what the faculties have in common, and this sketch provides clues for the most difficult task left to the reader by the absence of the third volume: questioning how she might have spoken of the faculties' interrelations. She did provide some indications, though, and she did supply the cornerstone for her construc-tion, namely, the claim that the faculties are not hierarchically related. Nonetheless, though thinking can neither move the will nor supply judg-ment with rules for linking particulars and universals and thus does not reign over will and judgment, it does have a certain priority—or, to use the terms of Arendt's political theory again, a certain authority. Thinking presents the other two faculties with "desensed" thought objects, invisi-bles, afterthoughts; it presents the will with images of the future, and it presents judgment with images of the past. The past and future "exist" only in the images given by thinking.[5] As willing and judging withdraw from the world present to the senses, they maintain their orientation (in temporal terms) by means of thinking's image-gifts.

In comparison to the other two faculties, judging withdraws least: it remains close to the particulars. And the judging person stays in the company of others, a spectator among spectators. Willing "takes a position" near but radically free from objects. The radicalism of its freedom is that it affirms or denies the very existence of objects. Thinking itself withdraws most completely from the world. But though its distance is greatest, thinking is linked to the world by language, and particularly by metaphor, in which thought is manifest and by which thinking is reminded, so to speak, of the world it has left behind. The Greek metaphor "wind of thought," for example, draws on a worldly appearance, the wind, to reveal thinking, to link it to appearances.

Arendt's discussion of metaphor paves the way for another stretch of the *via negativa*. Presupposing a link of thought with the world, she sought a metaphor to present thinking in its withdrawn condition, in its worldlessness. Metaphors linked to visual objects, for example, present thinking as a process coming to an end in a passive, contemplative beholding or intuition rather than as a resultless activity. Similarly, metaphors linking thinking with the other senses' objects impute to it a relation outside of itself; they present thinking as purposeful, intentional, cognitive. For thinking, which is concerned with itself, which is a purposeless end in itself, there is no adequate metaphor, Arendt suggests, except perhaps the metaphor of life itself. The exception—"thinking is life"— is inadequate, however, when the question "Why do we think?" (no more answerable than "Why do we live?") comes up.

Arendt leaves the question "Why do we think?" hanging and takes another tack. It we do not think for the purpose of knowing or cognizing or, for that matter, if there is no purpose to thinking, "What makes us think?" (1:129ff.). Considering this question, she discerns two basic types of "professional thinkers": on the one hand, there are those who are moved to think by wonder that things are as they are, and, on the other hand, there are those who fear that things as they are are hostile. The wonderer stays put, while the fearful thinker either retreats to a stoical safe distance or tries to convert hostile things into thought-things, into creatures of a spirit or *Geist* with which he or she can be reconciled. As she reflects on these possibilities, Arendt notes that they involve "confessions of need" and that her own contribution to the catalogue of needs, the need to search for meaning, is no less vague and general than the others. Even though it is obvious that Arendt's sympathy lies with the wonderers, the point of her inconclusive historical excursus is not to praise wonder: "Our question 'what makes us think?' is actually inquiring about ways to bring [thinking] out of hiding, to tease it, as it were, into manifestation" (1:167). So, the problem of how to present the thinking activity has not been solved; and it is at this impasse that Arendt begins again, turning to her model of a thinker, Socrates, "to represent for us the actual thinking activity" (1:167).

But, as we noted before, Socrates is not entirely satisfactory either. This is not only because he (unlike Everyman) was a noble nature, but because his *eros* was for wisdom, beauty, justice—all lovable, positive concepts—and the consequence of such an *eros* is that all unlovables— evil, for instance—are overlooked, considered mere privations of the positive concepts, rootless nothings. Like the majority of western thinkers, Socrates provided no example of real confrontation with evil; his "no man does evil voluntarily" is not confrontational. Neither of the two problems that inspired Arendt's inquiry—Is thoughtlessness a condition of evildoing? What is the thinking activity in itself?—can be resolved as long as the thinker's noble nature or the thinker's moral maxim are still at work in the inquiry.

The movement of Arendt's work, the manifestation of her thinking style, is perfectly of a piece with this nonresult. She carefully presents what thinking is not; she discusses the manifestation of thinking in language but shows why it cannot, qua activity, account for itself metaphorically; and then she turns to Socrates as a representational figure and refuses even this mode. Like Penelope, Arendt undoes her weaving when a finished product threatens to emerge. Thinking is not revealed on the frame.

2

Arendt's unravelling procedure, her *via negativa* march, makes the last section of the "Thinking" volume a very startling experience (2:197ff.). The "positive statements" made by Socrates, a man who was not much given to positive statements, are woven together to present thinking—finally, to say what thinking *is.*

First, she explicitly warns that Socrates' claim for thinking—it is "a dialogue between me and myself"—was a "translation into conceptual language" by Plato of Socrates' discovery of "the essence of thought" (1:185). We have to unfreeze the conceptual language and imagine how Socrates discovered that he could do with himself what he had done with others—examine what he had said, talk things through—and how he discovered that in order to do this he had to keep his thinking partner fit and friendly (1:188). We do not have to consider Socrates' nature or the objects of his *eros* but only these original discoveries, which anyone can make. But even if we imaginatively reenact Socrates' discoveries, what assures us that we have found the thinking activity itself? An internal dialogue is activated when I say to myself, "What do you mean when you say——?" But what makes me ask? Arendt's "What makes me think?" question is bound to recur vis-à-vis internal dialogue, and it seems we are to answer, "It is natural for me and myself to talk—once we discover that we can." This answer seems implicit in Arendt's claim that "thinking is a natural need of human life" (1:191). But even if we accept this, does it help us with the further question: what makes us *not* think? What makes us deny or never feel a natural need of human life? And if, in circumstances where thinking is possible (short of torture or total terror), some think and some do not think, are we not cast back on some prior condition, like the nobility or ignobility of people's natures, for an explanation? Arendt notes that among Socrates' students were the future tyrants Alcibiades and Critias, who were not content with the nonresults of Socratic dialoguing. A resultless quest for meaning can "at any moment turn against itself," Arendt admits, but she does not say what might prevent this from happening.

If we establish a faculty's autonomy, Arendt's admission implies, we must look outside of the faculty for a check on the faculty's potential for self-destruction. Again, the interrelations among the faculties become crucial. Arendt remarks in her second volume, "Willing":

> Just as thinking prepares the self for the role of a spectator, willing fashions it into an "enduring I" that directs all particular acts of volition. It creates the self's *character* and therefore was something understood as the *principium individuationis*, the source of a person's specific identity [as opposed to his or her talents or abilities, which are given by nature]. (2:195)

This passage indicates that we cannot take the "positive statement" that "thinking is a dialogue between me and myself" as anything more than a partial statement, one that leads not only to other faculties but to those elements from which the "thinking ego" is so carefully distinguished— like "the self." If thinking did not prepare the self for the role of spectator, for judgment, we would have no reason to hope that this "good for nothing" activity could survive the charges periodically laid against it by those who consider it a kind of disease. If we accept that "thinking is a *natural* need of human life" (my italics) we are invited to travel back over the *via negativa* Arendt lays down, to go in the opposite direction: to reunite the thinking ego with the self, the soul, and the senses through which we apprehend the particulars we judge.

The "Thinking" volume ends with a metaphor, taken from a parable by Franz Kafka. Arendt presents a "thinking ego" that moves between a past and future that have nothing to do with historical or biographical time, the self's domains. Her metaphor of past and future flowing toward each other, colliding, is a "time construct . . . totally different from the time sequence of ordinary life."

> It is because the thinking ego is ageless and nowhere that past and future can become manifest to it as such, emptied, as it were, of their concrete content and liberated from all spatial categories. What the thinking ego senses in 'his' dual antagonists are time itself and the constant change it implies, the relentless motion that transforms all Being into becoming instead of letting it *be,* and thus incessantly destroys its being present. (1:206)

As Arendt shows in her reflections on metaphor, mental activities cannot be described except in metaphors that draw on everyday life and worldly appearance. But in this metaphor of "between past and future," which presents thinking not as a response to Being (as Heidegger did) but as a response to Time,[6] we have Time emptied of concrete content and liberated from spatial categories, Time *totally different* from the time sequences of everyday life. The metaphor has escaped the world of perceptible phenomena; and, in a way, Arendt recognizes this, for she comments that the metaphor is "valid only within the realm of mental phenomena"—that is, the realm of invisibles, of things only metaphorically phenomenal (1:209).

Representing an invisible in its invisibility or an ineffable in its ineffability is a special talent of poets and storytellers, the conveyors of Meaning, not Truth. In *The Concept of Irony* Kierkegaard captures Arendt's difficulty as she tries to present the Mind: it is like trying to paint an elf wearing a magic cap that makes him invisible. Such a talent is very rare in a modern philosopher and such an embarrassment to common sense that those who possess it often display it only in their private notebooks. Those with daily cares to struggle with hardly want to follow away-from-the-world metaphors that offer no guidance, no standards, not even any content. To this attitude Franz Kafka himself once offered a little cautionary tale:

> A man once said . . . If you only followed the symbols you would become
>   symbols yourselves, and thus rid of all your daily cares.
> Another said: I bet this is also a symbol.
> The first said: You have won.
> The second said: But unfortunately only symbolically.
> The first said: No, in reality; symbolically you have lost.[7]

3

The codetta of the "Thinking" volume prepares us very well for the opening of "Willing," for we have been alerted to the difficulty involved in "locating" a mental faculty: picturing the unpicturable. And we have also been reintroduced to the theme of temporality in the form that frames the second volume and probably would have framed the third volume of *The Life of the Mind.*

"Willing" begins with a warning: the faculty of willing is even more difficult to discover than thinking; its very existence went undiscovered for centuries. Once discovered, it was not a pleasing concept. For thinkers the contingency it entailed seemed to be "the ultimate of meaninglessness," the opposite of tranquilizing notions of Necessity. Even more basically, the Will's will to do is disturbing to thinking's pleasure in doing nothing.

At the beginning of "Willing," Arendt sets out the claim that the lack of a notion of Will among Greeks and the achievement of such a notion among the Christians are tied to time. Because the discovery of the Will is datable and because so many arguments from thinking's point of view have tried to obscure the discovery, Arendt felt that her exposition had to be historical. The technique of trawling the opinions of "professional thinkers" with a question for a net, which is introduced in the "What makes us think?" excursus of the first volume, is the major technique of the second volume.

Because the historical method dominates the second volume, it is not immediately apparent that the types of thought movements underlying "Thinking" are replayed in a contrasting key in "Willing." There are four basic types of movements in the first volume: a *via negativa* argument to establish the autonomy of the faculty; a movement that shows how the faculty, though autonomous and withdrawn, is linked to the world (for thinking: by metaphoric language); a presentation and commentary on a representational figure (Socrates); and, finally, "positive statements." There is a definite historical task in "Willing," and many of the first movement distinctions have already been made, so the order of movements in the second volume is different. As in "Thinking," Arendt begins with negative argument, this time historically framed; she moves, again, to a discussion of the faculty's withdrawal and relation to the world through action. But the metaphorical leap to "positive statements" emerges from the first two movements, and the representational figures come at the end of the volume, providing a bridge to the unwritten "Judging" volume.

The major problem is to distinguish willing and thinking (and, by implication, judging) because willing's autonomy has to be rescued from thinking's hostility; the whole *via negativa* movement of the second volume is spurred by reflections on *homo temporalis*. We can put this matter simply: when thinkers emphasize the past within the context of a cyclical time theory—that is, when the future is seen as an actualization or consequence of the past—no mental "organ" for the future, no Will, is posited; but, on the other hand, when they emphasize the future within a linear sequence of events thought to be possible, an "organ" for the future is considered essential. If a thinker holds that the Will is primarily among the mental faculties, it is likely that he or she will also claim that the future is the primary "tense" of time. But we should make a qualification (to note the first step on Arendt's *via negativa*): past-oriented thinking within the context of a cyclical time theory lacks a notion of Will but has a notion of choice among givens, a notion that often invokes the process of fabricating with an end or project in mental view. The *liberum arbitrum,* the Latin equivalent of Aristotle's *proairesis,* is a faculty for deliberating about and choosing among means appropriate to a particular end, like good health, or an ultimate end, like living well. The *liberum arbitrum* is dependent on means given by nature, and thus it is not autonomous; it does not involve "recoil" on itself or self-motivation.

Arendt's first step, which sets the Greek *proairesis* aside and notes the difficulties inherent in a past-oriented time theory—nothing genuinely new can arise out of a choice among givens—prepares for her second step, toward post-Hellenic discussions of the Will. St. Paul had recognized a conflict between I-will and I-can, which he described as a conflict between the spirit and the recalcitrant flesh, but Augustine, "the philosopher of the Will," went further and recognized a conflict within the Will itself: "In every act of Will, there is an I-will (*velle*) and an I-nill (*nolle*) involved" (2:89). Augustine understood that the Will commands itself— "thou shalt will"—and responds by both willing and nilling. The double response is the sign of the Will's freedom from itself, within itself; because the Will neither wills nor nills completely, it is not a slavish command-obeying faculty. What must precede any particular volition is not a choice of means, but a resolution of this internal conflict. Unlike St. Paul, Augustine did not think that only grace could still internal conflicts. Love, he said, "the weight of the soul," brings peace (2:95).

Augustine attributed autonomy to the Will, but he also granted the Will rulership over the two other faculties he took to be fundamental, Intellect and Memory. Both Aquinas and Duns Scotus questioned this claim; they were less interested in the nature of the Will itself than in the relation between Will and Intellect. Arendt takes the next step on her *via negativa* by mediating this controversy. She asks us to accept that the Will is not a choosing faculty and not a master/slave contest in which the master is either spirit (St. Paul) or intellect (Aquinas). Then we are asked to take a clue from Duns Scotus: even though the Will is free of internally or externally given commands, neither self-obedient nor obedient to intellect, it is not without limit, not omnipotent. The past, what has happened and therefore become absolutely necessary, is beyond the reach of the Will. The autonomous Will causes volitions, without being coerced; but these volitions cause effects or actions the Will cannot undo. Scotus denied that every sequence of events has been necessarily and not contingently caused, so that he was able to retain conceptually the obvious fact that even if we are free to do this or that and free to affirm or disaffirm our deeds, we are still not free to undo deeds.

Arendt found in Duns Scotus a thinker who could give her a way to reformulate an insight she comes to in her discussion of thinking. If you clearly distinguish cognition and thinking, truth and meaning, you need not equate necessity and meaning. And to break with the equation of meaning and necessity is to break with metaphysics and take seriously— that is, be able to judge—action. To put the matter another way: that something has happened and is thus necessary is not in itself meaningful; what people say about what has happened, how they judge it, how they represent it in stories—these are meaningful. Again, it is when we look for the limitation of mental faculty that the importance of the faculties in their interrelations emerges. Thinking's quest for meaning can "at any moment turn against itself"; Will's internal conflicts can be so unresolved that some Necessity suggested by thinking looks like salvation. What, if not a notion of Necessity, can aid the Will?

With her consideration of Duns Scotus, Arendt initiates the second thought movement of "Willing": she comes on a way of portraying Will in its relation to the world. As thinking is related to the world by metaphoric language, willing is related to the world by action. But, as metaphor fails fully to reveal the thinking activity itself, so action fails to expose the willing activity itself; so Arendt borrows an insight of Duns Scotus' to make a "positive statement." As there is pleasure in the thinking activity as sheer activity, there is pleasure in the willing activity as sheer activity, independent of action. For Duns Scotus, this willing-pleasure, purified of all transient needs and desires, is an intimation in this life of the state of blessedness he felt would be ours in the afterlife. "Transformed into love, the restlessness of the will is stilled but not extinguished; love's abiding power is felt not as the arrest of motion . . . but as the serenity of a self-contained, self-fulfilling, ever-lasting movement" (2:145). As Arendt uses Kafka's parable to present thinking as an unending lover's quest in contentless time, she uses Duns Scotus' image of future blessed-ness to present the willing activity as an unending movement in objectless space, in the space of a love that does not absorb or possess or desire objects but only wills them to be.

A crucial distinction must be noted here. Love is will transformed: the conflict of I-will and I-nill becomes a harmonious balance, "Love as a kind of enduring and conflictless Will." Will thus transformed into Love has a "weight," a "gravity," that allows it to shape the self's character, to train the self to make decisions between different projects. But these projects are not natural givens; they are thought-things, like Justice. Thus Arendt claims that people become just by loving Justice. However, it is action that stops (rather than transforms) the Will's internal division. When we act, we cease willing (2:101–102). The price for action, it follows, is loss of that freedom in which I-will and I-nill are active: *mental* freedom. But action can gain people the freedom in political terms that Arendt considers in the final pages of "Willing."

4

After presenting her image of Love's character-shaping stillness, which so forcefully evokes her image of dialogic thinking's capacity to shape the self for judgment, Arendt turns to her representative figures. These are the revolutionary eighteenth-century "men of action." But first Arendt provided a reflection on two modern thinkers, Nietzsche and Heidegger, who reactivated the old hostility between thinking and willing.

It was precisely the failure of the I-can in the face of what has happened, the past, which Duns Scotus had accepted as the Will's self-limitation, that Nietzsche railed against. The Will's inability to will backward haunted him and prompted him to the cyclical time theory he called "Eternal Recurrence." Nietzsche could say "yes" and "amen" to what has come to be in the world only if all values could be mentally changed or "transvaluated," that is, only if the Will could have *mental* omnipotence. He repudiated the Will's worldly connection, action, in favor of its internal action.

In the late work of Martin Heidegger the repudiation took a different form: he portrayed thinking as a "function of Being," a kind of voicebox for Being, and equated the thinking activity with "doing." The only history that there is is the "History of Being," which is a rectilinear history but certainly no history of spontaneous human action in the world. Rejecting Nietzsche's effort to present the Will as a destructive agent of *mental* change, an omnipotent assaulter of thought-things, Heidegger spoke of "a thinking that is not a willing," a thinking that can recognize its own source, Being, as the determiner of men's destinies (2:178). Each in his own way, these thinkers accepted, even wondered at, the world as it is; but they wanted to "make history" mentally or have history made mentally. Arendt felt that to find out anything about action *in the world,* we have to look to a period prior to the modern mentalization of all activity.

Arendt's representative "men of action," like her representative thinker Socrates, are in a certain sense flawed as models. Socrates left us without a real confrontation with evil; the men of action without a real appreciation of novelty, spontaneity, contingency. Arendt presents the men of action standing between the historical past (revolutionary liberation) and the future (the tasks of constitution framing); she has them looking in this moment through the archives of tradition for their future guidance in what she calls "foundation legends." The American Founders realized that they were not going to found "Rome anew," but they were not ready to conceive of their "new order of things" as something genuinely new. New beginnings carry with them an element of arbitrariness and contingency that is dizzying: when a new regime is launched, there is a traditional temptation to mask the unpredictability with an appeal to the past. The "foundation legends" do not picture freedom, they invoke a repetition, a return to paradise lost.

Arendt sought an image of "how to restart time within the inexorable time continuum" (2:218). Each free action turns immediately into a cause in the time continuum; explanations are sought that link the action to what preceded it and thus deny its freedom. Drawing on Augustine's notion that humans and time were created together, Arendt suggests that humanity was created "to make possible a beginning." She speaks of "the novel creature who *as* something entirely new appears in the midst of the time continuum of the world" (2:217).

The creation of the world and of humanity was an absolute beginning as Augustine imagined it, but each individual's birth is a beginning in the sense that it interrupts a causal chain and begins a new series of events. The human is that creature, unlike all other creatures, who lives in time and is able to reach into the past and into the future, to bind together his or her beginning and end. The human's capacity to know his or her own beginning and to know that as an individual he or she will come to an end is Will. What Arendt wants for political theory is an image of the "faculty of beginning" that accords with the future-directedness of Will but is not caught up in the perplexities caused by the conflict of I-will and I-nill. It is the Will's conflict that shapes the self's character; the sheer activity of the Will is the principle of human individuation, the principle that, so to speak, sustains for the future the capacity of beginning that is each person's by virtue of birth.

Arendt considers both thinking and willing as activities that do not have direct results in the world. Their remoteness from the world is the condition of their freedom; nothing external to them binds them or coerces them.

> [It] is the miracle of the human mind that man at least mentally and provisionally can transcend his earthly conditions and enjoy the sheer actuality of an exercise that has its end in itself. (2:145)

Athough without result in the world, these activities are not without result in the individual; and Arendt suggests, in the last sentence of "Willing," that our pleasure—or lack of pleasure—in the freedom of the mental faculties is something only an exploration of the faculty of Judgment can illuminate. This exploration should hold the key to understanding what made Socrates' disciples turn against the quest for meaning and what has made thinkers and men of action turn against the arbitrariness or contingency of willing; it should bring us back to the self, the self that thinking prepares for judging and that willing shapes and individuates.

5

Given the structure and the basic elements of the two existing volumes of *The Life of the Mind*—both reflections of a thinking style—we should be able to imagine the structures and elements of the unwritten "Judging." We have guidelines: there are reflections on Judgment in *The Life of the Mind* and its appendix, in Arendt's earlier books, and in unpublished notes and seminar papers. What can be made with these materials is not, obviously, Arendt's "Judging." Had Arendt lived to undertake the final third of her book, she might very well have changed her mind about what she had written; her "Judging" might have surprised her. What can be made is an order of the fragments we have, an outline, which is consistent with the procedures, the patterns, the questions, the principles, of the existing volumes. Perhaps, with this ordering, we can take up the problem that helped launch Arendt's work: in what way do mental activities condition us to abstain from evildoing?

There are two principles articulated in "Thinking" and "Willing" that ought to be set out as constructing principles. First, Arendt not only avoided but tried to block off any path that would lead to a denial of the mind's freedom. Of any such path, she would have said with Duns Scotus, *quia hoc nullo modo salvat liberatum* (that is not the way to save freedom). The axial principle will have to be: Judgment must not be coerced—not by "truth," philosophical or scientific, not by violence, intellectual or political, and not even by the beauty of things, natural or fabricated.[8] Second, Arendt wanted to save the mental activities from mutual hostility, to avoid constructing them as warring parties. With good government in the mind the faculties will check and balance each other. If thinking foregoes the equation of Necessity and meaningfulness, then the Will, the seat of contingency, will not seem its mortal enemy. We can suppose that when thinking is hostile toward judgment, a similar way can be found out of that deadlock. This hostility, as we shall see, has traditionally focused on the fact that judging deals with particulars that, as Kant said, "as such contain something contingent in respect to the universal" (1:237). We will also have to consider the long-standing quarrel between willing and judging and seek a similar accommodation.

As we have seen, it is by a *via negativa* argument that the domain and hence the freedom of a faculty is established. As in the case of willing, historical terms seem appropriate to judging. Arendt thought that the faculty of judgment became "a major topic for a major thinker" only with Kant (1:215). If we survey the thinkers' approaches to judgment and consider judgments' manifestation in the world, it would be consistent with Arendt's thought movements to turn then to a representational figure who can show us a way to the mental activities their manifestations do not provide. Arendt wrote two long essays about Karl Jaspers and his "unerring certainty of judgment." Jaspers was for her a man whose judgment remained secure in the historical context where Adolf Eichmann's thinking ceased. Finally, to complete the outline of judging, we will have to find an image, a "positive statement" about judging in itself as sheer activity; this image will be like the image of thinking in "the quiet of the Now" and like the image of willing in the serenity of an "everlasting movement." It will, we can infer from the first two images, be an image of loving.

6

In order to consider the Will, Arendt has to emphasize *homo temporalis*, the human being who has had a beginning and is going toward an end, and to do this she has to turn away from cyclical time theories. A different sort of time speculation stands in the way of her consideration of Judgment: a rectilinear time theory in which the future, so to speak, calls events toward itself. In such a future events are judged by history as the determinants of progress. Confronted with theories of this sort, Arendt asks: "Who shall be the judge, History or Man?" and answers, with Kant, "Man." In a passage at the end of "Thinking" concerned with the questions involved in relating theory and practice she notes:

> Since Hegel and Marx, these questions have been treated in the perspective of History and an assumption that there is such a thing as Progress of the human race. Finally we shall be left with the only alternative there is in these matters—we can either say with Hegel: *Die Weltgeschichte ist das Weltgericht* [*World History is Last Judgment*], leaving the ultimate judgment to Success, or we can maintain with Kant the autonomy of the minds of men and their possible independence from things as they are or as they have come into being. (1:216).

Arendt suggests that in order to consider Kant's alternative we would have to examine the concept of history, tracing it back to its Greek source, the noun *histor:*

> [The] Homeric historian is the *judge*. If our faculty of judgment is our faculty for dealing with the past, the historian is the inquiring man who

by relating it sits in judgment over it. If this is so, we may reclaim our human dignity, win it back, as it were, from the pseudo-divinity named History of the modern age, without denying history's importance but denying its right to be the ultimate judge. . . . Old Cato has left us a curious phrase which aptly sums up the political principle implied in the enterprise of reclamation. He said: "*Victrix causa deis placuit, sed victa Catoni*" ("The victorious cause pleases the gods, but the defeated one pleases Cato"). (1:216)

The political principle implied in reclaiming judgment's autonomy is freedom from Success, from the Future hypostasized; but the mental principle has to be "independence from things as they are or as they have come into being." This is what we attain with the first step of a historical *via negativa*—by distinguishing judgments from the Greek *phronesis* and from the sense of taste.

The Greeks had what Arendt describes as

a kind of insight and understanding of matters that are good and bad for men, a sort of sagacity—neither wisdom nor cleverness—needed for human affairs. *Phronesis* is required for any activity involving things within human power to achieve or not to achieve. (2:60)

This concept, *phronesis,* which is a kind of practical reason (as opposed to theoretical reason), points to an ability to measure or see proportion in political as well as artistic matters. It was linked by Aristotle with *proairesis;* it is an ability to weigh up the various ends compelling desire and choice. *Phronesis,* in Arendt's understanding, was only a forerunner of the notion of judgment because it was tied to given ends and means, without the necessary recoil, and because it was tied to desire, a source of unfreedom. Kant's great achievement was to treat judgment as something other than a kind of reason and something other than a ruler over desire. For Arendt what is most significant about *phronesis* as a forerunner of Judgment is its link with persuasion:

When free men obeyed their government, or the laws of the *polis,* their obedience was called πειθαρχία, a word which clearly indicated that obedience was obtained by persuasion and not by force.[9]

Persuasion—what Kant called "wooing the consent of others"—is the communicative mode or manifestation of judgment.

While the eighteenth-century notion of taste marked an ability distinct from reason, it too lacked the recoil proper to judgment. It was a commonplace of the period to note that taste was different from Reason and lacked Reason's universalism. The idiosyncracy of taste—and the possibility that we must say of taste *non disputandum est*—was what Kant's conception sought to address. Taste, for Kant, was not a form of cognition, not an ability residing in the senses, not the sense of taste. Particulars that are tasted affect us immediately; there is no dispute, not even any real communicability here. Judgment involves a step back: we represent to ourselves (and this involves imagination) the now-absent particulars we once sensed:

> You chose as it were those senses by which objects in their objectivity are given to you. . . . This operation of imagination prepares the object for the 'operation of reflection.' And this operation of reflection is the actual activity of judging something. (2:266)

When we "sense" an object inwardly, having imagined it, we do what the *sense* of taste does, we choose.

> But this choice itself is once more subject to another choice: you can approve or disapprove of the very fact of [something's being] *pleasing*, it is subject to approbation or disapprobation. (2:267)

Something is pleasing and then *the pleasure* is either approved or disapproved. What we do when we communicate our pleasures and displeasures in the mode of approbation or disapprobation is tell our choices and thereby choose our company. We woo the consent of others to choices we have made at least in part because they are communicable.

To put the matter summarily, judging involves sensing; imaginative representation of the sense object when it is absent, which is responded to with pleasure or displeasure; and an operation of reflection in which there is approbation or disapprobation. The reflexivity of Judgment, its recoil, is the last stage, where we have a pleasure in our pleasure that is also a pleasure in the freedom of our judging faculty. The manifestation of the judging activity's recoiling is communicating approbation or disapprobation. The two-in-one of thinking is the "me and myself" in dialogue; the two-in-one of willing is the I-will and I-nill. Judging's recoil is different: it is the activation of a "me and you (plural)." When we judge, we imaginatively make others present in ourselves—Kant spoke of "enlarged mentality"—to make, so to speak, an interior public space "by comparing our judgment with the possible rather than the judgment of others, and by putting ourselves in the place of any other man" (#40).[10] To do this mental touring, we presume (and Kant actually tried to prove) that others who judge will share our judgments, and we try to disregard as much as possible our own subjective conditions and our sensations.

It is particularly noteworthy that our most private sense, taste, rather than sight or hearing or touch, should be the sense from which judgment is derived. We do not represent to ourselves the taste *sensation*, but rather the it-pleases or it-displeases, our immediate response, so that it is, as Arendt remarks, "as though you sense yourself, like an inner sense" (2:266). Taste's idiosyncratic nature seems to be an argument against deriving judgment from it, but Arendt found in Kant's own questioning of the derivation one observation she thought strongly supported his conclusion:

> The true opposite to the Beautiful is not the Ugly but 'that which excites disgust.' And do not forget that Kant originally planned to write a Critique of Moral Taste. (2:266)

In this remark of Arendt's there is an important clue to the problem she first sets out in the "Thinking" volume, to which we as yet have no clear answer: what conditions us against evildoing? The answer would *not* be, if we followed Kant's discussion, art collecting. Kant thought that those who take an interest in the beautiful forms of nature (as opposed to "artificial forms") are much more often "good souls" than are "connoisseurs in taste." One's relation to nature's beautiful forms is immediate, he argued, while "a beautiful representation of a [natural] thing" is grasped mediately, that is, as a representation (#42). Art works can present as beautiful what is ugly and displeasing in nature—war, disease, and so forth. But artworks cannot, Kant argued, present the disgusting:

> For this singular sensation, which rests on mere imagination, the object is represented as it were obtruding itself on our enjoyment while we strive against it with all our might. (#49)

People who have spent all their lives surrounded by beautiful representations of nature have been sheltered from what cannot be represented, the disgusting, and have not had occasion to strive with all their might against it. In his *Lectures on Ethics* Kant remarked that:

> Anyone can see that an action is disgusting, but only the man who feels disgust at it has moral feelings. The understanding sees that a thing is disgusting and is hostile to it, but cannot be disgusted; it is only the sensibility which is disgusted.

We can infer from this that when people do not strive against a disgusting action, they have lost their moral feeling; or, in Arendt's terms, if they do not communicate displeasure and disapprobation, they have lost their judgment. And this is what Arendt thinks when she describes Eichmann's visits to the killing centers at Chelmo, Minsk, and Treblinka. She relates his disgust and horror at what he saw and then his striving not against these disgusting actions but against his own feelings of disgust, his (in Arendt's phrase) "innate repugnance toward crime."[11] Once he had blocked off his disgust, he no longer judged, no longer put himself in any other person's place. And no examples in his environment, no communicated judgments of others, stood in his way:

> As Eichmann told it, the most potent factor in the soothing of his conscience was the simple fact that he could see no one, no one at all, who actively was against the Final Solution.[12]

The spectre of Eichmann very clearly lay behind Arendt's effort to separate Kant's reflections on judgment from his notion of the will as practical reason (which we will consider below). What she had wanted to eliminate from willing is the element of duty so crucial to Kant's *Critique of Practical Reason*. To the astonishment of everyone in the Jerusalem courtroom where Eichmann was tried, the man not only claimed that he had tried to live according to the Kantian categorical imperative but produced a nearly accurate statement of it. Eichmann admitted, as Arendt reports, that

> from the moment he was charged with carrying out the Final Solution he had ceased to live according to Kantian principles, that he had known it, and that he had consoled himself with the thought that he no longer 'was the master of his own deeds'. . . . [But] he had not simply dismissed the Kantian formula as no longer applicable, he had distorted it to read: Act as though the principle of your actions were the same as that of the legislator [the Führer] or the law of the land [the Führer's law].[13]

When Eichmann gave up his capacity to judge, he identified his will with the Führer's will. Eichmann made it very clear why he had put his Führer's orders above his own will: "[Hitler's] success alone proved to me that I should subordinate myself to this man"[14] Eichmann reversed Old Cato's pleasure in defeated causes: the successful cause pleased Eichmann; whether it was right or wrong did not matter.

In Kant's view, the faculty of judgment is not the faculty that considers right and wrong; this, for Kant, is the province of practical reason, of what he called will. Arendt firmly separates will from practical reason in her "Willing" volume, and, as she studied the *Critique of Judgment,* she left aside Kant's attempts to link judgment to practical reason. She did not, in other words, follow Kant, as he tried to go beyond what he called the "empirical interest" we take in beautiful forms and in the company of others, "an inclination proper to human nature" (#41), to any transcendental derivation of this interest. She stayed on the empirical level and explored our "social inclination" as a potentially political experience: She questioned what taste has to do with the company we keep.

When we judge, Kant held, we must be disinterested because "All interest presupposes or generates a want, and, as the determining ground of assent [or approbation], it leaves the judgment about the object no longer free" (#5). This disinterestedness (or, to use the term Arendt applied to the historian, impartiality) of judging is its freedom; it is the activation of the "me and you," the overcoming of *self*-interest. Arendt notes, interpreting Kant again, that

> Because we call something beautiful, we have a *'pleasure in its existence'* [not just in its beautiful form] and that is wherein all interest consists. (In one of his reflections in the notebooks, Kant remarks that the Beautiful teaches us to love without self-interest [*ohne Eigennutz*]). And the peculiar characteristic of this interest is that it 'interests only in society.' (2:270)

What we have here is an image of judging as a disinterested love to put together with the image of thinking as an eros for meaning and the image of willing, transformed into love, willing objects to continue *being*. Here, we take pleasure in the existence of objects that *have come to be* as such. What this means is that in the quiet of saying "this is beautiful," we feel at home in the world and that we have been born to take pleasure in the world. There is in our judging activity a harmony. Kant spoke of harmony of imagination and understanding, a "free play of the faculties," to which Arendt, I think, would have added: a harmony of "me and you." If people become just by loving Justice (as Arendt says in "Willing"), they become capable of impartiality by loving the Beautiful.

This disinterestedness that loving the beautiful can teach us is fundamentally a social experience. Considering the link Kant had established between our love of the beautiful and our sociability, which rests "as it were [on] an original compact dictated by humanity itself " (#41), Arendt writes:

> It is by virtue of [the] idea of mankind, present in every single man, that men are human, and they can be called civilized or humane to the extent that this idea becomes the principle of their actions as well as their judgments. It is at this point that the actor and the spectator become united; the maxim of the actor and the 'standard' according to which the spectator judges the spectacle of the world become one. The, as it were, categorical imperative for action would read as follows: Always act on the maxim through which this original compact can be actualized into a general law. (3:271)

Kant was filled with enthusiasm for the French Revolution not because he approved of the revolutionary mode of action—he did not—but because he was hopeful that the enthusiasm of all spectators, including himself, would contribute to a "cosmopolitan existence." As Arendt notes, there was a clash in Kant between "the principle according to which you act and the principle according to which you judge," because Kant's principle of action, his categorical imperative, would not allow him to sanction violent overthrow of a legal structure. Her own maxim stills the war between willing and judging which Kant experienced. "Had Kant forgotten because of his 'moral duty' his insights as a spectator, he would have become what so many good men, involved and engaged in public affairs tend to be—an idealistic fool" (2:261). In order to insure that 'moral duty' not stand in the way of or clash with judging, Arendt simply abandoned the categorical imperative.

As she formulates her own maxim for judging and acting, Arendt invokes the thought of the man we will take as a representative figure—Karl Jaspers. Kant had projected into the "far-distant future" his idea of a compact of mankind; he viewed a united mankind as a possible result of human history, a notion of progress Arendt rejects. Following Karl Jaspers, she thinks of the unity of mankind as a 'present reality,' the present result of the "one world" that modern technology has ushered in. In her essay "Karl Jaspers: Citizen of the World" Arendt puts the maxim for judging and action thus: "Nothing according to the implications of Jaspers' philosophy, should happen today in politics which would be contrary to the actually existing solidarity of mankind."[15] What Arendt did in her lectures, and presumably would have done at length in "Judging," was to consider how we *experience* the solidarity of mankind—in and through judging's activity. Our empirical interest in communicating our judgments is the sign of a *present* human compact.

To see how this link between enlarged mentality and humanity's solidarity comes about in practice, we should look at Jaspers as a model practitioner of judgment. Like Socrates and the men of action, Jaspers is ideal as a model of practice but flawed as a model for theoretical reflection on practice. His theoretical error was to believe

> that the intimacy of the dialogue, the 'inner action' in which I 'appeal' to myself or to the 'other self' . . . can be extended and become paradigmatic for the political sphere. (2:200)

The mental faculty we have that extends to the political sphere is not thinking but judging, and this is why acting and judging can have the same principle. But in practice Jaspers, whose "unerring certainty of judgment" astonished Arendt, was inviolable to the temptations of his times—as a man who was not tempted to do evil, he was the opposite of Eichmann, who was not tempted *not* to do evil—and she attributes this inviolability, this independence of judgment to "a secret trust in men, in the *humanitas* of the human race."[16] Such a trust is the precondition for judging freely—and, we can infer, for acting well.

Being able to choose your company by communicating your choices and wooing the consent of others is for Arendt a manifestation of *humanitas;* humanitas is, so to speak, the trait that underlies the "enlarged mentality." She cites Cicero's statement: "I prefer before heaven to go astray with Plato rather than hold true views with his opponents [the Pythagoreans]." Cicero's willingness—so like Cato's—to give up the truth for good company marked him as a nonspecialist:

> The humanist, because he is not a specialist, exerts a faculty of judgment or taste which is beyond the coercion which each specialty imposes upon us. . . . [For him] the question of freedom, of not being coerced, [is] the decisive one—even in philosophy, even in science, even in the arts. Cicero says: In what concerns my association with men and things, I refuse to be coerced even by truth, even by beauty.[17]

Arendt's statements indicate that she would have brought a different approach to the problem considered by Kant: why are the "connoisseurs of taste" not notably moral? She would not, it seems, have distinguished artificial and natural beauty and recommended the latter. What she thought was that a person possessed of *humanitas* has the means to check potentially destructive interest in beautiful objects. For judging too can be excessive.[18] We have already noted that thinking checks judging, but we still need to inquire about the relation of thinking and *humanitas*.

We have looked at a personal quality, *humanitas*, that signals a link between the enlarged mentality of judging and the solidarity of humankind. Humankind's unity, we saw, is to provide judging with its "standard" as it provides action with its principle. But in what sense is humankind a "standard"? When we judge particulars we need a *tertium comparationis*. Kant's "idea of mankind," insofar as it is an idea, is supplied to judgment, according to Kant, by Reason—it is a regulative idea. But in order to preserve the autonomy of the judging faculty as it judges particulars, we need another sort of *tertium comparationis*—one supplied by thinking. We need a particular that contains in itself a generality; we need what Arendt calls "representative figures" or what Kant called examples of humanity in men.

Arendt described the reflective procedure involved in an unpublished 1971 lecture (now with the Arendt papers):

The example is that particular which contains in itself, or is supposed to contain, a concept or general rule. How, for instance, are you able to judge, to evaluate, an act as courageous? In judging you say, spontaneously, without any derivation from general rules, this man has courage. If you were a Greek, you would have 'in the depth of your mind' the example of Achilles. Imagination is again necessary; you must have present Achilles though he is certainly absent. If we say of someone he is good, we have in the back of our minds the example of St. Francis or Jesus of Nazareth. The judgment has *exemplary validity* to the extent that the example is rightly chosen.

This spontaneous appeal to examples depends on prior choice, a right choice. How do we make this prior choice? It is here, it seems, that we see finally how judging is what Arendt calls a "side effect" of thinking. We are prepared to make particular judgments spontaneously by having *thought* about the question "What is courage?" and the question "What is goodness?" and settled on representative figures, examples—as Arendt settles on Socrates when she asks, "What is thinking?" Thinking's gift to judgment is these thought-things, these absent-made-present exemplary figures, which meaningfully represent for us "that which otherwise could not be defined."

When humankind is a present reality and not simply an idea or a projection into the future, the exemplary figures of all peoples are available for all people; we need not be Greeks to have in the depths of our minds Achilles or Socrates. Jaspers understood this when he set out to write *The Great Philosophers,* a world history of philosophy:

> Just as the prerequisite for world government in Jaspers' opinion is the renunciation of sovereignty for the sake of a world-wide federated political structure, so the prerequisite for . . . mutual understanding would be the renunciation, not of one's own tradition and national past, but of the binding authority and universal validity which tradition and past have always claimed.[19]

The opposites of "binding authority and universal validity" are guidance and exemplary validity. The "presence" of humanity *in the judger,* what Kant called "esteem for self (for humanity in us)," is the precondition of our ability to choose our examples: "man's dignity demands that he is seen, every single one . . . in his particularity, reflecting as such, but without any comparison and independent of time, mankind in general" (2:272).[20] Will shapes the character; judging shapes the *humanitas,* "the valid personality which once acquired, never leaves a man."[21]

7

Arendt's entire political theory—which, although it is not systematic, is a coherent whole—focuses on freedom for action and speech. In *The Life of the Mind* she is concerned with mental freedom, considering both the mind's freedom from the world and the freedom of each faculty within the mind. Conceptually, it is obvious what the two freedoms have in common: spontaneity and plurality, or indeterminacy and autonomy. But in practice, empirically, the connection is not so obvious, although it might well have been clear if "Judging" had been written. The way in which Arendt adopted Kant exhibits her concern for the empirical realm, in contrast to Kant's concern for the transcendental. She tried to show that judging and acting have the same principle, which is not transcendental, but empirical: we must act and judge in ways that do not violate the actually existing solidarity of mankind. "A secret trust in man, in the *humanitas* of the human race" animates action and judgment. Trust in *humanitas* is another way of saying trust in the love people have for meaning, the love they have for the existence of things and people, and the communicative pleasure they take in reflecting on those things and people.

This trust, paradoxically enough, was what the trial of Adolf Eichmann taught Hannah Arendt. When she wrote of *The Origins of Totalitarianism* shortly after World War II, she was still a "stateless person" and believed that the totalitarians had brought "radical evil" into the world. She renounced the "radical evil" notion with her idea that it was not a "radical" or original fault but thoughtlessness that characterized Eichmann, who shared with all people "innate repugnance for crime." But what made Eichmann not-think? We still face this question.

Arendt gives no answer in the existing pages of *The Life of the Mind*. But if thinking in its search for meaning gives to the will and to judgment invisibles, thought-things and examples, then we might suppose that when such gifts are refused, when a person neither wills nor judges, the mental need for those thought-things disappears. Thinking may be "good for nothing" in the world, but in the mind it is good for guidance—not legislation, but guidance.[22] Unless thinking has provided these examples, having asked, "What is courage?" and, "What is goodness?" the character and the personality are not shaped; unless thinking continues to provide examples, other forms of guidance or legislation *can* take over: truth, necessity, the law, or even the Führer's will. But thinking does not stop itself. It stops when people, having given up willing and judging, feel no internal need for thinking. It is difficult, if not impossible, to think when the other faculties are constrained.

Arendt always maintained that no serious political understanding could be expected from Philosophers who kept aloof from politics or who thought that philosophy ought to rule in the political realm and who offered Truths or Standards to the many unphilosophical souls.[23] When she turned at the end of her life to philosophy, to what she called, remembering her university studies with Heidegger, Husserl, and Jaspers, "my first amour,"[24] she did not abandon her criticism. What she does in *The Life of the Mind* is to show how a philosophical investigation of the Mind can offer political theory a portrait of the thinking, willing, and judging faculties *in their freedom*. When in the political realm there is no freedom for the manifestations of will and judgment, acting and speaking your judgments, the wonder is that the mind can still be active. Were it not able to be free *in itself*, this would not be so.

4

King Solomon Was Very Wise— So What's His Story?

A Lecture Celebrating Solidarity, 1981

1

In his play *Mother Courage*, Bertolt Brecht has the Cook, a get-along-as-best-you-can opportunist, sing out a catalogue of the "Great Souls of the Earth." The first stanza goes like this:

> King Solomon was very wise,
> So what's his story?
> He came to view his life with scorn,
> Yup, to wish he'd not been born;
> So, said he: all is vanity.
> King Solomon was very wise,
> But long before the day was out
> The consequence was clear, alas;
> His wisdom brought him to this pass.
> A man is better off without.

Ginny Jenny, a prostitute with heart of uncertain metal, takes up a hurdy-gurdy and sings the same stanza in the *Three Penny Opera*. Brecht, master plagiarist and self-plagiarist, gave the stanza to two different audiences, one in Berlin and one in Zurich, in what he suspected would be two years opening on great and horrible novelties: in 1928, on the brink of the Great Depression, and in 1939, on the brink of World War II.

In Brecht's plays the *Kleinevolk* are not slow to realize that the wisdom of kings, no matter what its source, is corruptible and eventually will be corrupted. They know that such wisdom, though it may do the mighty for a while at eventual great cost, will not do the unmighty at all. The second insight is the one Brecht stressed in 1939 by adding a stanza to the Cook's song that had not been part of the *Three Penny Opera* "King Solomon's Song." It goes like this:

God's Ten Commandments we have kept
And acted as we should.
It has not done us any good.
All you warm ones by your fires
O help us in our need so dire!
The Ten Commandments we have kept
And long before the day was out
The consequence was clear, alas:
Godliness brought us to this pass.
A man is better off without.

There is nothing distinctly modern about the predicaments of Brecht's *Kleinevolk;* Mother Courage makes her living and loses her children in the seventeenth-century Thirty Years War. One can also imagine that the thirty thousand Israelites forced into labor by King Solomon for the building of a temple to Yahweh in Jerusalem were not impressed to know that their king had instituted his corvée after having had wisdom bestowed on him by the Lord. And one can imagine that the soldiers conscripted into Solomon's army felt their obedience to the Ten Commandments to be ill-rewarded when their king disobeyed Commandment One and Yahweh's wrath was taken out on them. Shortly after King Solomon's son Rehoboam declaimed publicly, "My father imposed a heavy yoke upon you, but I shall add to your yoke; my father chastised you with lashes, but I shall chastise you with scorpions," the Israelite subjects revolted in a manner far from the godliness they had found they were better off without. But even if the Brechtian themes have been around as long as the Ten Commandments themselves, their urgency is always renewed as each generation contributes its distinctive types of corruption in high places and calamity in low places.

I am going to take up Brecht's "man is better off without" challenge in a way that would no doubt strike him as over-serious or under-ironic, for it seems to me that there *are* wisdoms we'd all be better off without, unless they are accompanied by a wisdom we'd be better off with. The story of King Solomon, as the Old Testament tells it, is rich with illustrations of wisdom gone awry, and I will take it as a launch in an effort to delineate some insufficient wisdom types, biblical and Greco-Roman. To put the matter another way, I am going to look at how wisdom for making judgments has been conceived and ask why judgment was not a topic for philosophical investigation until Immanuel Kant wrote his *Critique of Judgment*. This tour of judgment theories will bring us to the *Critique of Judgment* and to late and little-studied political writings of Immanuel Kant, writings published at the time of the French Revolution. In Kant's late writings I think we can find gestures at describing the wisdom for judgment we'd be better off with, a wisdom of which everyone has a share. It's not surprising to find these gestures at the beginning of the era of popular revolutions; and to reflect on them and explore them further, I will turn to the revolution of our immediate historical moment, the one now (1981) going on in Poland.

2

So, what was King Solomon's story?

This king, son of David, beloved of the Lord, had two sorts of wisdom—earthly and heavenly. He received his heavenly wisdom in the traditional Near Eastern manner; God gave it to him in a dream by night after he had humbly offered a prayer: "give . . . thy servant an understanding heart to judge thy people, that I may discern between good and bad." Solomon was given wisdom to keep God's statutes and God's commandments. On the other hand, the king had earthly wisdom: nature wisdom for classification of plants and animals, encyclopedism, skill in riddles, and, most importantly for his monarchical success, genius for public administration and what we now call management. The two wisdoms, it seems, did not overlap.

In piety and gratitude and to fulfill a promise made by his father, Solomon raised up a temple in Jerusalem for Yahweh. His reputation for wisdom in judgment had already spread through the land, and the temple so much further enhanced his glory that neighboring people came to marvel. The Queen of Sheba, a very clever woman and good at riddles, who came to test Solomon's wisdom, praised him ("Happy are thy men, happy are these thy servants, which stand continually before thee, and that hear thy wisdom") and then bestowed lavish gifts on his household. But in his capacity as ruler and administrator the king also introduced novelties that made the people of Israel much more "like unto the other nations" than they had ever been before: he kept a standing army, built fortifications—you can see the walls in Jerusalem today—divided his kingdom into administrative districts, promoted trade, and established a treasury. All of this, as a line of antimonarchist prophets pointed out, was ominous.

But for any reader of 1 Kings who wonders why this king, this judge and ruler, wise in God's commandments and worldly wise, was so foolish as to turn away from his God to foreign gods and take one of the most spectacular falls from worldly power in all of history, the text has no clear answer—in either its chronicle parts or its redactions. There is the usual Old Testamentarian suggestion that one should *cherchez la femme*. In this case, there was not one Eve but seven hundred of them, Solomon's wives and concubines. They corrupted Solomon, introducing him to the rites and religions of their native and sometimes conquered lands. But we do not learn why Solomon was susceptible. There is also the prophetic and Deuteronomistic charge that Solomon was hubristic, both because he accumulated wealth, Egyptian chariots, and golden ornaments for his rather Canaanite and pagan palace complex and because he arrogated unto himself the prerogatives of rulership and judgeship that were the Lord's alone. The prophets thought that human kingship had been a mistake from the first and that its dreary history was a history of God's wrath at the people of Israel for ever requesting a king. But Solomon, wise above all others and aware that his own father, David, a man of humble origins, had been chosen by the Lord for virtues that King Saul had lacked, should certainly have been able to think, long before Lord Acton did, that "power corrupts and absolute power corrupts absolutely." The wisdom—and the warnings—Solomon had received from Yahweh were of no help to Solomon, who in his retirement—so the legend goes— wrote the melancholy verses in Ecclesiastes to which Bertolt Brecht alludes:

> The thing that hath been it is that which shall
>   be; and that which is done is that which shall
>   be done; and there is no new thing under the
>   sun.
> I the Preacher was king over Israel in Jerusalem.
> And I gave my heart to seek and search out by
> wisdom
>   concerning all things that are done under heaven:
>   this sore travail hath God given to the sons of man
>   to be exercised therewith.
> I have seen all the works that are done under the
> sun;
>   and, behold, all is vanity and vexation of the
> spirit.

3

The early Christian apostles, who had learned the antimonarchist prophetic lesson well enough to render unto Caesar what was Caesar's and concentrate their attention on the rigorous charge their Lord had given them to live an unworldly life in this world, said again and again, "Judge not lest ye be judged." However, even though they had eschewed the troubling mixture of politics and religion on which the prophets had laid blame for the division and civil war among the Israelites, the Christians were not well defended against the temptation to judge as others judged, by human standards. The apostles had to warn the Christian fellowships repeatedly lest the members judge any but the faithful and lest they judge by any standard except faithfulness. St. Paul was most adamant:

> But with me it is a very small thing that I should be judged of you, or of man's judgment; yea, I judge not mine own self. For I know nothing by myself; yet I am not thereby justified, but he that judgeth me is the Lord.

In writing this, Paul was echoing the thought that follows on the "judge not that ye be not judged" imperative in the Gospel According to St. Matthew: "For with what judgment ye judge, and with what measure you mete, it shall be measured to you again." But Paul also added to this Synoptic tradition an element important to the little Christian communities living dispersed and powerless among non-Christian peoples. He wrote to the Corinthian fellowship about how they should keep their company pure:

> For what have I to do to judge them also that are without? Do not ye judge them that are within? But them that are without God judgeth. Therefore, put away from among yourselves that wicked person.

The Christians were to ignore the pagan swindlers and fornicators; their only charge was to judge and expel from within their own fellowship anyone who behaved like the pagans—and then to let God judge the pagans. Differences of custom among the faithful were to be ignored— "why do you pass judgment on your brother?"—and the failings of the faithful but weak breathren were to be borne; however, the distinction between the faithful and the unfaithful was to be respected absolutely. "I speak to your shame. Is it so that there is no wise man among you? No, not one that shall be able to judge between his breathren?" What does not proceed from faith is sin—and that is that.

This Pauline tradition has come forward at every time that Christians have been tempted to let mingle in their theology a Greekish mode of thought. In the Pauline tradition God's judgment is the only judgment, God's power the only power, God's will the only will. But opponents of this tradition, borrowing from an argument laid out in Plato's *Euthyphro*, have argued that if what is right is right only because God judges it so and does it, then God's judging and doing are arbitrary. The right, so this argument goes, must be right in and of itself—God must do what is right because it is right. But the specter raised by this argument is that rightness can be apprehended without faith in God and his power.

To this Greekish argument many within the Scholastic tradition offered thunderous and complex refutations. Duns Scotus declared that "the justice of God will be coextensive with the power of God." But no voice of protest was stronger than Martin Luther's as he, commenting on Paul's Epistle to the Romans, reaffirmed that "gracious election of God" or predestination is what makes a man good. No works of man avail for his salvation at all.

> For the fact is that there neither is nor can be any other reason for [God's] righteousness than His will. So why should man murmur that God does not act according to the Law, since this is impossible?

There is no Law and justice except God's will: "God is He for Whose will no cause or ground may be laid down as its rule and standard; for nothing is on a level with it or above it but it is itself the rule for all things."

Those Greekish types within the Christian tradition who objected to this mode of thinking emphasized not God's will but his knowledge: God knows the good and wills it. People should do likewise: know the good and then will it. St. Thomas Aquinas, writing just the kind of argument Luther abhorred, put the matter this way:

> The will never aims at evil without some error existing in the reason, at least with respect to a particular object of choice. For, since the object of the will is the apprehended good, the will cannot aim at evil unless in some way it is proposed to it as good; and this cannot take place without error. But in the divine knowledge there cannot be error. God's will, therefore, cannot tend towards evil.

That no man knowingly, without error, does evil is a Greekish notion; it was elaborated by both Plato and Aristotle, and Aquinas is here under the influence of the Aristotelian way. Aquinas, if I may presume to argue for him for a moment, would have said that what King Solomon mistook for a good—worldly power and an acquisition—was an evil. But those who adhere to what the theologian Karl Barth calls biblical or theological ethics say to such concern with knowledge what they say to all ethics of human standards—in effect, "vanity of vanities."

4

I have not recalled these intricate disputes in order to incite anyone to the sort of religious civil war that was going on in France when the first great modern theorist of human judgment, Michel de Montaigne, wrote his *Essais* or going on again in Germany when Mother Courage had no time for theories of judgment. Rather, I want to use these disputes to frame several generalizations even broader than the ones I've made already. Within the biblical or theological ethics tradition the problem of judgment is this: how to accord one's judgment with God's. The dispute within the Christian tradition is over whether this according comes from faith alone or also requires knowledge. To put the matter another way, the problem is whether the good and right are what the faithful do in obeying God or whether the faithful, through knowledge, do the good and right. The second alternative, which I have said is rather Greekish, overlaps with the problem of judgment as it was posed within the mainstream of the Greco-Roman tradition: namely, how to relate theory or knowledge and *praxis* or doing. Let me say a bit more about this Greekish problem—by way of introduction to the kind of wisdom for judgment I think we would be better off with.

Within the Greco-Roman tradition reflections on judgment were contained within the boundaries set by two questions: what is the good, and how could one, knowing the good, not do it? The first question was simply answered: the good is what one's intellectual vision, one's *nous*, apprehends. If this answer seems circular, that is probably because we do not share the assumption that made it seem straightforward to Plato and Aristotle, the assumption that people are intellectually fitted for the world in which they live and thus for a vision of the good. They do not, therefore, have to work at such a vision; the forces that organize the world will draw them to it, up out of the cave or from potentiality to actuality. Them—but not all of them. Plato and Aristotle also tried to explain why anyone should fail to see the good and thus fail to do it. They were as vexed about bad knowing as the biblical ethicists are about bad willing; ignorance is the Greek version of mortal sin.

Bad knowing was the cause of bad doing. And bad knowing meant either (in the Platonic mode) usurpation of the intellect by the appetites or (in the Aristotelian mode) insufficiently complete or actualized knowing that could not rule the appetites. Those who did know well and completely, on the other hand, did as they knew. Judgment, thus, meant deducing the appropriate means from knowledge of the end. Judgment did not concern ends but only means; it was not directed at ideas or principles but at deduction from ideas or principles, application of theory in practice. The ones who judged rightly were the ideal knowers, the philosophers (for Plato) or the men with practical wisdom (for Aristotle). These were not, needless to say, the Many.

We modern folk are so accustomed to the idea that divine judgments are at least up for interpretive judgment and not just revealed and to the idea that principles of organization and classification are at least up for theoretical judgment and not just intuited that we hardly realize how difficult it was for the first great theorist of judgment to entertain these ideas. This was Michel de Montaigne, critic of both religious dogmatism

and philosophical authority, advocate of versatility in judgment and close-
ness to *honnestes et habiles hommes*, the *Kleinevolk* given not to applying
artificial and externally located standards of judgment but to *self*-knowl-
edge. Montaigne hoped to be neither a "slave to precepts" nor a slave to
science but a cultivator, as he said, of "the seed of universal reason
imprinted in every man who is not denatured." The freedom for judgment Montaigne thought that each individual could, with great efforts
of self-formation and careful habituation, achieve for himself or herself
was not, however, something that he thought could be an achievement
of a community or an achievement for community. The discouragement
Montaigne felt whenever he contemplated the dreary political situation
in which he lived, the horror of the religious wars and the corruption in
almost every high place in France, cast him back on himself alone—
respectful of the common people but isolated from them. The case was
different with Immanuel Kant.

5

Kant realized that judgment, *Urteilskraft* as he called it, judgment-
power, is neither a matter of obedience nor of applying theory to *praxis*,
neither a matter of will nor of knowledge, neither of practical reason nor
of pure reason. But this realization did not come to him as he wrote his
major ethical work, the *Critique of Practical Reason*. Rather, it came when
he wrote the last of his trilogy of critiques, the *Critique of Judgment*. As an
ethicist, Kant was at the headwaters of both the Judeo-Christian and the
Greco-Roman mainstreams. If one has in mind the categorical imperative—act so that the maxim of your actions can be acceptable as a law for
all mankind—one really does not have to make judgments. The only
problem is the Judeo-Christian one of doing or willing the obvious. But
Kant also posed his categorical imperative in the theory-*praxis* terms that
are central to the Greco-Roman tradition. As he said, when a man "asks
himself where his duty lies, he is not in the least embarrassed for what
answer to give himself: he is instantly certain what he must do." In ethics,
"what is right in theory must work in practice." It will work without
conscious linkage through judgment; it will work "instantly." Reverting
again to the Judeo-Christian framework, Kant could claim that there is
all the difference in the world between judging man "as he appears, i.e.
as experience reveals him to us"—that is, "by an empirical standard
(before a human judge)—and judging him "according to the standard
of pure reason (at a divine tribunal)."
  In ethics the relations of the divine to the empirical and of theory to
practice are not problematic. Everywhere else they are. In the pages of
the *Berlinische Monatsschrift*, in 1793, after the first phase of the French

Revolution, Kant published an essay called "On the Old Saw: 'That may be right in Theory but it won't work in Practice.' " He first discusses the Aristotelian problem of theoretical completeness or actualization of knowledge and then remarks:

> However complete the theory may be, it is obvious that between theory and practice there must be a link, a connection and transition from one to the other. To the intellectual concept that contains the rule, an act of judgment must be noted whereby the practitioner discusses whether or not something is an instance of the rule. And since we cannot always lay down rules for judgment to observe in subsumption (as this would go on *ad infinitum*), there may be theoreticians who, for lack of judgment, can never be practical: physicians or jurists, for example, who have been well schooled but do not know what to do when they are summoned to a consultation.

What is lacking in the impractical physician or jurist is not a deduction from complete knowledge of an end but an act of judgment, of a separate faculty, that involves discussion, in relating generalizations and particular cases.

In reflections such as these, Kant had already seen more complexity in the relation of theory and practice than Aristotle saw: what is needed is not deduction but an act of judgment involving discussion. Kant went even further when he drew a crucial distinction between determinate judging and reflective judging. There is one set of problems when one judges determinately, subsuming a particular case under a general rule, and quite another when one starts with particular cases and goes in search of a rule. The two types of judging are different and require different talents. Here is a description from Kant's *Anthropology* of the differences as they relate to action:

> The domestic or civil servant under orders needs only to have understanding. The officer, to whom only a general rule is prescribed, and who is then left on his own, needs judgment to decide for himself what is to be done in a given case. The general, who must consider potential future cases and who must think out rules on his own, must have Reason. The talents necessary for such different uses are very distinct.

But what Kant here calls Reason is what he elsewhere calls reflecting judgment—thinking out or discovering the rules. As though aware that by confining judgment to the subsumption operation, the officer's talent, he is slighting the reflective operation, Kant generates another term in the *Anthropology*—intelligence or mother wit (*Witz* in German; *ingenium* in Latin). This is the faculty of discovering the universal for the particular. But notice that Kant finds this wit very mysterious:

> Mother wit belongs, as a distinct talent, to the liberality of disposition in the mutual exchange of ideas (*veniam damus petmusque vicissim* [we grant and plead for mutual goodwill]). Wit is a characteristic of the understanding which is hard to explain. It is like a favor given to you which contrasts with the strictness of judgment (*judicium discretivium*) in the application of the general to the particular (that is, of the concepts of class to those of the species), which not only hampers the faculty of assimilation, but also the inclination to use the faculty.

Kant then delineates three domains of this intelligence or wit, three modalities of this faculty he calls a "natural gift." First, it is comparative or productive; its operation extends knowledge, unlike that of strict judgment, determinate judgment, which is more corrective than extensive. "The activity of the comparative intelligence is rather like play; while that of judgment is more like business. Intelligence is primarily a flower of youth, judgment a ripe fruit of old age. He who unites both to a high degree in a product of the mind is perspicacious (*perspicax*)." Kant realized that the young, who are less fixed in their ways and more open to novelties, who have little invested in what has already been said by others and more need for adventure, are the always new world of judgment. Second, intelligence or wit can operate as sagacity or the gift of investigation:

> Discovery requires a natural gift of preliminary judgment (*judicium praevium*) as to where the truth may indeed be found; it requires the ability to hit upon the clues, and to use the least appearance of relevancy, in order to find or construct what one is seeking. . . . There are people of talent, who, so to speak, with divining rod in hand track down the treasures of knowledge.

Third, there is a talent for invention, called genius. The genius does not imitate or follow rules—though he or she must have skills; rather, the genius produces what is worthy of imitation or exemplary.

Determinate judgment must combine with each of these talents to bring them to their full power: it must correct the errors of playful comparative intelligence; it must temper the investigative talent with procedures for testing its hypotheses or flashes of insight; it must, as Kant says in the *Critique of Judgment*, "clip the wings" of genius to keep it from producing uncommunicative objects or "original nonsense." But it is important to note two facets of Kant's description: first, determinate

judgment may inhibit reflective judgment, and, second, reflective judgment "belongs to the liberality of disposition in the mutual exchange of
ideas." And let me add a third observation (to which we will return): each
of the three talents of intelligence or wit is concerned with novelty—
producing novel conjunctions or comparisons of particulars, investigat-
ing in novel ways, inventing novelties. Novelty is precisely what determinate judgment does not deal with, for novelty defies immediate subsumption under a rule. A reflective judge can never say there is nothing new
under the sun in King Solomon's mode or, in the Platonic-Aristotelian
mode, that theory can be complete and applicable to any case. Further-
more, to draw the web of these reflections together, it is when we deal
with novelties that mutuality or exchange of ideas is essential. Alone,
without—so to speak—a judging community, we would be unable or
perhaps just uninspired to search through unfamiliar particulars for
their meaning or their rule.

6

The most arresting and important example in Kant's writings of how
a judging community comes about in a context where a great novelty
defies immediate classification is his description of reactions to the French
Revolution:

> It is simply the mode of thinking of the spectators which reveals itself
> publicly in this game of great revolutions, and manifests such a universal
> yet disinterested sympathy for the players on one side against those
> on the other, even at the risk that this partiality could become very
> disadvantageous for them if discovered.

Kant's appreciation for those who, like himself, were filled with enthusiasm for the revolution even though their partiality cost them oppro-
brium, as it cost him, was what he called a "genuine enthusiasm"—that
is, an enthusiasm of the sort that "moves only toward what is ideal and,
indeed, to what is purely moral, such as the concept of right." Such
enthusiasm "cannot be grafted onto self-interest."

> The revolution of a gifted people which we have seen unfolding in our
> day may succeed or miscarry; it may be filled with misery and atrocities
> to the point that a sensible man, were he boldly to hope to execute it for
> a second time, would never resolve to make the experiment at such
> cost—this revolution, I say, nonetheless finds in the hearts of all specta-
> tors (who are not engaged in this game themselves) a wishful participa-
> tion that borders closely on enthusiasm, the very expression of which is

fraught with danger; this sympathy, therefore, can have no other cause than a moral predisposition in the human race.

No determinate judgment—the revolution is in accord with the purpose of the human race or it is not—but the "mode of thinking" of the spectators impressed Kant. His conclusion, therefore, does not seem warranted: why must we assume that a moral disposition in the human race is the chief cause of the spectator's sympathy? As a moral thinker, an upholder of the categorical imperative and the concept of duty, Kant's judgment on revolutions in general was not at all sympathetic:

> If a violent revolution, engendered by a bad constitution, introduces by illegal means a more legal constitution, to lead the people back to the earlier constitution would not be permitted; but, while the revolution lasted, each person who overtly or covertly shared in it would have justly incurred the punishment due to those who rebel.

Kant arrives at this position by taking the formalist route: there can be no principle of action favorable to revolutions, for they are illegal and illegality cannot be made into a principle or a maxim for all men. But he also adds a second argument against revolutionary action—and this one is not dependent on the requirements of his concept of duty. Revolutionary action, he argues, requires secrecy, and secrecy is inimical to public life: what cannot be publicized must not be permitted. With this second reason we are back in the domain of judgment, out of the domain of the categorical imperative. But here we must consider not cognitive judgment but aesthetic judgment—the judgment of spectators.

Disinterestedness in the objective existence of things and communicability are the hallmarks of aesthetic judgments. Interest in Kant's terms "presupposes or generates a want," and it is thus characteristic of merely sensual inclinations, which call for gratification by objects, or of commands concerning objectively existing goods, worthy objects of desire. The beautiful, unlike both the sensually pleasant and the morally good, pleases people freely *in the judging,* for it is not really the beautiful object *per se* that pleases but the harmony in the mental faculties of the judge. The free play of the faculties is in Kant's terms, universally communicable, and this means that the effect resulting from the free play of faculties is common to people as a *sensus communis.* When we expect that others will agree with our aesthetic judgments, we appeal to this *sensus communis.* Kant argues (against the skeptics) that cognition implies communicability, or harmony between cognitions and objects, because how could it be otherwise if objects are constituted in cognition? But he also argues in the *Critique of Judgment* that the state of mind of people as they make judgments, the relation of their faculties, the mood or feeling in them, must also be communicable—and this implies a common sense. To put the matter in other terms: we do not judge in solitude; we always appeal to others by invoking them imaginatively or by actually seeking out their agreement. So why not conclude that what is manifest in spectators' sympathy is just this: the joy in solidarity, in sharing of appreciation, sharing of judgments?

There is another condition of judging aesthetically that bears directly on Kant's attitude toward the French Revolution, and if we look into this condition we may see more about the spectator's attitude. The relation between mental faculties in aesthetic judging is not the same as their relation in cognition. In aesthetic judging imagination has understanding in its service and not vice versa as in cognition. In cognition imagination is set in motion by the senses, it collects the manifold of sense intuitions, and, in turn, it sets in motion the understanding that judges or unifies the manifold in concepts. In aesthetic judgments the imagination is not determined by the understanding's concepts or laws. Imagination does conform to the understanding's law, but freely, as a matter of subjective agreement, not because it *ought* to. Kant illustrates this difference in the relations among the faculties with the empirical observation that things bearing blatantly the marks of designers are repugnant to taste; the concept of purpose dominates the imagination, constrains its free play. It is characteristic of contemplation of the beautiful that it lasts over time and does not fall into utilitarianism: "we linger over the contemplation of the beautiful because this contemplation strengthens and reproduces itself."

> All stiff regularity (such as approximates to mathematical regularity) has something in it repugnant to taste; for our entertainment in the contemplation of it lasts for no length of time, but it rather, in so far as it has not expressly in view cognition or a definite practical purpose, produces weariness. On the other hand, that with which imagination can play in an unstudied and unpurposive manner is always new to us, and one does not get tired of looking at it.

Variety is the spice of aesthetic contemplation, the entertainment of the mental powers. And it is not much of a leap to the idea that novelty is the spur of political judgment in the reflecting not the determinate mode.

7

But, one may argue, if you aestheticize political affairs or turn them into a matter of reflecting judgment, you will have no way to say what is good and what is bad, what moral and what immoral, within these affairs. Appreciation of novelty for novelty's sake, one may argue, could easily be a step in the direction of horrendous novelties. I certainly do not disagree. But that is not what I am suggesting. When Kant tried to demonstrate the unity of morality and politics, he did so by eliminating politics, making it a subdivision of the moral, a reflection of the moral disposition and destiny of the race. I simply want to suggest that the differences in our manners and modes of judgment must be appreciated and each must be recognized for the importance of its contribution to our lives. Application of a moral rule and contemplation of what does not, as we initially apprehend it, have a rule are two different processes. My point is that contemplation of novelties or reflecting judgment must have its day in the sun for us to achieve what no religious concept of duty and no philosophical concept of theoretical intuition can ever bring about—community, sharing of judgments. Before the divine tribunal and in the arena of logical demonstration there is no need for debate, discussion, comparison, investigation, invention.

Because he left aside his own philosophical procedure when he invoked the concept of duty, Kant could find himself in the awkward position of at once appreciating the French Revolution as a spectator among spectators and condemning participation in revolutionary action. Kant himself had had to search for the categorical imperative, reflecting on the many varieties of happiness theories in order to find the rule of their insufficiency. But he then set up the categorical imperative as *the* rule and left aside questions about the judgment involved in applying the rule; he made the application unproblematic, automatic. Having opened a space for judgment between understanding (*Verstand*) and reason (*Vernunft*), he closed it again—for actors, if not for spectators. Having found a middle ground between the natural realm and the revealed divine realm, he abandoned it.

The conceptual space for judgment has been closed many times since as hopes for complete theoretical knowledge in politics and convictions about the hidden divine or at least inexorable processes behind historical particulars have marched on in ways both Kantian and un-Kantian. But events, as always, continue to send tremors through the most stolid and fixed of conceptual habits. One need only open the morning newspaper.

There, this morning, amidst joyless financial reports and dire economic prognostications, I read a report by Stefan Bratowski, chairman of the Polish Union of Journalists. Of the recent events in Poland, Mr. Bratowski writes:

> The only thing Polish society is tired of is tiredness. The atmosphere here is nervous, but it is not explosive. . . . [During the recent work

stoppages] there was no tumult. There was a picnic with shows by comedians and with lectures by management systems specialists.

The picnic and the comedians have many precedents in the history of revolutionary political initiatives. Remembering this, one can see that speaking of disinterestedness and communicability or publicity in connection with political action does not imply "aestheticizing" politics in any narrow, disciplinary sense of the word. It is not romantic to recall the joyfulness and *esprit de carnival* of political action—and not just revolutionary action, for political action in general implies new beginnings, novelties. Fine—but what about the management systems specialists?

Here is Mr. Bratowski's explanation—a reflection on the old saying that "it may be right in theory, but it won't work in practice":

> Political life in Poland can yield a leader in one day. But management needs many months or longer to adequately test a person's talent. The very practice of management means that you must create a system to discover, develop and promote skillful people. . . . In many ways Poland is suffering an old European disease—the university thinkers know economics, but they never ran a business. They don't know the real practice of management, or industry or commerce. They love to build castles in the clouds without any idea of how to reach them. . . . A university lecturer, named minister of prices, a man of goodwill and a high-brow, managed to panic the Polish market in one week.

Mr. Bratowski goes on to make the sad and misguided lament that "one can't simply import a Friedman or a Samuelson from the United States" to help out the Polish society as it tries to overcome its weariness. That is, he sees the difference between a political leader and a management systems specialist, or, as Kant would have it, between those gifted for reflecting judgment and those trained for determinate judgment, but he does not seem to appreciate the former. In this he is, as I have tried to indicate, a traditionalist, sharing the traditional disinclination to respect or even acknowledge the judgment faculty. He wants civil servants and officers—and it would be foolish to argue that Poland would be better off without them; but he neglects the leaders yielded up each day by the Polish society, or he takes them as a matter of course. But no equalitarian society could be better off without these.

I have been talking about Kant, a thinker of the time of the paradigmatic revolution, and I have done so because in that time, prior to management systems, he attempted to draw distinctions between modes of judging with precision and care. Here is Kant in his *Anthropology from a Pragmatic Point of View*, drawing distinctions, finding general principles, making judgments—and respecting the faculty that respects no distinctions of wealth or power:

> People with common sense [*sensus communis*] are familiar with the principles relating to practical application (*in concreto*). Scientific people are familiar with the principles themselves prior to their application (*in abstracto*). The understanding, which belongs to the first cognitive capacity, is sometimes called horse sense (*bon sens*), whereas the understanding belonging to the second cognitive faculty we call perspicacity (*ingenium perspicax*). Some praise [horse sense] fanatically and represent it as a storehouse of treasures hidden in the depths of the mind. Sometimes we even interpret the dictum of horse sense as an oracle. . . . [However] so much is certain, that, whenever the answer to a question rests upon general and innate rules of the understanding (the possession of which is called native intelligence or wit), we may be sure that seeking for studied and artificially established principles (school learning), and forming a conclusion accordingly, is less reliable than gradually coming to a conclusion from the grounds of judgment which lie in the dark recesses of the mind. This may be called logical tact, in which reflection looks at the object from many angles and produces the correct result without being aware of the acts occurring within the mind during the process.

Statements of how determinate judgment, cultivated and trained, needs reflecting judgment, a matter of native intelligence or wit, and of how the two modes could relate and complement each other are implicit in these distinctions.

8

It has very often been announced that mere human judgment would not stand between us and chaos if we decided that we were better off without the Ten Commandments pure and simple or that we were better off without a science of ethics pure and simple—that is, if we said that neither obedient willing nor good knowing is sufficient for us. This is because human judgment has seemed a matter of defiant or arrogant subjectivity, irrationalism, each person his or her own god, atomism, anarchy. This fear is, I think, based on a profound misunderstanding, for the remedy of which Kant made many suggestions. It is based on the idea that judging both is and should be imposition of order from above, from without, by application of standards, commandments or generalizations to cases, determination. A claim like Rosa Luxemburg's—that you learn revolutionary action in a revolution as you learn swimming in the water—sounds like a formula for drowning rather than what it is: a claim that you must make judgments as you go, reflectively. Kant made it clear that we are never less alone or arbitrary or subjective than when we are doing just that: searching, reflecting, establishing rules and meanings. Such activity would not and could not take place in solitude; it is community-founding by definition. People trained for applying rules with knowledge of the principles involved are crucial to any society. But from them we do not receive playful reflection, imagination, enthusiasm; they will not gather the people for picnics, they will not call for the comedians; and they cannot bring about Solidarity.

5

Cosmopolitan History

> History, the great mistress of wisdom, furnishes examples of all kinds: and every prudential, as well as moral precept, may be authorized by those events which her enlarged mirror is able to present to us.
>
> —David Hume, *History of England*

1

When President Harry Truman announced on August 6, 1945, that "the greatest achievement of organized science in history" had devastated the cities of Hiroshima and Nagasaki, commentators felt justified in proclaiming the commencement of "The Atomic Era." Since the days when this slogan graced the world's newspaper headlines, the habit of signaling epochs, which had become widespread after World War I, has become even more deeply entrenched. We now regularly label and announce seasons and decades of historical time; we characterize periods with the names of our energy sources and inventions; we invoke recent frightening events when we feel history is about to do what we are not sure it can do, "repeat itself." When we are uncertain about whether an invention, an event, or a crisis warrants elevation to turning-point status, we use the adjective that serves both pride and panic, "unprecedented." At times our habit helps us reaffirm human progress, and at times it expresses a despair that feels each longed-for wave of the future sweeping yet another generation into the category "lost." Periods of mourning prepare for periods of redefinition and vice versa.

This habit of epochal thinking, which could be dismissed as nothing but a predictable trait of The Age of Advertisement, the triumph of public relations over politics, looks like something we are not sure exists, a *Zeitgeist*, if it is compared to the habits of recent European philosophy and historiography. There too epoch-definition is crucial, and there too it serves both hope and despair.

Many philosophical critics have brought into adamant question optimistic visions of the Story of Mankind. They have rejected the notion that this story unrolls like a carpet up the grand staircase of Evolution or *Weltgeschichte* [World History]. The simplest form of this critique rests on a reversal: what was seen as going ever upwards is presented as going down fast. Cultures may rise, but they then must fall. Such cyclical images of birth and decay have been with us since the Greeks, persisting through centuries of linear Christian eschatological speculation; crises bring them to the fore. It was Scipio, weeping over his enemies, the Carthaginians, as he burnt their city to the ground and then uttering the insight that "all cities, nations and authorities must, like men, meet their doom," who inspired Polybius to his influential cyclical vision. Polybian reflections abound in Spengler's *Decline of the West,* which was finished in the wake of World War I. And they are obvious in Paul Valéry's famous letters called "The Crisis of the Mind" (1919):

> Elam, Ninevah, Babylon were but beautiful vague names, and the total ruin of those worlds had as little significance for us as their very existence. But France, England, Russia . . . these, too, would be beautiful names. *Lusitania,* too, is a beautiful name. And we see now that the abyss of history is deep enough to hold us all. We are aware that a civilization has the same frailty as a life.

Beneath the optimistic visions of the twentieth-century Christian and evolutionary theorists this analogy of a life and the lives of civilizations rests in a different form. Both Teilhard de Chardin and Julius Huxley invoked it. Others, like Reinhold Niebuhr, Karl Barth, and Nicholas Berdayev, have also used the analogy, though they have been careful to emphasize the evil of this world as they imagined future individual and species triumphs of the spirit. Those Marxists who still adhere to notions of history's dialectical forward march envision an agent of liberation in terms of the analogy—the proletariat acts like an individual.

The cyclical vision of history given such forceful modern formulation by Spengler has also been adapted to the optimism of evolutionary theories. Arnold Toynbee, for example, imagined the ups and downs of civilizations as ultimately headed upward. But, even though the social-evolutionary concern for periodization and progressivism lingers in Toynbee's work, he and a small number of other historians—Huizinga, Alfred and Max Weber, Teggert and Hinze—did offer a fundamental challenge to habits of historiography in the years between the wars. They included in their stories both "defeated" or "minor," "pariah" peoples and non-European peoples. That is, they did not see History as just one story, analogous to the unfolding of one life. Their aspiration was for cosmopolitan history. And further, they wrote with great self-consciousness about how their own historical moment influenced their conceptions of history: in a moment when progress seemed mocked by World War I, they tried to revise the prevailing notion that history is written, so to speak, looking down on previous periods of lesser development.

It was the absence of an analogy between individual lives and civilizations that made the post–World War II work of the French *Annales*
historians so troubling to the optimistic. Distinguishing among layers or
strata of history, Fernand Braudel and his colleagues emphasized not the
surface of "event history" or even the middle range of slow long-term
socio-economic change, but the deepest layer, the *longue durée* of history
changing so slowly as to be nearly "immobile." Beneath the events and
tendencies that can be gleaned from human records, lies the *profond* of
relations among populations, land, disease, climate. Braudel assumes that
until the eighteenth century and its economic and technological change
the vast majority of people in the world lived in or near this *profond*. That
is, he assumes that peasant life in all regions of the globe was similar
and similarly circumscribed, unchanging. Modern Western European
experience, it follows, is separated from this *longue durée* and its *mentalité*
as if by chasm, and its peculiar—perhaps even aberrant—characteristics
should not be used to measure the earlier periods. Indeed, Braudel seems
much more inclined to measure the modern period against the earlier
and to suggest that, if we but had the proper deep perspective on our
fast-changing world, we could discover that it too is really relatively
immobile. All history, Braudel suggests, is really very slow history, and
humanity is never the master of its destiny.[1]

Individuals are of as little significance in this type of "slow history" as
they are in those of the French "structuralists" and "post-structuralists"
who have cast into question traditional ways of writing the "history of
ideas." Perhaps epochs, Michel Foucault and others have argued, are
separated by chasms of *discours*, of ways of conceptualizing. Perhaps there
is real discontinuity in history—a plurality of stories, a garden of forking
paths; perhaps the people of one epoch are separated from those of
another by more than the years and levels of development that traditional
historians have found in both the stages of individual lives and the Ages
of Man. To the distress of historians who put the wills and actions of
individuals or the achievements of a generic (although certainly not
genderless) "Man" at the center of their narratives, these recent critics
have proposed archaeologies of discrete, causally unrelated *epistemes* and
notions of history as a process without a subject. To "humanists" writing
either linear or cyclical histories the French materialists and epistemic
historians are "antihumanists."

The debate between the "humanists" and the "antihumanists" is an
important element of the recent enormous ferment over History and the
possibility that History has lessons to teach. The two world wars, the first
of which was supposed to make the second impossible, and the second
of which has laced our lives with fears for a possible third, have induced
in lay people and scholars alike the sense that our lives, the life of

the species, hang on historical understanding. The habit of epochal definition, which reflects this sense, takes many forms, but the questions behind those forms are the same: are the phenomena of our century without historical precedent, unununderstandable in our learned historical languages of continuity and causation? Are the causes and consequences of those events, *au fond,* controllable by human action? These questions persist even when historical theories go in directions that seem to minimize them. That is, they persist even when events are judged with the measure of *durées* beyond the vision of present actors or when they are judged as epiphenomena of epistemes or processes; and they persist when events are judged as though they were signs of an invisible but nonetheless coming epoch of barbarism or of spiritual upsurge. The deep past and deep structures do not swallow these questions; and signs of the future—for better or worse—do not still them.

In this essay I would like to take up four historical visions that are neither traditionally humanist nor antihumanist. These visions do not depend on analogies between individuals and civilizations in either linear or cyclical frames. And they do not posit layers or strata of history into which both individuals and civilizations are set: although, as I will try to show, they do tend toward the cosmopolitanism that is, I think, the most important feature of *Annales* historiography. The visions were articulated in the years immediately after World War II, in a stunned, still moment of what Hannah Arendt then called "bitter realization that nothing has been promised us, no Messianic Age, no classless society, no paradise after death."[2] This was a moment of commencement, like the Year One of the French revolutionaries, but also a moment undefined, empty, out of time even though produced by six years of unfathomable misery, twelve years of Hitler's Reich, sixteen years of Stalinism. The European "economic miracle" and the American and Soviet cold war closed this moment over quickly enough, but those who tried then to understand what had happened in their lifetimes still have, I think, much to teach us.

2

In the years immediately after the war, Karl Jaspers wrote *The Origin and Goal of History* (1949) and began a never-completed series of volumes called *The Great Philosophers.* Martin Heidegger, who had announced in his 1947 "Letter on Humanism" a turn (*Kehre*) from his prewar work, wrote a series of essays culminating in "The Question Concerning Technology" (1949). Theodor Adorno and Max Horkheimer, exiled in America, collaborated on *The Dialectic of Enlightenment* (1944 and 1947).

Hannah Arendt completed *The Origins of Totalitarianism* (1951), a work that set the questions for her succeeding essays, collected in *Between Past and Future* (1961), and another book, *The Human Condition* (1958). Theoretically incompatible as they certainly are in almost every other respect, these works are, nonetheless, informed by a common vision of Western history. To put the view in very summary terms: these thinkers saw the centuries from Plato to Nietzsche as one epoch, and they saw themselves as standing on the threshold of another—an undefined and only vaguely imaginable new era.

In this vision the Western tradition commenced with the shift from early Greek to Platonic and Aristotelian philosophy; in this shift were rooted "the dialectic of enlightenment," "the forgetfulness of Being," and the "rationalization of Western science." Through the Medieval and Renaissance mergers of Greek and Judeo-Christian thought, this history continued with various transformations up to the decisive turning point of the seventeenth-century scientific philosophizing of Descartes and his heirs. Science and philosophy together prepared the ground for the tremendous eighteenth- and nineteenth-century advances in technology as well as for a novel self-consciousness that then manifested itself in the philosophical history or historical philosophizing of Hegel and his critics, the post-Hegelians, Marx, Kierkegaard, and Nietzsche chief among them. A fundamentally new era, a new commencement, was prepared by the triumph of technology and the post-Hegelian "end of metaphysics." On the threshold of this new era Jaspers called for a "new way of thinking," Heidegger for thinking rather than metaphysics, the Frankfurters for "a radical critique," and Arendt for "a new science of politics." Each of these thinkers held that the world had been made one in technological terms and that this unity meant that the path peculiar to Europe had come to a great fork: either the Europeanization or technologization of the earth would continue unchecked until ultimate disaster resulted, or Western people, in a moment of unprecedented self-consciousness, realizing that their technology imperiled the earth, would make a new turn, an unprecedented turn. Which path would be taken was not predicted—neither a new cycle nor a linear advance was expected; and these thinkers, importantly, disagreed completely about the individual or collective sources whence new initiatives might spring forth in response to the crisis.

In the philosophical tradition that prevailed after the war in England and America, the vision these thinkers shared was classified as "speculative" or "formal" philosophy of history in contrast to "critical" or "material" philosophy of history. That is, it was argued that these thinkers, like latter day Hegelians, were seeking a dominant pattern or key cause in history rather than concentrating their attention on the nature of historical inquiry and the problems of historiographical method. But this distinction itself and the facility with which it was widely accepted were part of the historical situation Jaspers, Heidegger, Arendt, and the Frankfurters addressed. While they did not reject concern for historiographical method, they did refuse to think of history as that which is written by historians; and they did refuse to place epistemological questions at the center of a philosophy itself, except insofar as they viewed philosophy as *fallen*, in a historical situation, into epistemology. However, speculative philosophy of history in the Hegelian manner was not their alternative. They saw Hegelianism as the culmination of a tradition to be overcome—and not overcome with new systematic speculations about the patterns or essential moving forces of history.

For those who distinguish speculative and critical philosophies of history, Heidegger in particular looks like a direct descendant of Hegel. Heidegger appears to have echoed the Idealist claim that Western history is the history of Western philosophy and, further, that the history of Western philosophy is no mere history of human thoughts but the unfolding of something rather like the Hegelian *Geist*—that is, *Seinsgeschichte*, Being-as-History. In such a caricature of his views Heidegger appears as a speculator who has presented humans as minds on Being's marionette strings.

More than any other of the postwar thinkers under consideration here, Heidegger struggled with the philosophical language of the long epoch from Plato to Nietzsche. He experimented with many ways of formulating the question he thought had gone unasked in this epoch—the *Seinsfrage*, the Being-question. Since Plato, he said, philosophers have distinguished between Being and beings or essents. But they have not questioned Being itself; they have only approached Being *via* their questions about the origin, nature, or unity of beings. The various ways in which the Being/ beings distinction has been drawn have all assumed that Being is simply the supreme or original essent, a unique kind of essent lying before or beyond all other essents, an object to be conceptualized or correctly represented in a special, privileged modality of the true knowledge relation people have sought with all other objects. All ways toward Being have been ways from beings and for the sake of knowledge of or power over beings.

For the Greek thinkers prior to Plato, Heidegger argued, there was no gulf between knowing people—the type of essent characterized by possession of reason—and Being. The rift that arose with Plato's philosophy was not, however, simply an error on Plato's part—either in Plato's own terms or in Heidegger's. In his postwar efforts to compass the history of metaphysics, Heidegger attributed the rift to

Being. Being withdrew, concealed itself; the epoch of Western meta-physics is Being's *epoche* or hiddenness.

Heidegger himself acknowledged that the notion of *Seinsgeschichte* represents *Sein* as something like another variation on the metaphysical notion of a supreme supersensible object to be grasped in its historical agency, in its effects. Heidegger despaired of representational thinking itself as he struggled with his dilemma: how to present Being's "presencing" in a language not informed by the humanistic history of "oblivion to Being." The problem is rather like the one Kierkegaard once invoked to describe Socratic irony: how to present an elf wearing the magic cap that makes him invisible. Heidegger resorted to his many lexigraphical and linguistic inventions to indicate the ways in which man and Being historically have concerned each other. For example, to present the contemporary configuration of man and Being that is technology, he coined the term *Ge-Stell* (enframing) and used it to meditate on what he called the *Er-eignis*, the event or belonging and appropriation to each other of man and Being. These words were intended to gesture toward or hint at a fundamental relation—not a humanistic form of knowledge, but a form of belonging. Heidegger imagined that the *Ge-Stell*, the technological frame as the present particular form of belonging, might, if properly understood, reveal the promise of a redemptive vision of man and Being in their true *Er-eignis*.

Heidegger's notion of *Seinsgeschichte*, at first glance such an Idealist-looking notion, is not as far removed from the vision of Adorno and Horkheimer as the latter, always critical of Heidegger, supposed. Heidegger noted in his 1947 "Letter on Humanism" that the "Marxist view of history (*Geschichte*) is superior to all other historical accounts (*Histoire*)," because it presents the modern experience of homelessness, alienation (*Entfremdung*) in a technologized world. Heidegger reflected that:

> The essence of materialism is concealed in the essence of technology, about which much has been written but little has been thought. Technology is in its essence a destiny within the history of Being and of the truth of Being, a truth that lies in oblivion. . . . As a form of truth, technology is grounded in the history of metaphysics, which is itself a distinctive and up to now the only perceptible phase of the history of Being. No matter which of the various positions one chooses to adopt toward the doctrines of communism and to their foundation, from the point of view of the history of Being, it is certain that an eventual experience of what is world history speaks out of it.[3]

Heidegger thought that in his "Theses on Feuerbach" the young Marx had gestured toward a conception of new beginnings that only needed to be put in proper perspective:

> it has been demanded of philosophy that it no longer interpret the world and prowl around abstract speculations, that it rather succeed in practically changing it. Except that the worldchanging, so thought, requires in advance that thinking transform itself, since also behind the demand already mentioned stands a changing of thought.[4]

Over this analysis—thus abstractly stated, without specification of *what* transformation thinking would have to work upon itself—Heidegger and the Frankfurt Marxists would not have disagreed.

The postwar vision of Adorno and Horkheimer involves a critique of Marxism that places crucial emphasis on ideology and culture, or, more broadly, on "the patterns of thought." Although they did not abandon the Marxist project of a critique of political economy, they did refocus that project into a critique of technical civilization; and behind this civilization, they argued, lay "instrumental reason," no mere superstructure but the very source of technical civilization. The aim of critical theory, as it is presented in *The Dialectic of Enlightenment* and the works immediately succeeding that book, was an appeal to the potential consciousness of people who could transform capitalist society, who could become enlightened about the restrictions on enlightenment operating in the long epoch from the Greeks to the post-Hegelians. The Frankfurters did not consider revolution the natural result of historical necessities, contradictions; if a revolution was to come, it would have to commence with a rupturing of the historical chains enslaving theoretical reason. Jürgen Habermas once referred to *The Dialectic of Enlightenment* as a "philosophization of *Capital*"[5]—and that is what Heidegger in his own context called "a changing of thought."

In their *The Dialectic of Enlightenment*, a work with the significant subtitle "Philosophical Fragments," Adorno and Horkheimer reject the systematization of history and philosophy that they consider to be the legacy of German Idealism. Along with this critical departure, they reject the distinction with which Idealist histories of ideas traditionally began—namely, the distinction between *mythos* and *logos*. They analyze Homer's *Odyssey* in order to criticize the notion that in Homer's time there was a mythic, prephilosophical unity of man and nature, subject and object, from which later disunities arose. Wily Odysseus, they claim, was the prototype of "enlightenment" efforts to liberate man from nature. This Greek "bourgeois" dominated his own nature, making sacrifices and repressing immediate needs, in order to dominate nature; his cunning was "rational calculation," his craftiness "instrumental reason." But even though they see the emergence of subject/object, man/nature distinctions in Homer's tale, Adorno and Horkheimer also argue—and in this they are not far from Heidegger—that the early Greek philosophical concept of nature, *physis,* did not involve distinguishing of mind or dominating subjectivity from the world of objects. Centuries of transformation had to come before matter was viewed in the seventeenth century as "natural and disenchanted," of "no internal significance," mere stuff to be dominated, used and abused, by instrumentalizing subjects. Like Heidegger, Adorno and Horkheimer locate the foundations of modern technology in this period of Baconian "knowledge is power."

Hannah Arendt originally conceived *The Human Condition* as a completion of *The Origins of Totalitarianism;* it was to present a critique of the Marxist philosophy of history and of Marxism's historical perversion in Stalinism. But although she and the Frankfurters rejected the Marxist view of history, they did so for different reasons. She, too, called for a new way of thinking about politics, but not because she expected theoretical reason, liberated, to prepare the way for revolution. She wanted, rather, to show how traditional ways of thinking have obscured from view the source of political renewal and revolution—action, deeds—and contributed to the expectation that historical processes and governments, not the ways in which people think and act, are the essential concern of political theory.

Arendt viewed Marx as the crucial theorist of labor, and it is the purpose of her book to distinguish action from labor and work. Arendt's distinction among the modalities of the *vita activa* are drawn in basically two ways: first, she locates labor, work, and action in their relations to the public (political) and private (household) spheres; and second, she sketches the transformation of these relations and spheres from classical Greece to the post-Hegelians. She shows how labor, originally the least public and least valued activity, came to be viewed by Marx as the highest ranking human activity, and how labor, further, came to be construed by Marx as a kind of work or fabrication and ultimately as history-making. Arendt argues that our era is one in which action, "new beginnings," have virtually disappeared. Action is "an experience for the privileged few," and those few are scientists or technologists, acting into nature, not citizens acting in the public space.[6] Or, to put the same conclusion in other terms: she argues that we no longer know what history is. The central element of Arendt's critique of Marx is that, following in a tradition that began with Plato, he postulated a history-fabricating force—the class struggle—and thereby failed to understand politics. For her,

Nothing, indicates more clearly the political nature of history—its being a story of actions and deeds rather than of trends and forces or ideas—

than the introduction of an invisible actor behind the scenes whom we find in all philosophies of history, which for this reason alone can be recognized as political philosophies in disguise.[7]

In Arendt's view the epoch from Plato to Nietzsche was one in which politics was not taken seriously, or in which political action was misunderstood as the effect of an extrapolitical agency—a God, Providence, Nature, an invisible hand, a *Weltgeist*, a class struggle, or, she said in criticism of Heidegger, a *Seinsgeschichte*, Being-as-History. The corollary to this philosophical faith in extrapolitical agencies has been political faith in states—whether those be city-states led by philosopher-kings, sovereign states with divine dispensations, dictatorships of classes installed by historical necessity, or states that in secularizing times have manufactured a manifest destiny.

Although they took very different attitudes toward history, Arendt and Heidegger did, however, agree about the original Platonic rift with which our metaphysical tradition commenced. When Being, in the Platonic formulation of *Idea*, was separated from beings and beings were construed as appearances, mutable imitations of Being, actions came to join beings in the realm to be transcended by the philosopher's contemplative gaze. In the last years of her life, as she attempted to complete *The Life of the Mind*, a complement to her earlier work on the *vita activa*, Arendt tried to describe thinking as a self-reflexive interior dialogue, not a still, contemplative gazing at the highest object, Being. Like Heidegger, she wanted to overcome the quest for a true relation between thinking and Being-as-object. But this was not because she thought that the Being-question had gone unasked in metaphysics; it was because she understood thinking as a purposeless, unintentional (not related to objects) interior conversation. Thinking, she said, is not instrumental knowing or cognition, not truth-seeking; thinking seeks *meaning*, and never reaches an end to its quest.

Like Heidegger, Arendt focused her attention on how thinking, after being reduced to scientific cognition by the Cartesians, had with Nietzsche become associated with willing and the will-to-power. But she followed her discussion of Nietzsche with one of Heidegger himself in which she argued that he, like Nietzsche, identified thinking and willing.[8] That is, she repudiated, as she had since *The Human Condition*, the idea that a change in thinking implies a change in acting or brings on such a change in acting. She wanted to preserve for thinking the condition she felt it required: withdrawal from the world of action for its self-reflexive dialogue. If thinking and action are related, she claimed, it is through the mediation of judging—a "side effect" of thinking. For judging, appearances or particulars, including actions, are the elements of a story, history. What thinking gives judging is not truth formulas or rules but memories of its wide travelling through time and space, its dialogic quest for meaning: thinking frees judgment to face particulars as such and to search reflectively for what generalities may unite them.

Between Arendt and her teacher Karl Jaspers there was no disagreement about the centrality of judging; but his sense for the ranges to which thought must go in order to prepare for judgment was greater—geographically, if not temporally. The key to Jaspers' endeavor in *The Origin and Goal of History* is the statement with which he opens his book: "By virtue of the extent and depth to which it has transformed human life, our age is of the most incisive significance. It requires the whole history of mankind to furnish us with standards by which to measure the meaning of what is happening at the present time."[9] Heidegger, the Frankfurters, and Arendt would have agreed that the meaning of the present requires for its measure the whole history of humanity, but Jaspers was the one postwar European philosopher who thought of humanity in un-Eurocentric terms. The notion that ours is the era in which European patterns of thought and technology are reaching the non-European world with unprecedented force and consequence was shared by all these Europeans. But Jaspers was the one philosopher who, following the empirical work of Alfred and Max Weber, looked for the origin of this situation in world history, not just European history.

Jaspers, writing not a philosophy of history designed to present a moving force or idea but what his chief philosophical mentor, Immanuel Kant, had called "history with a cosmopolitan intent," formulated an Idea (in the Kantian sense) of the origin and goal of world history. The origin he named "The Axial Period" and located in the centuries from 800 to 500 B.C., when Confucius and Lao-tsu lived in China, when India produced the *Upanishads* and Buddha, when the prophets appeared in Palestine and Zarathustra taught in Iran, when in Greece there were epic, lyric, and tragic poets, historians, philosophers. The Axial Period, which began while the main geographical regions—China, India, and Greece—were dotted with small states and city-states and laced with commercial travellers and itinerant teachers, ended in the anarchy that ushered in mighty empires and enormous efforts at technological and organizational planning. But, although the Axial Period ended with rigidification, during it the great individuals, who lived unknown to each other in the three main geographical regions, had induced an irreversible "forward leap" for humanity.

This overall modification of humanity may be termed spiritualization. The unquestioned grasp on life was loosened, the calm of polarities becomes the disquiet of opposites and antimonies. Man is no longer enclosed within himself and thereby [is] open to new and boundless possibilities. He can hear and understand what no one had hitherto asked or proclaimed. The unheard-of becomes manifest. Together with his world and his own self, Being becomes sensible to man, but not with finality: the question remains.[10]

Far from thinking that the question of Being had gone unthought in this age, Jaspers imagined it asked in the most multifarious ways—and never answered, as it cannot be, definitively.

Jaspers believed that the Axial Period is still the historical matrix from which world civilizations take their bearings. And he hoped that this ultimately mysterious—not empirically explainable—moment of world-wide commonality could give humanity an image of a goal, a new commonality, from which bearings could be taken for the future.

> The history of mankind visible to us took, so to speak, two breaths. The first led from the Promethean Age [the genesis of speech, tools, and the use of fire] *via* the ancient civilizations to the Axial Period and its consequences. The second started with the scientific-technological, the new Promethean Age [of the seventeenth century] and may lead, through constructions that will be analogous to the organization and planning of the ancient civilizations, into a new, a second Axial Period, to the final process of becoming-human, which is still remote and invisible to us.[11]

Jaspers did not live in expectation of the new Axial Period; he simply posited it as a "regulative Idea" (in Kant's term), and he did not imagine that the history of philosophy in itself provided any forward-moving impulse that would lead in this direction. *The Great Philosophers,* begun after the war, is not a chronological history of philosophy. Jaspers considers the great philosophers as "contemporaries in the realm of a single, unbroken present, comprising three millenia . . . in a timeless area of human kinship."[12] They are "a great community" that lived during the epoch initiated with the Axial Period and embracing all the centuries to the end of the nineteenth. Jaspers' purpose is communication:

> listening, learning and loving, we shall try to gain admittance to this community, to be at home among the philosophers, and we shall succeed to the extent that philosophy had become our concern. . . . What concerns us is not historic knowledge about philosophy but philosophy itself as it comes to us in all its power from the great philosophers.[13]

The Great Philosophers is thus as wide in its geographical range as *The Origin and Goal of History;* Jaspers writes of "world philosophy." And he considers as philosophers not only the cast of characters usually found in textbooks but also the "paradigmatic individuals," Socrates, Confucius, Buddha, and Jesus of Nazareth, whose importance for "the history of man" has been greatest. The most important individuals for the history of philosophy have been the "seminal thinkers," Plato, Augustine, and Kant. But Jaspers also considers those he classifies as metaphysicians and religious visionaries, creative orderers and makers of systems, and rebellious awakeners and negators.

Although Jaspers was as critical of the limitations of Greek philosophy as the others under consideration here, he did not use his non-Greek originary figures to point out the Greek "error"—whether that be metaphysics as oblivion of Being, instrumental reason, or unseriousness about politics. He was an eclectic who made judgments about all the great philosophers with the measure of his ideal—worldwide communication. His vision is synthetic—or better, dialogic, communitarian—and his most critical expositions were reserved for those philosophers who were exclusionary or intolerant of others. He classified the great philosophers neither by historical period nor by affinities in their philosophical assumptions or *Weltanschauungen* but by their importance for the great community of philosophical concern, their place in an ongoing, perennially renewed conversation. He felt that the philosophical community, thus understood, could be exemplary to any present—or future—cosmopolitan philosophical community.

3

What the thinkers I have considered here had in common is a "sense of an ending." They judged their own era to be fundamentally disconnected from the long epoch preceding; they were able to imagine real historical discontinuity; and they could use the word "unprecedented" in a strong sense of both the particular events of World War II and the general event of modern technology. Because, to use a phrase of de Tocqueville's that Hannah Arendt was fond of citing, "the past no longer casts its light upon the future," the past had to be understood for the purpose of present life as what we *are no longer.* This is not to say that the past is "dead" or that we are not affected internally or externally by past developments; it is to say, rather, that to learn from the past we have to begin with the realizations that it is *other* and that its meanings must be *sought*—they are not going to be revealed to us or in us with the unfolding of an inevitable process. As the past is understood as other, the false expectations fettering our vision are removed; as we are, so to speak, cast loose upon the world, we can appreciate the world, all the peoples of the world, as potentially affected by a condition that the West has reached. How this condition that has come about in the West will affect others is unknown.

Throughout this essay I have been stressing this common vision of world history, this epochal vision. But it is as important to note that the philosophical orientations of the thinkers I have considered are in other respects quite different. Heidegger, Adorno, and Horkheimer have been among the most influential midcentury sources for the "antihumanist" mode of thought. Heidegger's turn (*Kehre*) from concern for *Dasein*, human being, and for human consciousness or subjectivity to his later concern for *Seinsgeschichte* and the Frankfurters' turn from concern for a historically necessitated proletarian revolution to their later concern for a cultural-ideological nexus that all but completely determines all human thought and action, making it seem like little but the product of such a nexus, have aided those who call into question the humanist preoccupation with human initiatives. Arendt and Jaspers, on the other hand, are much closer to "humanist" efforts to reassert freedom and the possibilities for human "new beginnings." These differences are very stark if each of these thinkers is approached with questions about how and by whom the present moment of historical transition or threshold is to be judged.

It is interesting to note that Heidegger, struggling with the legacy of German Idealist philosophy of history, and Adorno and Horkheimer, struggling with the legacy of Marxian materialist philosophy of history, came to consider poets and artists as the individuals capable of liberated vision. In his late essays, Heidegger presents the poets—and particularly Hölderlin—as "attuned" to Being and possessed of (perhaps possessed *by*) language true to Being. In the technologizing world, Hölderlin writes:

> But where danger is, grows
> The saving power also . . .

And Heidegger comments: "Could it be that [Being's] revealing lays claim to the arts most primarily, so that they for their part may expressly foster the growth of the saving power, may awaken and found anew our vision of that which grants and our trust in it?"[14] Adorno and Horkheimer for their part tried to imagine how artists in the role of culture critics could be both of modern technological culture and critical of it as harbingers of something new—how they could practice "immanent critique." They were more preoccupied with the epistemological problems so important to contemporary analytic thought than any of the other thinkers we have considered, for their concern was with the status and means of social *science.* But artists are, for them, exemplary practitioners of "negative dialectics"—not producers of systematic positive visions, but novel in their complex role as critics of the old visions rooted in the nexus of instrumental reason. Both Heidegger and the Frankfurters assumed that those whose work grew from *techne,* from craft traditions rooted in premetaphysical or proto-instrumental cultures, could speak from experiences of making quite different from those who have produced or are completely ensnared in advanced technological civilization.

Because their focus was on the advanced "capitalist" and "socialist" societies of the West, the Frankfurters developed their approach to world history from the Western point of influence. Heidegger, too, considered the end of metaphysical philosophy as "the beginning of the world civilization based upon Western European thinking." But he also tried to imagine how Western European thinking might—in a dialogue over the language of such thinking—be touched by non-European thinking. His hope for such a possibility waned after the immediate postwar years, however, as is obvious in his 1953–1954 "Dialogue on Language between a Japanese and an Inquirer." In this dialogue, Heidegger speaks of conversations he once had with the Japanese Count Kuki:

I: . . . He could say in European languages whatever was under discussion. . . . It was I to whom the spirit of the Japanese language remained closed—as it is to this day.

J: The language of the dialogue shifted everything to European.

I: Yet the dialogue tried to *say* the essential nature of Eastasian art and poetry.

J: . . . the language of the dialogue constantly destroyed the possibility of saying what the dialogue was about.

I: Some time ago I called language, clumsily enough, the house of Being. If man by virtue of his language dwells within the claim and call of Being, then we Europeans presumably dwell in an entirely different house than Eastasian man.

J: Assuming that the languages of the two are not merely different but are other in nature, and radically so.

I: And so a dialogue from house to house remains nearly impossible.[15]

Heidegger's hope for the "nearly impossible" faded as he came to feel that the process he called "the complete Europeanization of the earth and man" continued.

Arendt and Jaspers, by contrast, did not single out artists or poets as the ones standing in a unique relation to the epoch past or to present possibilities. They did not view language as the "house of Being" or consider thinking as responding to Being; and they did not try to reconstitute theoretical reason in a liberated, truly enlightened form. Both shared the democratic idea that thinking is (in Arendt's phrase) "a possibility for every one" or that (in Jaspers' phrase) "philosophy is for everyman." The internal communication that they felt thinking to be is not fundamentally compromised by epochal conditions; it is a perennial possibility: people discover it by carrying on in themselves the conversations they have had with others, so that plurality is the precondition for individual thinking. The subject/object dichotomy so crucial in different ways to Heidegger and to the Frankfurters, is not part of this description of thinking as an internal conversation between (in Arendt's formulation) "me and myself." Similarly, although they certainly realized the rarity of action in the modern world, they both assumed that action in its spontaneity is possible in all political-cultural conditions short of total terror or "total domination." Jaspers felt that such action needed an Idea of the goal of history for its guidance, as he felt that thinking needs the exemplary "great community" of philosophers for its guidance. Arendt put much more stress on the political conditions for thought and action. Thinking needs leisure for its withdrawal, and action requires a public space opened by prior actions and guaranteed by fundamental rights of speech and assembly.

But both Arendt and Jaspers saw in the potentiality of a relation between individual internal conversation, dialogic thinking, and unlimited communication among individuals the only hope in a technologizing world. The political analogue to such a hope is a relation between the achieved and preservable particularities of cultural and national experience and creatable communication among these particularities. As Arendt puts it: "Everything then seems to depend upon the possibility of bringing the national pasts in their original disparateness, into communication with each other as the only way to catch up with the global system of communication which covers the surface of the earth."[16] Such a vision has much in common with earlier, Enlightenment cosmopolitanism. But it is not traditionally "humanistic," in the sense that it is not built upon a philosophy of Man. In Arendt's words again: "A philosophy of mankind is distinguished from a philosophy of man by its insistence that not Man, talking to himself in the dialogue of solitude, but men talking and communicating with each other, inhabit the earth."[17]

The cosmopolitanism of the Enlightenment, which fostered such a library of armchair travelogues and histories, was predicated on the assumption that people are fundamentally the same, Man. History, to use David Hume's metaphor, is like a mirror: it shows present Man his single story, his universal precedents, and the singularity of the story reinforced the sexism of the "Man." The postwar cosmopolitan philosophers began, on the other hand, from an assumption of plurality—be it plurality of cultures, "houses of Being," or people "talking and communicating with each other." They opposed projections of subjectivities onto these pluralities—mankind as One, civilizations as individuals writ large, history as a single man's life-story; and they opposed reductions of these pluralities to objective processes and trends. "Plurality preserved" as the aim of cosmopolitanism was a philosophical novelty. The assault made on plurality by world war, totalitarianism, and advanced technologies fostered this novelty; the emergence onto the stage, so long dominated by white European males, of not just the other Axial Period peoples but feminist movements and "Third World" peoples, recipients of European technologies, have since made the novelty urgently in need of further concern.

In the works considered here, the assumption of plurality was tied to a critical effort as reconceiving thinking itself—thinking as it had been thought about in the long epoch of Western philosophy. Not thinking as a subject's way of relating instrumentally or contemplatively to objects, but thinking as dialogic, essentially communicative—and thus essentially tied to human plurality—is what these reconceptions invoked. Of those I have considered here, Jaspers is the one who most coherently and conscientiously integrated his concern for communicative thinking with his cosmopolitanism—in his work the former leads directly to the latter. But if the epoch all these thinkers anticipated is to be marked by a new cosmopolitanism, a philosophy of humankind, a global historical sensibility, it will not be because any one of the historical analyses discussed here—or any other not discussed here—is adjudged the Truth, for past or future. The challenge of an uncertain, transitional epoch is to hear the common elements in works that we can listen to, following Jaspers' example, as though they were in conversation with each other. Such conversations of the immediate postwar years give us neither labels for the period nor grounds for either hope or despair but, rather, clues to the closure in the European tradition that has made cosmopolitan history a possibility for us.

6

What Are We Doing
When We Think?

1

There are many ways to describe generally the course of European philosophy in the last three hundred and fifty years. Each of the fine intellectual historians of the last fifty years—from Burtt and Whitehead to Hazard and Foucault—has helped us see different themes of continuity and discontinuity. For purposes that I will sketch in a moment, I would like to emphasize the alternations between methodological conflict and methodological cohesion. What I have in mind is not alternations between skepticism and dogmatism. Rather, I am referring to ways of being concerned about—to borrow a phrase from Hannah Arendt's *The Life of the Mind*—"what we are doing when we think."

The two most momentous movements from conflict to cohesion came in the early seventeenth and late eighteenth centuries. When they became known, René Descartes' philosophical and scientific achievements were challenged from many directions, but he did instigate a period of methodological cohesion in many quarters with his *Discours sur la méthode* (1637). This work along with the uncompleted *Regulae ad directionem ingenii* (1628), placed the question of method, the question of what we should be doing when we think, at the center of philosophical activity. The problem before philosophers, as they struggled for liberation from church doctrine, was how "people" by themselves and for themselves, can attain truth. Immanuel Kant slowly arrived at the project of his mature years amidst the conflicting claims to truth of just such protestant philosophizing—the conflicting "isms" of the Enlightenment. The doctrinal dimension of Kant's achievement was vehemently challenged, but his transcendental method, summarized by the word *Kritik,* dominated for a century the work of all thinkers who wished either to extend or to subvert Kant's philosophy.

After World War I there was once again a period of methodological disarray; and once again the hope was widely shared that a dominant methodological tendency might emerge. There was a renewal of interest in Kant—several forms of neo-Kantianism flourished—and in Hegel and Marx; but the strongest bid for predominance came from positivistic intellectual schools in which scientific methods were held up as the ideal for philosophical work. In a sense Cartesianism had a new day. But the forms of positivism were many and diverse: historicism, psychologism, sociologism, mathematical-logicism, and so forth—each with its own key for understanding the universal "man."

Among the many varieties of scientific philosophizing propounded in the 1920s, phenomenology had an important place. But, as Edmund Husserl developed it and made it progressively more Cartesian, phenomenology had much less impact than had seemed possible in the early 1920s, when Husserl's slogan "back to the things themselves" seemed to offer a way to avoid the positivistic reductions. However, as Martin Heidegger revolutionized it, phenomenology has had an enormous impact. In philosophical hermeneutics, sociology, anthropology, psychology, psychoanalysis, and literary theory the descendants of the adjective "phenomenological" are ubiquitous.

The Heideggerian methodological revolution—a revolution that began in the late 1920s with *Sein und Zeit* and continued in a new form after World War II—certainly has not had a breadth or depth of effect comparable to those produced by Descartes' and Kant's innovations. Agreement about method has not been its result. Indeed, Heidegger's questions about method were so radically posed that he ended in repudiation of "method" as Descartes and Kant had understood it. But Heidegger did incite a revolution of great importance, and I would like to suggest how and why that is so. I will proceed by presenting first a context for viewing this revolution and then a description of it. These projects will prepare the way for some reflections on the work of one of Heidegger's most illustrious students and critics, Hannah Arendt. By focusing my attention on Arendt's adaptation and critique of Heideggerian "phenomenology," I hope to be able to point out a way to answer my title question—what are we doing when we think?

2

Let me try to prepare for my presentation of Heidegger's revolution by sketching with very broad strokes the historical and philosophical contexts of Descartes' and Kant's methodological innovations. I am going to suggest correlations between these two thinkers' images of what the mind should be doing and their images of what ideal political arrangements might look like; later I will try to justify this approach.

René Descartes, European traveller and mercenary soldier in the armies of Duke Maximillian of Prussia and others, was a spectator by temperament. He lent himself to causes, hired himself out to courts, cultivated no ties of family, nation, or religion. In a period of class breakdown, clashing cultural traditions, religious wars, new scientific advances, and voyages of discovery, he stayed aloof. His philosophical goal, he says in his *Discours,* was to tear down the house in which he himself lived, to rid himself of all the ideas, customs and examples he had acquired but learned to find inconstant and full of errors. "I . . . reached the decision to study my own self," he claimed. "Never has my intention been more than to try to reform my own ideas, and rebuild them on a foundation that would be wholly mine." Descartes' hope—for himself—was complete control, exemplary absolute monarchy in his isolated mind.

To discover a new foundation and rebuild his house, Descartes needed a method. "By 'method,' " he wrote, "I mean rules so clear and simple that anyone who uses them carefully will never mistake the false for the true, and will waste no mental effort; but by gradually and regularly increasing his knowledge, will arrive at the true knowledge of all those things which he is capable of knowing." The method is one of spatial organizing: "Method consists entirely in the order and arrangement of those things upon which the power of the mind is to be concentrated in order to discover some truth. And we will follow this method exactly if we reduce complex and obscure propositions step by step to simpler ones and then try to advance by the same gradual process from the intuitive understanding of the very simplest to the knowledge of all the rest."

Immanuel Kant, who was famous for never leaving his home town, Königsberg, but travelling widely in his imagination, entered right into the conflict of systems that flourished in the cosmopolitan Enlightenment. His hope for a "broad highway" that *all* people could walk on was expressed in the method he called "transcendental." Behind (or "transcendent to") all the conflicting philosophical systems, Kant assumed, lie general mental structures: forms of intuition (space and time), categories of the understanding, and Ideas of reason. Kant proceeded like a diplomat who hopes to be able to show warring parties that their wars hide their common interests and prospects for peace. Antithetical systems, critically reduced to their origins in mental activity, could be reconciled or synthesized.

Kant's critical method was focused not on an ideal hierarchy of ideas that present knowledge but on the interplay of mental faculties as they legislate in our lives and produce knowledge. The method involved a spatial mapping of the mental faculties, but its main project was to represent those faculties interacting and, so to speak, alternating their rule over one another. Kant searched for a dynamic model—and that meant, of course, one in which temporality was included—for what might be called mental republicanism.

The political problem of Kant's day was not the diversity of customs and religions among the aristocracies of postfeudal Europe but the existence in all regions of similarly rigid sociopolitical hierarchies that could not accommodate the aspirations of people desiring to be free. Correlatively, the philosophical problem was not to institute a hierarchy of ideas in a new universal science but to revolutionize all hegemonic old metaphysical systems and let emerge into the light the structural universals of mental life. Kant's practical political views were complex: he was filled with enthusiasm for the French Revolution, but he advocated political reformism and enlightened monarchy. His heirs and critics often displayed similar ambivalences, but none failed to see the possibility that Kant's method had presented: namely, the possibility that how we think and how we act—the course of mental development and the course of historical development—are related determinatively. Hegel and Marx disagreed completely about the "direction" of this determinative relation, but both set its exploration as their task.

Martin Heidegger, an intellectual cosmopolitan but a fervent German nationalist, published his *Sein und Zeit* in 1927. He shared with many Europeans of his generation the sense that World War I had made monstrously evident the spiritual decline, social deterioration, and political corruption of the *fin de siècle*. In the 1920s, a period when both progressive experimentation with constitutional democracy and conservative nationalistic retrenchments were rife, Heidegger stayed away from direct political involvements. But he was not a diplomat and not a spectator (later, he actually signed on with the Nazis and then never repudiated his involvement). He was trying to summon in himself and in others the will to resist all the forces of decline and deterioration that seemed so obvious in the wake of World War I. Like so many of his generation, he was at once passionately utopian and quite convinced that only a philosophical revolution would or should bring renewal.

In his understanding the forces to be combatted were not basically socio-economic or political, they were philosophical. They stemmed from a centuries-long oblivion in the European tradition to the "question of the meaning of Being." This oblivion, Heidegger argued, was the source of the modern malaise; the cure was a method for recovering and asking anew the question of the meaning of Being. Heidegger viewed philosophers as—if I may adopt Shelley's phrase—the secret legislators of mankind. Their legislation has not been what it should have been, but it might be truthful in the future.

Heidegger's student, Hannah Arendt, a Jewish refugee from Nazi

Germany and a radical democrat, came to disagree with her teacher about both his analysis of the modern malaise and his proposed legislation. In the wake of world War II, as her eighteenth year of political statelessness came to an end, she offered a massive analysis, informed by Marxism but not Marxist, of the socio-economic and political elements of the modern situation. This is *The Origins of Totalitarianism*. In her later theoretical work she explored the political antidotes to totalitarianism—republicanism, participatory political structures. But even though she departed radically from Heidegger's teaching, she nonetheless learned much from his methods. Specifically, I will argue that she adopted for her own purposes the *Zeit* side of Heidegger's two-sided project, *Sein und Zeit;* she adopted the phenomenological method of analyzing *homo temporalis*.

3

I will return later to Hannah Arendt's critical adoption of Heidegger's method. But let me first try to present that method, indicating as I do how it evolved after the publication of *Sein und Zeit*.

Heidegger's *magnum opus* is a fragment. The original plan called for two divisions, but only one was published; and of the published one, only two of the three planned parts appeared. In very general terms what this state of affairs means is that Heidegger's guiding question—what is the meaning of Being?—was asked in only one of the ways he had planned to ask it. In the existing parts of *Sein und Zeit* Heidegger questions how *Dasein*, human being, distinguishes human particular being from that of any other being by asking this question. That part of the project involves an extensive and highly original analysis of human beings in their everyday lives and in their questioning reflection, in their "inauthentic," and in their "authentic" ways of being. Heidegger had intended to present his analysis of authentic, reflective life, his analysis of *Dasein* questioning, as the necessary preface to his own raising of the Being-question *per se*. But, as I noted, this sequel was not written. And Heidegger later concluded that it could not be written as the continuation of *Sein und Zeit*. He did not repudiate the book, but he did conclude that he had been—more than he understood at the time of writing *Sein und Zeit*—rooted in the very methods he was trying to overcome—those of Descartes and Kant. He felt that he had been too much of a subjectivist, too much a part of the modern tendency to focus on the human creative power of thinking and thus that he had missed human beings as part of the "history of Being" as respondents to Being rather than questioners of Being.

It seems to me that the most appropriate way to present Heidegger's early methodological revolution is to adopt his guiding assumption:

namely, that both human existence and the process of human consciousness are temporally structured. They draw on and memorialize the past, present the present, and reverberate with expectation of the future. As Augustine said in his *Confessions,* time *is* for people their three activities: expecting, attending, remembering. Accordingly, I will draw out the three dimensions of Heidegger's work in temporal terms—though I should note here what will soon be obvious, that the linearity of this analytical technique is artificial, for each modality of time involves the others.

What most forcefully strikes any reader of *Sein und Zeit* is—to borrow for my purposes a phrase of Frank Kermode's—its "sense of an ending." Heidegger felt himself to be at the end of an historical epoch, and he felt his work to be contributing to the end of philosophy—or, more accurately, to the end of metaphysics in its oblivion to the question of the meaning of Being. From Kant's heirs and critics—from Hegel, from Nietzsche and Kierkegaard, and from Dilthey—Heidegger had learned to view philosophical activity as historically situated, to see it in its "historicity." In Heidegger's understanding the past presses on the present like a force; it does not stretch out behind us like a road once travelled.

Using the metaphor that had been introduced into modern thought by Descartes, Heidegger describes his work:

> Just because we have ventured upon the great and long task of pulling down a world grown old and rebuilding really and truly anew, i.e. historically, we must know the tradition. We must know more, i.e. in a manner more stringent and binding than all ages and times of upheaval before us. Only the most radical historical knowledge can make us alive to the extraordinary character of our tasks and preserve us from a new wave of mere restoration and uncreative imitation.

As in Freudian psychology the key to overcoming a compulsion to repeat is locating an original trauma, so the key in Heideggerian phenomenology to overcoming the compulsion to repeat the age-long but newly apparent oblivion to the question of the meaning of Being is describing man's original misconstrual of the question. Accordingly, Heidegger tried to remember anew Plato and Aristotle, the two thinkers who gave the tradition its philosophical language. It is his claim that throughout the tradition the metaphysical lexicon derived from Plato and Aristotle has obscured human experience; it has been uncritically laid over real experiences, like a grid over unexplored terrain.

Implicit in Heidegger's sense of an ending is his sense of how to describe and thematize the structures of actual present experience. The key here is reflexivity. *Dasein,* human being, insofar as it is presently authentic is reflective: *Dasein* both questions and questions its questions. *Dasein* is that being who asks the meaning of Being and questions the question. What we are doing when we think is thinking thinking. The central and revolutionary claim of *Sein und Zeit,* it seems to me, is that this reflexivity is—in Heidegger's terms—"temporalizing temporality" (*Zeitigung der Zeit*). It is the articulation in thinking of our Being-in-time. What we are doing when we think is authentically existing in temporality.

Philosophical activity thus reflexively structured cannot be systematic in the Hegelian sense. It cannot conclude, totalize, synthesize; not its results—its new edifice, to use the Cartesian metaphor—but its method of building is its *raison d'être.* For there is no divorcing the methodological process—the questioning how—from what is questioned. Particularly in the works published after World War II, Heidegger stressed this notion of thinking activity as always *unterwegs,* underway.

That Heidegger learned from the example of Socrates is obvious; he called Socrates "the purest thinker of the West." But unlike Socrates, Heidegger took as his *agora* the entire European philosophical tradition. In the reflexivity of thinking the whole of the past as we have it in language is present—and thus questionable. When a thinker resorts to the *idées reçues* of the metaphysical tradition, he or she thwarts the authentic questioning process, the reflexivity of thought. And he or she cannot, then, discover the interior source of the reflexivity—that structuring experience Heidegger calls *Sorge,* care.

What decisively distinguishes Heidegger's method from Kant's is that, although he made a Kantian search for the necessary conditions of thought, he found the conditions not in fixed, spatially conceived structures of thought—forms, categories, or ideas—but in the living experience of *Sorge,* care, and the temporalizing structures of care. "The Totality of Being-in-the-world as a structural whole has revealed itself as care," Heidegger writes. "In care the Being of *Dasein* is included."

This brings me to the third temporal dimension of Heidegger's method—the future. "As Care," Heidegger claimed, "*Dasein* is essentially ahead of itself." The future does not stretch out ahead of us like a road not yet travelled; it is as it is expected or anticipated, cared-for. Heidegger's sense of human possibility is summarized in the analysis of Care. All the merely spatial ways of being-*in* or being-*with* that constitute everyday life can be overcome in caring-*for.* We can care for things and the tools of our practice; we can care for people (Heidegger calls this "solicitude"); and, most crucially, we can care for the very question of the meaning of Being. The ultimate possibility of human life is to give Being its meaning or disclose Being's meaning. Again and again, Heidegger identified *care*ful thinking with willing futureward, with being resolute: "The authentic future is revealed in resoluteness."

Heidegger had hoped to break away from the subjectivism of the modern philosophical tradition—and he did break with the Cartesian autarchic mind and the Kantian emphasis on universal mental legislation in both the theoretical and ethical domains. But his analysis of Care led him to a subjectivism of a different sort; he imagined an isolated self as structured by Care. *Dasein* is given, by virtue of birth and life-towards-death, the possibility of disclosing the Being that mere inauthentic life in the world conceals. But resolute Selfhood is the condition for the actualization of this possibility. What we are doing when we think is giving meaning by ourselves and for ourselves alone to the Being that in the long tradition had been considered not a possibility *for humanity* but a given, the origin *of Dasein.*

Heidegger's invocation of the solitary Self was no less fervent in his later work, but it took a very different form—one that he thought relieved the Self of its egoistic subjectivism. He presented thinking as a kind of receptivity to Being—hearing the "call of Being." The emphasis he had placed on the future and on the possibilities inherent in questioning the meaning of Being gave way to an emphasis on the past, on what has been given to man. *Denken ist andenken*—thinking is remembering. *Denken ist danken*—thinking is thanking for what has come to be. *Denken ist nachdenken*—thinking is following Being, *after*-thinking. In Heidegger's later work the thinker is presented in his or her authenticity as a preserver and conserver, a celebrant of Being, a guardian of Being. Heidegger did not revert to the Cartesian vision of absolute monarchism for thought; he ceded monarchy to Being, and he became Being's humble servant.

4

In Hannah Arendt's *The Origins of Totalitarianism*, as in her *Between Past and Future* essays and *The Human Condition*, there are many echoes of Heidegger's analysis of everydayness and of his search for the temporal structures of everyday life. She began in these works from what she thought was the revolutionary importance of *Sein und Zeit*. As she wrote in 1946: "Heidegger's philosophy is the first absolutely and uncompromisingly this-worldly philosophy." Arendt, too, wanted a this-worldly philosophy—but one without the hubristic purpose of "fundamental ontology," of making Being meaningful as human selfhood.

Arendt clearly saw in the phenomenon of totalitarianism the institutionalization of inauthenticity as Heidegger had described it. She wrote about the perverse misuse of the past in Nazi race ideology—with all its nonsense about ancient Teutonic purity and national greatness; she

described the horrendous misuse of the future in the Nazi millenarian-
ism. These analyses of ideological perversity, which grew from her analyses of the socio-economic and political disintegration produced with the
triumph of the European bourgeois mass-man and his imperialism, led
her to view totalitarian terror as temporal meaninglessness. She called
the concentration camps "organized oblivion" and presented in powerful
passages the destruction in camps of people's worldly future security—
their human rights; of their past experiences—their moral personalities;
and of their present lives—their unique identities. What disappears in
a totalitarian regime is any form of human action, any spontaneous
"beginning of something new." All is functioning—blind obedience,
empty moment to empty moment.

   Like Heidegger, Arendt was attempting to understand a condition of
obliviousness, forgetfulness; she later called it thoughtlessness or banality. But what she thought had been forgotten was not Being; it was the
meaning of politics and human action. However, even though her this-
worldly question was utterly different from Heidegger's and stood as a
repudiation of his allegiance to the Nazis she used his methods. In her
theoretical works of the 1950s she proceeded Heideggerianly: she
mapped out the different spaces of everyday life—the household, the
social, the political realm—and then she explored the temporal modalities
of the activities that constitute each space.

   Her well-known distinction between work and action, for example,
rests on her presentation of these activities as, respectively, past-oriented
or memorializing and future-oriented or self-disclosing. People make a
world where what they do can live on in everyday things and works of
art, stories. People act, show who they are, disclose themselves together
with others; and their *polis,* their political realm, is their "organized
remembrance." Labor, the third form of human activity Arendt analyzed,
is timeless in the sense that its alienation, particularly in modern conditions, isolates each present moment from the past and the future, from
remembrance and anticipation. People laboring become objects among
objects; or, in Heidegger's terms, objects are only *zu-handen* to laborers,
not *vor-handen* as they are for those who work, fabricate. In each of
these analyses Arendt transformed a Heideggerian insight by making it
political and by making it relate to men and women in the plural.

   The only authentic present-tense activity presented in *The Human Condition* is the activity of "thinking what we are doing." But this present-
tense understanding marks the great difference between *The Human
Condition* and *Sein und Zeit.* Heidegger's question is the question of Being's
meaning; Arendt's is the question of the meaning of the *vita activa* and
its modalities. Her perspective is not ontological, and she makes it quite

clear that the traditional philosophical perspective, which Heidegger had both shared and portrayed as resolute Selfhood, is not her own.

She had learned from Heidegger the importance of "historicity," of people's temporal situatedness, of their "temporalizing temporality," their existence as temporalizing beings. She knew that this key element of Heidegger's thinking had brought him rich insights into the general intellectual and experiential tendencies of his time. But she had learned from her own experience as a "stateless person," a political refugee, that "the political realm" was absent from Heidegger's view. His view, the view of a contemplative—even though of a contemplative who had not defined thinking as contemplation of a given reality—was rooted in a tradition that had, since the trial and death of Socrates, found the *polis* hostile and political action intolerable but that also was full of successors to Plato's alliance with the tyrant Dion of Syracuse. She thought that Heidegger's tradition-boundedness had become more and more pronounced after the war, particularly when he began to speak of events as part of the "history of Being." This, she felt, signalled his lapse into a Hegel-like vision of historical determinism.

Arendt did not take the opposite view—as did Sartre, Merleau-Ponty, and Camus—and claim that only in acting does action become meaningful or understandable. She was not—after the war or ever—an existentialist or activist. What she did, rather, was to ask anew about "what are we doing when we think," in order to see how thinking can come close to the political realm, how it can be practical—which is not at all the same as pragmatic or involved in policy-formation.

Her questioning went on for many years. Soon after she completed *The Human Condition*, she thought of writing the complement—a study of mental life—to go with her study of the *vita activa*. But she did not undertake the project until late in the 1960s, and then she did so under the influence of her reflections on Adolf Eichmann's trial, published as *Eichmann in Jerusalem*. She began her last work, *The Life of the Mind*, by questioning whether thinking in some way keeps us from evil-doing; that is, she was in search of a link between thinking and acting.

Implicit in the sections of *The Life of the Mind* that Hannah Arendt lived to write, "Thinking" and "Willing," there are two very different ways to conduct such a search. It seems, first, on the evidence of the posthumously published sections, that Arendt intended to present the faculty of judgment as a link between thinking and doing. She claims, in a very tentative passage, that judging is a "side-effect" of thinking; that those who have stopped to think—and that means in her terms stopped to generalize, to deal in general ideas—are prepared mentally to see particulars in their generality. She held that judging is a process of reflectively moving from particular events and actions to the general principles appropriate to them; and she contrasted this process to the kind of judgment that had been emphasized in traditional philosophy—that is, the application of an already maintained general principle to a particular event or action, a deductive procedure. Judging does not link thought and action by classifying or categorizing actions; it does not apply rules. But, on the other hand, judging does not approach each particular that comes along as though nothing had preceded it. Judging searches for general principles by comparing particulars with other particulars—ones that have gained what Arendt calls "exemplary validity" for judgment. To say "this is good" of some deed or possibility for action, judgment makes reference to the exemplary goodness it regards as "embodied" in some deed or doer or deeds. This is Arendt's conception of how the past is present in our mental life: we have in our memories the products of previous reflection or thinking, and we use these to essay a present particular. If we did not live in political realms of "organized remembrance," we would not share such reservoirs of exemplary validity.

Arendt's gestures toward a theory of judging present one way to link thinking and action; but her last work also contains another way. Or, let me be more honest and say that it suggests to me, as I read it, another way. I am going to depart now from Arendt's portrait of "The Life of the Mind" in order to consider its implications as I see them.

5

Let me begin, once again, by setting a general historical and philosophical context. Different historical conditions permit different conceptions of what we are doing when we think. This statement is not intended as a statement of determinism, a claim that thought is determined by material conditions—that it is part of the "superstructure." I mean by "historical conditions," rather, the entire range of material, experiential, and intellectual products and activities of a particular time. A thinker thinks in his or her time and cannot leap out of that time; even mystical visions and experiences of *unio mystica* reflect the mystics' earth-bound starting point; and revolutionary ideas are revolutionary in relation to what they revolutionize. There certainly are what might be called "archetypes" of philosophical thought—patterns, schematisms, relations that recur again and again in response to the questions that make up *philosophia perennis*. This has been so and will be so as long as people distinguish spatially between inside and outside, invisible and visible, and temporally between what has been, is, or will be and what is timeless or eternal, what is changing and what is permanent, what is many and what is one. But all of these staples of philosophical orientation appear in different forms in different times.

One of the questions that recurs again and again is the one that Arendt addresses—or began to address—in *The Life of the Mind:* what is the relation between thinking and doing, or, as we sometimes say, between theory and *praxis?* The question is usually phrased as: how does thinking determine or influence or guide action? And sometimes it is phrased the other way about: how does *praxis* determine or influence or guide thinking? Hannah Arendt's reflections on judging in the extant parts of *The Life of the Mind* are in this traditional form—although her exploration of judging, with its emphasis on reflective use of examples, which are, so to speak, generalized particulars, marks a departure from the traditional distinction between the general and the particular.

But there is another way to put the question of the relation between thinking and doing, and it seems to me that this way is implied in *The Life of the Mind.* Are there answers—so this way goes—to the question "what are we doing when we think?" that are incompatible with acting? Are there ways of thinking about thinking that preclude acting? or preclude taking acting seriously?

Plato was perhaps the first philosopher to suggest that the ideal mind (or, as he said, the *psyche*) should be structured just as the ideal *polis* is structured. The mind is the *polis* writ small. The hierarchichal functions of the mind are analogous to the hierarchical functions of the *polis;* the mind's ruling part, the reasoning part (*logistikon*), is to the lower functions of the mind as the ruler of the *polis* is to the lower functions of guarding and laboring in the *polis.* Down through the tradition this notion echoed. Hannah Arendt referred to it as "the tyranny of reason" and saw it as one of the key elements in the tradition's obliviousness toward genuine human action and failure to take politics seriously. It is a contemplative's notion, a philosopher's notion of how to order the *polis* for the sake of philosophy and the rule of philosophers.

But in modern thought, in accord with the subjectivism of the period, the analogy relation has been construed differently. The *polis* is the mind writ large. The ideal ordering of political affairs should reflect the ideal ordering of mental affairs. Thus, as I suggested, Descartes' mental monarchism, his hierarchy of ideas descending from the simplest to the most complex, was reflected in his support of political absolute monarchism and his ethical advocacy of "abiding by the customs of one's country." Kant, who believed so fervently in the ability of each and every person to legislate for himself or herself—by deducing the one principle, the categorical imperative, that should determine all actions—advocated a universal republic. Both of these thinkers conceived of action as what follows from a properly organized mental life; politics was subjectively grounded and universalized through the universal subject. Even Kant's support of the French Revolution—which was so much out of step with his philosophical convictions—was expressed in terms of a potential subjective universal: he called it the "universal enthusiasm" of the spectators. He approved the enthusiasm even as he disapproved, on theoretical grounds, the principle of revolution. The principle according to which he judged and the principle he accepted for action were antithetical, irreconcilable.

Martin Heidegger's disastrous affiliation with the Nazi party is a particularly shocking instance of reasoning from a way of thinking about thinking to a political conviction. Heidegger never publically repudiated Nazism; he maintained the position he took in his 1936 work *Introduction to Metaphysics*, namely, that the Nazi movement had an "inner truth and greatness." This inner truth and greatness was a resolute *will* to combat the inauthenticity, the technologization and alienation of modern man, a resoluteness in the face of "the peril of world darkening." A more thorough misunderstanding can hardly be imagined. And it came about because both the emphasis on thinking as resolute futureward Selfhood in Heidegger's early work and the emphasis on thinking as receptive, meditative past-oriented listening in Heidegger's late work marked ways to leave behind this world and its present—people's present—predicaments. These were ways not to "think what we are *doing*."

What Hannah Arendt presents in *The Life of the Mind* is an image of the mind's activity that neglects none of the temporal modes of our living. She wrote of three faculties, thinking, willing, and judging, that are, temporally, attentive, expectant, and remembering. The three faculties are interrelated, interactive—in Kant's sense they are "at play" with each other. None rules once and for all; each rules in its particular temporal modality. None prompts to action or is the sole source of mental motion. Each of the faculties is internally reflexive, self-moving. Thinking, Arendt says, is an inner dialogue between me and myself. Willing is an inner struggle between "I-will" and "I-nill," our "yes" or "no" of inner debate about what we should do. Judging is an inner discussion between what we, as individuals, like or approve and what the "others" in us—the exemplary others of our tradition and of our contemporary acquaintance—represent to us as worthy of approval.

Arendt's image of the mind is an image that looks more like a busy, talkative little participatory democratic *polis*, with executive, legislative, and judiciary functions, than any in the history of the tradition. She did not claim that the mind is or should be the *polis* writ small; and she did not claim that the *polis* is or should be the mind writ large. What her image implies, it seems to me, is the claim that our mind, if it is to be adequate to our world, if it is to be at home in the world, be worldly, this-worldly, can be no less activity-filled, indeterminate, and complexly articulated in time than our world.

Historically, Arendt argues in *The Life of the Mind,* philosophy began with Socrates' fervent devotion to exploring thinking. The Christian "existentialists" St. Paul and St. Augustine, living in expectation of redemption in the future, fervently explored willing and the freedom of the will. Kant brought the faculty of judgment for the first time into question philosophically. The most illustrious enthusiast for the French Revolution, for a revolution that brought into the world novel ideas and novel political institutions on a grand, cosmopolitan scale, spent the last years of his life writing a *Critique of Judgment.* We are heirs to these achievements.

But we are also people who live in a world in which the political visions of the great philosophers—visions that, I have been maintaining, grew from and reflected their visions of the mind's chief modalities—have little to teach us. Ours is a world rendered by events understandable only as *one* world in time—for the potentialities we know for political totalitarianism and planetary destruction by nuclear weapons are not potentialities understandable from the perspective of any one present way of life, inheritance from the past, or hope for the future. We *cannot* think what we are doing if we think how we are thinking in any provincial way. Accordingly, the provinces or faculties of thinking, willing, and judging— each of which has had its historical regnancy—cannot be viewed in isolation or exercised in isolation. To judge without judging what one's judgment implies for thinking and willing, to will without willing that one's acts be thought about and judged, to think without thinking that one's thoughts will affect one's willing and judging—these are pathways to obliviousness, worldlessness, and solitude.

When we think what we are doing, we are all refugees and democratic cosmopolitans. The only good thing that can be said about this condition is that when we think what we are doing we share the condition—all appearances to the contrary notwithstanding. What we are doing when we think is thinking this condition—this present condition—as the condition that enables us to think what we are doing.

7

What Thucydides Saw

Before contemporary history became an acknowledged subdiscipline of history and began to be practiced by professional historians, it was the province of people who had in common much practical political experience; they were sidelined activists, retired politicians and soldiers, exiles and refugees. The classical touchstone for the great contemporary historians of the modern period, from Machiavelli to Marx, was a work unique in its own time and a marvel of method and acumen: Thucydides' history of the Peloponnesian War. In our own century, so rich in histories of history and historiographical analyses, Thucydides' work has been the touchstone for a voluminous inquiry into the processes and achievements of historical consciousness.

Many of his emulators and most of his nonclassicist analyzers share certain crucial assumptions about Thucydides' history. First, they assume that he expected history to repeat itself and wrote a book that he hoped would be a "possession for all times" because it was a book of lessons. Second, they assume that he wrote convinced that "human nature" is constant and unchanging, unchangeable. Finally, they assume that he searched for ultimate causes of events and distinguished these from proximate or precipitating causes. Each of these interrelated assumptions is, I think, right in some ways and wrong in others.

In this essay I want to question these assumptions about Thucydides' work and try to demarcate the ranges of their rightness. By suggesting how these assumptions obscure Thucydides' method and practice, however, I want to bring into focus the elements of his political judgment that have, I think, been neglected outside of the specialized studies of classicists. My approach of Thucydides' work is in the service of a general reflection on assumptions that either inhibit or subtend political judgment. So my essay is designed as a contribution *to* historiography as well as *toward* a kind of inquiry that has always engaged political philosophers but seldom focused on the work of a political historian. Such an inquiry might be called "critique of judgment."

1

Among the most instructive of the many innovations that distinguish Thucydides from his predecessor Herodotus, the "Father of History," as well as from less well-known later Greek historians is his decision to undertake his history before the events that had caught his attention were enough underway to be known by his contemporaries as *a* war, much less by the name that they, and Thucydides' book, eventually received: the Peloponnesian War.[1] His own involvement as an Athenian citizen and as a commander may explain Thucydides' continued and retrospective interest in the war. The *History's* prologue presents these two ingredients of Thucydides' judgment, and I will take it as a starting point for this inquiry:

> Thucydides the Athenian wrote the history of the war fought between the Athenians and the Peloponnesians. He began the account at the outbreak of the war, when he came to believe—[1] judging from the acmes of preparation reached by both sides and [2] considering the already set or developing intentions of the other Hellenes to ally with the two powers—that it was going to be a great war and more worth writing about than any preceding it. This was the greatest disturbance in the history of the Hellenes, affecting also a large part of the non-Hellenic world, and, indeed, I might also say, the whole of mankind. I found it impossible, because of the remoteness in time, to acquire a really clear knowledge of the distant past or even of the history preceding our own time, but from the evidence gotten inquiring back as far as I can, I conclude that these periods were not great periods either in warfare or in other things. (1:1)

Two of Thucydides' categories (marked above as 1 and 2) for judging the war in both its novelty and its significance are presented in this prologue, employed in the rest of Book 1, and elaborated throughout the history. He first notes that the technological means and economic capacities for war of the two principals, Athens and Sparta, had altered fundamentally since their participation as allies in the Persian War. During the Persian War Athens became a "people of sailors" (1:18) and achieved technological supremacy; the Athenian navy was both vast and equipped with ships specifically designed for war, not converted from commercial use. Sparta was supreme on land. Both cities had reached points of military preparedness and experience in their respective domains unknown in previous wars. And both cities had augmented their wealth—Athens by exacting tribute from its allies and Sparta by promoting cooperative oligarchies amongst its allies—to the point of having

"defense budgets" of surplus capital. Thucydides takes these technological and economic factors as evidence or signs (*tekmerion*) from which to
draw inferences about the greatness and novelty of the war. The key
political factors he judges as already accomplished, visible, observable.
Both cities had already developed political alliance systems. Their political organization for largescale, inter-Hellenic war, rather than local wars
or pirating raids, had come about with the abandonments of tyranny as
a form of government. In tyrannies, Thucydides notes, the personal
security of the tyrant is "the chief political principle" (1:17), and from
such governments, dedicated as they are to safety and defense, no great
action ever comes.

These basic comparative categories of technological-economic development and political organization seem to have been in Thucydides' mind
at the outbreak of the war. His second invocation of the war's greatness
and novelty in the introductory section of Book 1 is retrospective, and
its comparative categories are existential. He speaks of the war in terms
of its spatial extension, its temporal duration, and its impact on human
institutions and human lives.

> The greatest war in the past was the Persian War; yet in this war the
> decision was reached quickly as a result of two naval battles and two
> battles on land. The Peloponnesian War, on the other hand, not only
> lasted for a long time, but through its course brought with it unprece-
> dented suffering in Hellas. Never before had so many cities been cap-
> tured and then devastated, whether by foreign armies or by the Hellenic
> powers themselves . . . : never had there been so many exiles, never such
> loss of life—both in actual warfare or in internal revolutions. (1:23)

Novelty and greatness, both anticipated or inferred and confirmed by
events, were Thucydides' chief concerns as a theorist of history. In his
history statesmen and citizens are judged by their capacities to do as
Thucydides himself tries to do—judge novelty and greatness clearly. He
praises good judgment or insight (*gnome*) in those few who possessed it,
and he devotes himself to understanding both what made it possible in
them—even if seldom purely so—as well as what produced its lack in the
majority. His own judgments or insights, he anticipates, would be difficult
for his defeated and exhausted country people to appreciate. Specifically,
he anticipates that after the war and in their retrospection his Athenian
readers would have lost whatever sense of the war's greatness they had
developed merely by virtue of their involvement, their interestedness.
Most people, he claims, "judge the war in which they are fighting as the
greatest of all wars, but when it is over, they find ancient events more
wondrous" (1:21). Previous wars, glorified in the songs of poets and

monumentalized in prose narratives full of mythic or fabulous elements, would strike the Athenians as greater than the Peloponnesian War, the war of defeat, unless Thucydides' own history, written from carefully assembled and accurately assessed sources, was heeded. His book was dedicated to the hope that the war and the war period would not be diminished or misunderstood retrospectively, that the glorious past of the Trojan War or the more recent victory of the Persian War would not overshadow the war Thucydides considered so significant in comparison with them.

Why did the judgment of greatness and novelty matter so? Thucydides' answer is given in the most commented on and explicated passage of the first book:

> And it may well be that my history will seem less pleasing because it lacks *to mythodes* [the mythic or fabulous element]: but it will be enough for me if my history is judged useful by those who may wish to view clearly both the past events and the future ones, which will happen sometime again, *kata to anthropinon*, in the same or in a similar way. For it has been composed not as a debate speech for hearers of the moment, but as a possession for all time. (1:22)

This passage is often thought to convey the message that there is never anything new in human affairs, that what has been will be again. Yet it seems very unlikely that Thucydides would deliver this message after he has taken such trouble to emphasize the novelty and greatness of the war. This war, he says again and again, is not the same as or similar to any events that preceded it; why should the future be made up of events like those of the war?

Those who interpret this passage in "eternal return of the same" terms and thus expect from Thucydides political universals for all time must overlook his emphasis on the novelty of the war. They must also translate the mysterious little phrase *kata to anthropinon*, left untranslated above, as "human nature being what it is" or "according to human nature" (as though the phrase were *kata to anthropeian physin*, [2:50.1]). Such interpretations hold that Thucydides assumed that human events will always be the same or similar and that this is so because they are all effects of a constant, unchanging human nature. He is held to have presented the historiographical equivalent of the notion attributed to the early Greek philosophers, namely, that natural events are fundamentally the same as causal effects of *physis*, that is, as occurring *kata physin*, according to nature.

But in this passage *anthropinon* is not an adjective qualifying "nature," "affairs," or any of the other nouns with which the adjective form "human" is combined elsewhere in the narrative or speeches parts of Thucydides' text. The unusual substantive, uniquely used here, must signal a particular meaning. One recent commentator on the text, Marc Cogan, recognizes the importance of the unique usage and translates the word "the human thing." He claims that it refers to the cause not of individual human actions but of the actions of nations, which are not simply individuals writ large with motivations analogous to those of individuals: *"to anthropinon* [is] a public, not a private principle of action."[2] But this interesting interpretation also creates a tension in the passage: how can Thucydides emphasize the novelty of the war and the war period while at the same time believing that all actions of a public sort have been and will be basically the same?

No tension arises in the passage if the troublesome words in it are translated in Cogan's way—"by those who may wish to view clearly both the past events and the future ones, which will happen sometime again, according to the human element, in the same or a similar way"—but interpreted quite differently. Like *to mythodes* in the first part of the sentence, *to anthropinon* is a narrative element that makes a story pleasing; it reflects the human belief—the erroneous human belief—that events recur in more or less similar ways.[3] The sense of the last sentence in the passage, thus prefaced, is: this history, which does not have the human (narrative) element, which is not a debate-speech urging the similarity of the present war and the wars of the past, but a possession for all times, shows those who wish to see clearly how to judge novelty and greatness. The message is: future events will always have novel aspects, and these are just the aspects that are crucial. It is not pleasing to try to judge past events or future ones without the common human assumptions of similarity or continuity, but this is just what a historian—and a statesman—must do. A work that emphasizes greatness and novelty and shows how to judge them is a possession for all time.

2

If Thucydides did not believe that future events would always more or less resemble past events, if, indeed, he thought that such a belief was a barrier to judging the greatness and novelty of events, then his own references elsewhere in the text to "human nature" and to similarities among events need to be explained. No reader of Thucydides' book can escape the conclusion that he wanted to reveal similarities among events and that he held certain events to be paradigmatic. Similarly, no reader can fail to grasp that Thucydides believed that human nature is a mixture of judgment (*gnome*) and passion (*orge*). But the stress that he put on differences among events—judged by means of criteria for novelty and greatness—points to his conviction that all events have novel elements and that some are without precedent, beyond paradigm. I also think that Thucydides had a corollary conviction that human nature, made up of judgment and passion, is not only changeable but susceptible to such disturbance that it becomes inhuman, unnatural.

The philosophical tradition that stems from Plato and Aristotle has as deeply shaped our understanding of the phrase "human nature" as Thucydides himself has shaped our understanding of the Peloponnesian War. Until modern classical scholars and archaeologists questioned his account, the war was as Thucydides said it was; it was a war in a book and of a book. Where the Platonic-Aristotelian tradition has held sway, "nature," *physis,* has been conceived as the tradition conceives it: an immutable and permanent essence. The contrary notion that "human nature" is contextual, defined by conditions, historical, is our legacy from Darwin, Marx, and Freud. But this contextual defining is still shocking to philosophical and religious transcendentalists, particularly when it arises not in the confines of evolutionary or socio-economic or psychoanalytic theory but in histories of human actions.

For example, when Hannah Arendt's *The Origins of Totalitarianism* was published in 1951, Eric Voegelin focused a critical review on her claim that "what totalitarian ideologies . . . aim at is not the transformation of the outside world or the revolutionizing transmutation of society, but the transformation of human nature itself."[4] Voegelin countered:

> "Nature" is a philosophical concept; it denotes that which identifies a thing as a thing of this kind and not another one. A "nature" cannot be changed or transformed: a "change of nature" is a contradiction of terms; tampering with the "nature" of a thing means destroying the thing. To conceive the idea of "changing the nature" of man (or of anything) is a symptom of the intellectual breakdown of Western civilization.

To this charge Arendt replied: "Historically we know of man's nature only insofar as it has existence, and no realm of eternal essences will ever console us if man loses his essential capabilities" in a "radical liquidation of freedom as a political and a human reality." Arendt did not deny that a God might know of man's nature in a nonhistorical way; but she wrote without aspiration to such a perspective—or lack of perspective.

Without any need to assess critically centuries' worth of transcendentalist views, Thucydides was in search of a historical way to present the effects of unprecedented situations on people. To do this, he distinguished between events that follow patterns and can be judged familiar—

more or less—from past precedents and those that are without precedent. As I noted, his criteria for judging events to be unprecedented are of two sorts: on the one hand, there are criteria of socio-economic and political novelty and greatness, and, on the other hand, there are criteria of existential impact. It is in relation to the second type of criteria that he presents "human nature" as contextual and susceptible to such disturbance that it becomes inhuman, unnatural.

In Book 3, in the middle of a horrifying description of the revolution or *stasis* at Corcyra and of the atrocities committed during it, Thucydides indicates that this was but the first of the many revolutions that convulsed "the whole Hellenic world" as opposing factions in cities everywhere sought alliances with either Athens or Sparta.

> And so, according to [the way of] revolutions [κατὰ στάσιν] many calamities [χαλεπτὰ] came upon cities—such as happen and always will happen as long as human nature is the same [εὡς ἂν ἡ αὐτὴ φύσις ἀνθρώπων ᾗ] but which are milder or harsher, and distinct in their forms, as outstanding changes in circumstances come about. For in peaceful and good times, cities and individuals have better judgment, not having been assaulted by unwished for necessities; but war, which robs men of easy satisfaction of their needs, is a teacher of violence, and it fits most peoples' passions to their circumstances. (3:82)

This passage presents the *stasis* at Corcyra as paradigmatic and indicates that there is a *stasis*-pattern, a sequence of events that can be called *kata stasin*, according to the way of revolutions. But it is important to note that Thucydides adds a qualification: "as long as human nature is the same." He then stresses that there are differences in revolutions of both form and impact and that in general there are differences between peace times and war times in terms of human judgment. These distinctions are later all too clear, for the *stasis* that takes place in Athens itself—after twenty years of war—makes the reader question whether the "teacher of violence" has not brought about the possibility the subjunctive clause forbodes.

But even in the conclusion of the description of Corcyra's *stasis* Thucydides suggests that there "human nature" had passed a limit.

> In this crisis, the life of the city being in total confusion, human nature defeated [its] laws—being accustomed to doing injustice against [the city's] laws—and took delight in showing its passion to be ungovernable and stronger than justice, an enemy to any authority. (3:84)

When human nature is no longer a mixture of judgment and passion because judgment has disappeared, or when (as Thucydides says in a neighboring passage, 3:83) the εὔηθες, unity or simplicity, that is the chief mark of excellent people, is nowhere to be found, it hardly makes sense to speak of "human nature."

The way in which Thucydides suggests the greatness and novelty of situations by assessing their impact existentially, their impact on human nature itself, is clearest in the plague narrative of Book 2. In this narrative language is strained to its limits. Thucydides claims that the plague was unprecedented, unlike any known disease, completely novel. Having catalogued the disease's many peculiarities and peoples' reactions to them, he then takes as evidence (τεκμήριον [2:50]) of its strangeness the fact that birds and animals avoided the plague-infected corpses or died if they fed on them. The horror of the plague was such, Thucydides notes, that "the character [εἶδος] of the disease defied description [λόγου], in every case the result of its assault being more calamitous than according to human nature [χαλεπωτέρως ἢ κατὰ τὴν ἀνθρωπείαν φύσιν]" (2:50). The last phrase of this passage has been variously translated: "beyond the capacity of human nature to endure" is the most common, though Hobbes's rendition—"being crueller than human nature"—has its exponents among those who think that Thucydides subscribed to what later became the Hobbesian notion that human nature is constantly cruel. But this passage can be interpreted to mean that the plague's assault was so calamitous that most peoples' natures did not remain human natures. Assaulted by the plague, many people ceased to be people—as nature so ceased to be nature that the birds and animals acted unnaturally. No scientific *logos* can present such conditions, for such *logos* is only of and in the natural realm.

The disruption of "human nature" defies descriptive language—it requires another kind of language, which verges on the "unbelievable." Just after his second introductory invocation of the novelty and greatness of the war and the presentation of the categories of spatial extension, temporal duration, and existential impact Thucydides offers a quite Herodotean list of inexplicable wonders (2:23). From the sober, scientific Thucydides, this list seems very odd. During the war, he writes, "old stories, handed down orally, but rarely confirmed by facts, ceased to be unbelievable" (1:23). The occurrence during the war of earthquakes, frequent eclipses of the sun, droughts resulting in famine, and "lastly, the apocalyptic plague, which was the worst violation and which destroyed a great part of Athens," made the old stories believable.[5] All these phenomena "assaulted together [ξυνεπέθετο] with the war."

In the two passages just cited (2:50 and 1:23), as in the "teacher of violence" passage (3:82), Thucydides uses the verb πίπτω (or a compound of it) to personify as calamity-producing assailants the unwished-for necessities, the plague, and the conjunction of war and natural disasters or portents. The Corcyra narrative also concludes with a personification (and a reference to "violation" comparable to that in 1:23): "For surely no man would honor revenge over piety, or profit over refraining from injustice, were he not violated by envy's strong force [ἐν ᾧ μὴ βλάπτουσιν ἰσχὺν εἶχε τὸ φθονεῖν]" (3:84). These personifications are not naive; they seem to reflect a conscious rhetorical strategy for gesturing beyond the realm of "scientific" description and analysis. They present the war and its, so to speak, allies as active, as agents. In a similar way, Thucydides sometimes draws on the traditional religious association of τύχη, "chance," and "befalling," expressed with the verb πίπτω.[6]

By personifying war and its concomitants, Thucydides draws attention to effects. He does not search for the "nature" of war. His question is not the one over which Albert Einstein and Sigmund Freud exchanged their famous 1932 letters: "Why War?" Thucydides also presents human agents, individually or collectively, in terms of their appearances. He speaks of judgment and passion not as capacities or faculties but as effects, actions or reactions. With this orientation Thucydides was quite self-consciously opposing traditional methods of analysis, which named certain faculties of the *psyche* like *nous, thumos, phren* as sources for thought, emotion, deliberation, or choice.[7] This was the tradition that Plato later elaborated with his discussions of the tripartite *psyche* and its three bodily locations. But Thucydides, who does not use the word *psyche* analytically, rejected the "faculty psychology" approach and wrote instead of judgment and passion as modes of action and reaction knowable only in their relations to events and contexts. There are two levels of battle in Thucydides' history: there is the battle of men against men, the allied Athenian forces against the allied Lacedemonian forces; and there is the battle between the "teacher of violence" (war, with its co-assailants: the plague, unwished-for necessities, natural disasters, and portents) and "human nature," the actions and reactions of judgment and passion.

3

Thucydides does not analyze "human nature" in faculty-psychology terms. He does, however, present the Athenians and the Spartans and other peoples as "character types" of relative—not absolute—constancy. In the opening books of the *History* the characterological contrast between the Athenians and the Spartans is obvious to all the people who make speeches and to Thucydides himself in his narrative voice. The Athenians are famous for their innovativeness, their love of everything new and challenging, and their restless pursuit of power. The Spartans are characteristically slow to act, cautious, conservative, inclined to focus their attention on difficulties rather than opportunities, but staunch, spirited, and rugged once engaged.

It is to manifestations of these typically Athenian and Spartan characteristics that Thucydides refers in one of the only two passages in the *History* that are noted by all commentators as *loci* for a distinction between proximate and ultimate causes. This first passage comes immediately after Thucydides' statement about how the conjunction of war and natural disasters and portents rendered old stories believable:

> And the war began when the Athenians and Peloponnesians broke the thirty years' truce concluded between them after the capture of Euboea. The reasons [τὰς αἰτίας] why they broke it and the ground of their quarrel I have set forth first, so that no one need ever have to ask for what cause it was that the Hellenes became involved in so great a way. The true explanation [τὴν . . . ἀληθεστάτην πρόφασιν], although it has been the least often advanced, I believe to have been the growth of the Athenians to greatness, which brought fear to the Lacedemonians and forced them to war. But the reasons [αἰτίαι] publicly alleged on either side which led them to break the truce and involved them in the war were as follows. (1:23)

The second passage, which concludes a long history of Sicily that emphasizes the greatness and novelty of that island, presents an analysis of the Athenians' motives for invading it:

> Such were the nations, Hellenic and barbarian, that inhabited Sicily; and such was the magnitude of the island the Athenians were bent on invading, craving—by the truest explanation—to dominate all of it, but wishing, at the same time, to aid in a seemly way their own kinsmen and their old allies [among the islanders]. (6:6)

The Athenians really wanted to add Sicily to their empire, but they covered their naked ambition with a costume of virtue—the wish to aid their kinsmen and allies.

In both these passages the immediate reasons offered by the combatants for their actions are contrasted with "the truest *prophasis*," Spartan fear of being conquered or ruled and Athenian ambition to rule. The analysis seems straightforward enough, and it accords well with the views presented by many of the speakers in Thucydides' history, who claim that it is "natural" for the strongest to want more and more and for everyone else to become aligned with or against the quest.

But this simple vision of *Realpolitik* and bipolarism is complicated by the fact that Thucydides' phrase "the truest *prophasis*" is, if translated according to normal Greek usage, something of a contradiction in terms. *Prophasis* normally means "pretext" or "excuse," and it has this meaning in many other places in Thucydides' text. The apparent *prophasis* is usually opposed to the underlying or hidden *aitia*: the "pretext" is not the true "cause." But, as many commentators have noted, Thucydides may have been drawing on the Hippocratic tradition in his analytic or diagnostic use of *prophasis*. In the plague narrative, for example, Thucydides notes (2:49) that the plague came on both the sick and the healthy. People who were already ill "all answered to this [plague]," "ἐς τοῦτο πάντα ἀπεκρίθη" (as a defendant answers to a judgment in court); but "others with no *prophasis* were suddenly seized while in good health, first with intense heat in their heads . . . ," etc. The word *prophasis* here has a technical meaning: precondition, prodrome. If it is this meaning that Thucydides is employing in the two passages on causality, then "the truest *prophasis*" does not mean "the truest explanation" (the usual translation) but "the truest precondition." And a precondition is not an ultimate cause; it is a form of proximate cause. Thucydides seems to be using *prophasis* in this way in his summary statement at the end of Book 1. After he has detailed the events leading to the outbreak of the war, he notes that even though hostilities had not yet begun, "the events which were taking place constituted annulment of the treaty and were the war's *prophasis*" (1:146).

In the plague narrative Thucydides specifically excludes from his own inquiry and leaves to others' investigations any discussion of the origin of the plague conditions: "I will tell the course of the disease, and from such a study, should it ever assault [ἐπιπέσι] again, it ought to be possible not to be ignorant, having foresight about it" (2:48). This statement seems to me to indicate quite clearly Thucydides' procedure throughout the *History*. Ultimate causes are not sought; particular precipitating events and preconditions, both specific and general, are. When ultimate causes are unknown or unknowable, it is not possible to make predictions about their effects, their "assaults," or about whether and how they might come again. But should they assault again, they will be recognizable to those who have studied their previous effects. To those who have come to appreciate the greatness and novelty of those effects will come the wisdom of expecting the unexpected.

The Athenians' greatness and the Spartans' fear of it were not, then, the ultimate causes of the Peloponnesian War. They were the general preconditions, the culmination of the socio-economic and political developments Thucydides outlines in Book 1. Similarly, Athenian imperial ambition was the crucial precondition for the invasion of Sicily. But behind these preconditions stood all the imponderables toward which Thucydides gestured with his personifications—war itself, plague, natural disasters and portents, chance, envy. The imponderable "forces" ranged against the combatants of both camps presented the supreme tests to human judgment. Ironically, before the war began, when they did not want it, the Athenians were quite well aware that the better part of judgment is respect for the unknowable and uncontrollable effects of war. With a Thucydidean personification, the Athenians warned the Spartans:

> Think ahead [προδιάγνωτε], before you get into it, how great a part is played in war by the unpredictable [παράλογον]. The longer it lasts, the more war loves to turn many things into matters of chance, which neither side can control—both sides must await the outcome in the dark. Most men rush into war, coming first to violence, which ought to be the last resort, and only later, after much suffering, to words. (1:78)

4

In Book 1, Thucydides contrasts his history, which he hoped would be a "possession for all times," with debate speeches designed to be pleasing for the moment. Three basic assumptions, I have argued, distinguish Thucydides' historical perspective from the perspective characteristic of debate speeches: he did not assume the continuity or repeatability of events; he did not assume the unchangeability of human nature; and he did not assume that the ultimate causes of human affairs are within human ken. He expected novelty, he respected the force of circumstances or contexts on human nature, and he realized that particular events and general preconditions can crystallize in many different ways, for reasons ultimately unanalyzable. Thucydides constructed the single and debate speeches in his history to show how difficult it is even for people of good judgment—those who shared at least some of his own assumptions—to hold their convictions and to lead others. On the other hand, he showed how bad judgment rests on the assumptions he rejected.

Pericles is the exemplar of good judgment in the first two books of the history. Grasping the significance of Athens' naval power, he persuades the Athenians to suffer the Lacedemonian attacks on Attic soil while they assemble their financial resources and deploy their armada. The Spartan commander Archidamus assumes that the Athenians will do what people who are attacked always do: meet the attack and not allow their land to be ravaged. Pericles' novel strategy succeeds, even though the Athenians are restive and he has to resort to canceling the public assemblies in order to keep his opposition under control. Later, when the Athenians have suffered the first year of the plague and watched their lands being destroyed, Pericles has to oppose the Athenians' desire to sue for peace. He calls the Athenians to assembly and seeks to persuade them to stay their course.

> When a great change takes place without advance warning, the disposition to persevere in what you have resolved gives way. What happens suddenly, unexpectedly, and in the highest degree against reason reduces one's determination to that of a slave. This is what has happened to you, especially in the plague. (2:61)

The virtues and graciousness of Athenian life, which Pericles praises so hopefully in the Funeral Oration, have been disrupted by the "great change" of the first years of war, "the one phenomenon that has proved stronger than our expectation" (2:64).

Thucydides clearly admired Pericles' resolution, but he did not comment directly on its result, which was that the Athenians gave up their efforts to seek peace and fought on. What he did emphasize was that with Pericles' death in 429 B.C. or even before it Athens was without good leadership. Books 3, 4, and 5 are dominated by Cleon's ascendancy in Athens and by many stories in which Athenian lack of judgment—and particularly lack of moderation, the virtue Pericles so often praised—is salient. As the war goes on and its violence escalates, the theme of "human nature" and the ways in which circumstances affect it emerges and echoes the plague narrative passages on the destruction of nature's limits. The significance for human judgment of this theme is highlighted in the debate between Cleon and Diodotus over whether to rescind the decision to punish the Mytileneans for their revolt with a mass execution of the male citizens and enslavement of the women and children.

The debate is multilayered: it concerns the importance of public debate in Athens, a distinction between arguments of rightness or justice and arguments of advantage or self-interest, as well as contrasting views of human nature. But the last level is fundamental. Cleon, the most violent of the Athenian leaders, argues that the Mytileneans revolted because, having been well treated, they turned insolent, as people always do when they find themselves suddenly and unexpectedly prosperous. The Athenians, he claims, should never have been solicitous of the Mytileneans' welfare: "for it is human nature to be contemptuous of the solicitous, but to be in awe of those who will not yield" (3:39). But, the harm having been done, the punishment should be a lesson to all the other allied cities. Cleon advocates the death penalty as a deterrent. Diodotus, on the other hand, presents a more general argument that "all men by nature err, both in public and in private life" (3:45), and no law or threat of punishment will deter them. Not only the prosperous, spurred by insolence, but the poor, emboldened by need, will transgress: "desire and hope are everywhere." The most advantageous course for ruling cities is to stop revolts before they start, or, when they have taken place, to punish the people responsible, not the whole population. Diodotus advocates a policy of prevention.

These two policies, different only in degree of severity, rest on two assumptions about human nature that differ in scope or genarality but not in substance. Ultimately, the similarities between the assumptions rest on another assumption, shared by both Cleon and Diodotus. The Athenians, in their Book 5 debate with the Melians—a debate that echoes in many ways the one over the fate of the Mytileneans—offer the base on which the assumptions about the nature of the ruled rest. They say of the rulers:

> Of the gods we believe, and of human beings we know clearly, that, whenever they have the power, they rule—by necessity of their nature [ὑπὸ φύσεως ἀναγκαίας]. And we, who neither made this law nor were the first to follow it after it was made, but, finding it made and expecting it to be in existence forever, use it—knowing that both you and others, if you had the power, would do the same. (5:105)

What all the debate speeches have in common is a vision of the constancy of human nature and a conviction that future successes will be as the past ones have been if policy reflects the vision. Thucydides did not oppose these assumptions about ruled and rulers with any more moralistic ones; he did, however, suggest their key political fault—underestimation of the impact of events, expected and particularly unexpected, on the human nature of perpetrators and victims alike.

Books 6 and 7 drive this point home. In an inertia of success, the Athenians decide to invade Sicily. But they do not understand that the war has been going on for years enough to have completely shifted both longstanding ties of alliance and kinship and socio-economic realities. They face in Sicily a "new world." And they do not anticipate that a Syracusan Pericles, Hermocrates, will have grasped the significance of Sicilian naval power and conceived a novel strategy: to outdo the Athenians on Athenian territory, the sea. Hermocrates first persuades the factious Sicilians to form a united front and organize for a close-quarters harbor battle in which the Athenian naval forte, maneuverability on the open sea, will be rendered a liability. When this strategy succeeds, Hermocrates persuades his Syracusan fellow citizens and their allies to refuse the Athenians the traditional escape of the defeated. The harbor mouth is blocked, and the Athenians, forced onto the land, are pursued to the bitter end.

In a certain sense and to a certain point history repeated itself in Sicily. The novelty of the repetition was that with quite Athenian innovativeness the Syracusans set out to defeat the Athenians as the Athenians had once defeated the Persians. The roles have not changed, but the players have. And the completely novel element was that the Syracusans and their allies did not allow the Athenians to survive their Marathon. Thucydides emphasizes the differences in his concluding statement about the greatness and novelty of the Sicilian victory and its existential impact:

> This was the greatest Hellenic action that took place during this war, and, in my opinion, the greatest action that we know of in Hellenic history: to the victors, the most brilliant successes, to the vanquished, the most calamitous of defeats—for they were utterly and entirely defeated, their sufferings were on an enormous scale, their losses were, as one says, total, for their army, navy, everything, was destroyed, and out of many only a few returned. (7:87)

Thucydides' Sicilian narrative is laced with stories of how sudden storms, eclipses of the moon, famines, and other assaults of the unexpected turned battles this way and that. The narrative is also dense with allusions to the assault of the plague on Athens. The imponderable forces for which Thucydides had such regard seem to ally for their greatest impact in this the greatest action of the war. As they are retreating after the devastating battle in the Syracusan harbor, the Athenians and their allies, who have already "endured sufferings too great for tears" (7:75), break ranks and kill each other in a contagion of fear and panic. Wild with hunger and thirst, they fling themselves into the river Assinarus to drink and drown under Sicilian volleys. Bodies are piled high in the riverbed to rot unburied, and the survivors of the carnage are herded as captives into a stone quarry, where for months they live without shelter and in such deprivation and despair that Thucydides seems at a loss to say any more than "they suffered everything one could imagine might be suffered by men imprisoned in such a place" (7:87). The reader hears an echo of the failure of language in the face of the plague, which was "more calamitous than according to human nature."

It is ironic that, as his army is being defeated by the Sicilians and by the combined assaults of war's unpredictabilities (*paralogoi*), Nicias, the pious and brave Athenian commander, beseeches the gods for aid. In a last valiant effort to keep his troops' hope alive, he argues that, even if the gods have had reason to punish the Athenians, they will now help those who "deserve their pity rather than their envy." To fortify his argument, he cautiously and vaguely invokes the repeatability of human affairs and the constancy of human nature: "Other men before us have attacked their neighbors, and, after doing what it is human to do, suffered what can be endured" (7:77). His invocation is general, but his precedent seems to be specific: he hopes that the Athenians will, as the Persians did at Marathon, escape from their defeat by retreating to the sea. Trapped by his awful precedent, he does not stand to fight but orders a night march toward the sea; and this fateful decision sends the army toward its unendurable suffering. The army's two divisions become confused in the dark, are separated, and cannot come to each other's assistance.

5

Throughout the middle books of his *History* Thucydides contrasts Athenian disunity with the unity Hermocrates the Syracusan inspired among his allies. Hermocrates' success was, pointedly, not a product of moral argument; rather, he gave his potential allies new interpretations of commonly held opinions about human nature and the unpredictability of the future. That is, he helped them to intellectual reconsideration and consensus.

Hermocrates is no more inclined than any other character in Thucydides' story to question the "law of nature" that people wish to dominate and, having dominated, to dominate further. But he shifts his hearers' attention to the corollary to this law that holds for those about to be dominated: "My criticism is directed not against those who wish to dominate, but against those who are more disposed to yield. For it is as humanly natural to defend against attackers as it is to dominate everywhere anyone who gives way" (4:61). Similarly, he takes the commonplace about the uncertain future that the Athenians had urged on the Spartans before the war began and makes it too into a call for unity. "The instability of the future rules in most things, and, although it is the most hazardous of all, it nevertheless appears most useful. For, fearing it equally, we are more inclined to approach each other with forethought [ἐξ . . . προμηθίᾳ]" (4:62).

It was his intellectual masterfulness, grounded in respect for forces large and unknown, that gave Hermocrates such an advantage over the Athenian invaders. He recognized the folly of thinking that "I am the ruler of chance [*tyche*], which I do not control, in the same way that I am of my own judgment" (4:64). The Athenians had committed just this folly when they set out for Sicily: "because of their present good fortune [*eutychia*], they expected to be thwarted in nothing, and believed, whether their forces were powerful or deficient, that they could equally achieve what was easy and what was difficult" (4:65).

Book 8, the unfinished book that is all that we have of Thucydides' post-Sicilian narrative, is a study of Athens disunified. Oligarchic leaders of great rhetorical skill and no civic loyalty emerge. They are characterized by their disregard for the vagaries of fortune and their authoritarianism. Thucydides presents them as evidence that the desire to rule over chance and the future and the desire to rule oligarchically or tyrannically over fellow citizens are linked desires.

Using their reserve finances and their remaining ships, the Athenians fought on after the Sicilian disaster. But the oligarchs who came to power in the city overextended these limited resources and lost a key campaign in Euboea. "When the news of what had happened in Euboea came to Athens, it caused the very greatest panic that had even been known there. Not the disaster in Sicily, though it had seemed great enough at the time, nor any other ever had so terrifying an effect" (8:96). The loss in Euboea finally did what even the Sicilian losses had not done: it penetrated the Athenians' unrealistic view of the dangers to which they had exposed themselves by expecting that their *eutychia* would repeat itself in the same or similar forms. In fear, awaiting a Spartan attack on the Piraeus, the home ground, the Athenians mounted a hasty defense and deposed the oligarchy, instituting rule by the Five Thousand with a new constitution. Thucydides comments laconically:

> Indeed, during the first period of this new regime the Athenians appear to have had a better government than ever before, at least in my time. There was a moderate co-rulership of the few and the many, and it was this primarily, that made it possible for the city to recover from the bad situation into which her affairs had fallen. (8:97)

Formally, this government was more stable than the Periclean democracy, which was dependent on Pericles' presence. But the formal achievement did not last: it had been born of fear and a political pendulum effect and not of a vision such as the one Hermocrates had articulated for the besieged Sicilians. Book 8 contains no speeches, no examples of judgment. What appear instead are treaty documents (among the few written sources in the *History*) that mark the huge shifts in alliance shaping the war around the new Athenian government as the Persians became more and more influential. The last phase of the war was in effect a second Persian War, with both Athens and Sparta vying for Persian support and the Persians shrewdly fostering false hopes and waiting for the Hellenes to destroy each other.

Thucydides does not try to show that moral corruption in Athens either gave rise to or arose from bad political judgment. For example, Alcibiades, who emerges in Book 8 as a model of corrupt self-interestedness, displays good judgment and prevents the Athenian civil war at a moment when the city's survival suits his own desires: "Alcibiades did his first great act of service to his country" (8:86). A corrupt man can make political judgments advantageous to the city in particular circumstances, just as a virtuous man—like Nicias—can make disadvantageous judgments. The great Aristotelian project of analyzing the true and proper relation between particular political judgments and virtue and of portraying the exemplary man of *phronesis*, practical wisdom, was not Thucydides' project.

Good judgment can result from a fearful paralysis of passion, as it did when the Athenians deposed the oligarchy, or from self-interested calculation, as it did when Alcibiades kept the Athenians from deposing the oligarchy by fratricidal war. But Thucydides presents as exemplary only good judgment that has a lasting effect because it includes reflexive interpretations of the intellectual conditions of good judgment. These interpretations can be shared; they are instructive to the community. Lastingly effective good judgment is a teacher of the intellectual conditions of good judgment; it unifies because it stems from and appeals to respect for the imponderables of human affairs, the unpredictability of the future and the fragility of human nature. Such respect is not presented by Thucydides as a product of moral virtue (though men of virtue, like Pericles, may possess it). It presupposes, rather, intellectual respect for the limits of intellect and also appreciation for novelty and greatness *in their contingency*. Those who can appreciate novelties know that the future will not be lacking in them, as those who can appreciate greatness know that its causes are ultimately beyond analysis. Like Thucydides himself, such people are storytellers rather than moralists.

Unexpected events, like the plague, and the teachings of the "teacher of violence" undid much of the good effect that Pericles' judgment had on the Athenians. But Pericles' example was heeded and used to new unifying effect and new strategic brilliance by Hermocrates in Syracuse. And both of these examples are available to others in Thucydides' story, a "possession for all times."

8

Innovation and Political Imagination

In both classical and early modern European political theory avoidance of what Aristotle called μετάβολαι περὶ τὰς πολιτείας (revolutions) was a dominant theme.[1] Descriptions of forms or types of rulership were central to political theories, and each description contained prescriptions for countering disruption and decay. Even when the eventual dissolution of all forms was assumed and even when, after Polybius, it became common to assume a cycle of rises and falls through all forms of rulership, political theorists foreclosed any effort to rush against fate with revolution. Montaigne, contemplating the havoc wrought in his homeland by religious civil war, called on the authority of the founding father of this political theoretical tradition: "Plato likewise does not consent to have the repose of his country violated in order to cure it, and does not accept an improvement that costs the blood and ruin of the citizens, ruling that it is the duty of a good man in that case to let everything alone and merely pray to God to lend extraordinary aid."[2] So distrustful was Montaigne of innovational reform that he argued for maintaining even bad laws if the price of reform was novelty and instability: "Of our laws and customs, many are barbarous and monstrous . . . [but] if I could put a spoke in our wheel and stop it at this point, I would do so with all my heart."[3]

Only after the era of the paradigmatic revolution, the one that rose up in Montaigne's homeland, did calls for innovation in political affairs take the form of calls for the genuinely new, not the old in new costume, for the unprecedented, not the renascent. Machiavelli, of course, had reflected long and approvingly on innovation; but his ideal was still innovation for the reestablishment of a classical form, for the attainment of a classical goal—a republic, a new Roman republic in Italy. Not until after the era of the French Revolution (the French Revolutions) was revolutionary scorn poured on the efforts of innovators to replay past grandeurs and antique precedents. As Marx said:

> Hegel remarks somewhere that all great, world-historical facts and personages occur, as it were, twice. He has forgotten to add: the first

time as tragedy, the second as farce. . . . The tradition of all the dead generations weighs like a nightmare upon the brain of the living. And just when they seem engaged in revolutionizing themselves and things, in creating something entirely new, precisely in such epochs of revolutionary crisis they anxiously conjure up the spirits of the past to their service and borrow from them names, battle slogans and costumes in order to present the new scene of world history in this time honored disguise and this borrowed language. Thus . . . the Revolution of 1789 to 1814 draped itself alternately as the Roman Republic and the Roman Empire.[4]

The nineteenth-century theorists had to find ways to present the revolutions they envisioned without the conceptual framework that had shaped the antique ideas of stability and order. The key to this antique conceptual framework was very simple: form controls matter in the political realm as in the artistic; the rulers form the matter of their subjects as an artist forms the cosmos from chaos. The nineteenth-century revolutionaries had to make an assault on the idea that a preexistent form determines matter, that the old controls the new and makes it like the old.

In this chapter, I am going to sketch, schematize, four images of political affairs in order to highlight what I will call the problem of innovation. The images come to us from Plato, Aristotle, Machiavelli, and Marx. Each of these thinkers, of course, offered many metaphors. But I am going to select out a metaphor used by all four, each in his own way, to present the problem of innovation. Each equated form with masculinity and matter with femininity; each used a metaphor of male-female relations to present political things. From this metaphor, rather than from metaphors of machines in equilibrium or disequilibrium, of organic bodies in homeostasis or disease, of geological layers in equipoise or in earthquake (the list could go on and on), I think we can formulate most clearly the problem of innovation as we have inherited it from Marx and his contemporaries. I am going to practice a mode of analysis that might be called political metaphorics, and toward the end of the chapter I shall try to reflect briefly on the advantages and disadvantages of this mode *per se.*

1

Both Plato and Aristotle worked from the assumption that there is or ought to be homology of structure among the three principal dimensions of reality: the cosmos, the *polis,* and the *psyche* of man. The basic differences between the two philosophers are, accordingly, the same in each dimension. Aristotle makes the difference in the cosmic dimension quite clear in his *Physics,* where he notes that Plato's system presupposed a Form, which is good and which, as a pattern to be imitated, is responsible for order in the world, since the cosmic Demiurge looks to the Form as he shapes the matter of the world. Aristotle's own construction requires not three basic types of elements (matter, form, and demiurge) but only two (matter and form). According to Aristotle, through a hierarchy of forms all matter strives to actualize the ultimate Form, called the Un-moved Mover. With this simpler construction Aristotle eliminates two Platonic tenets: first, that there is some random motion in the matter Plato's Demiurge formed; and second, that the psyches of plants and animals are self-moving or auto-motive. Plato had needed the first assumption to explain imperfection or evil whose source is recalcitrance in matter; and he had needed the second assumption to distinguish radically the origins of psyche from the origin of matter. For Aristotle imperfection or evil is simply incompleteness or a state of not-yet-being-formed, and matter and psyche are not radically but evolutionarily distinguished. The basic assumption of Aristotle's evolutionary construction is summarized in one sentence in the *Physics:* "The truth is that what desires form is matter, as the female desires the male and the ugly the beautiful—only the female and the ugly not *per se* but *per accidens*" (I, 9:20). (This last phrase means, of course, that the female and the ugly have no independent existence; they are steps on the way to the male and the beautiful, "accidents" of the fully-formed.)

Like Plato, Aristotle imagines matter as female. But Plato's female matter is always unruly, always disturbed by random motion, while Aristotle's is, although as yet incompletely ruled, yearning for rule. In Plato's human being the structural homologues to the three basic cosmic elements (matter, form, and Demiurge) are the three chief bodily locations and psychic functions: the head, which houses the immortal part of the psyche; the thorax, which houses the superior part of the mortal psyche; and the abdomen, which houses the inferior part of the mortal psyche, the appetites. Thorax and abdomen are separated by the midriff, says Plato, just "as the men's and women's apartments are divided in houses."[5] That is, the female or the material part of the human is divided from the male parts of form and Demiurge, respectively called "spirit" and "reason." In the *polis* the appetitive class, the artisan class, is similarly distinguished from the other two classes, the warrior-guardians and the philosopher-kings.

By contrast, Aristotle divides the psyche into three different parts or functions: the two rational parts (theoretical and practical) and the irrational one out of which the other two have developed.[6] The lower or worse function exists for the sake of the higher or better, just as do the lower classes in a state and the lower types of human activity in the individual. The systematic vision is, again, evolutionary:

> Also life as a whole is divided into business and leisure, and war and peace, and our actions are aimed some of them at things necessary and useful, others at things noble. In these matters, the same principle of preference that applies to the parts of the soul must apply also to the activities of those parts: war must be for the sake of peace, business for the sake of leisure, things necessary and useful for the sake of things noble.[7]

Both Plato and Aristotle attempted to describe the best, most stable form of government or rulership. Plato, of course, proceeded by imagining such a form, Aristotle by extrapolating it from a survey of all forms which had, to his knowledge, existed in the Greek world. Thus Plato tried to portray the best and Aristotle the relatively best form. As opponents of political innovation, both tried to analyze the sources of disruption or decay in the *polis*. Plato's analysis, which is in structural accord with his entire system, yields one chief source of instability: appetite or greed, which leads men to overstep the role and function for which they are by nature suited. The problem, in short, comes from the women's apartment. The imaginary republic declines when the guardians for some unexplained reason "bring together brides and bridegrooms unseasonably" and beget a faction of young guardians given to pursuit of wealth and in rebellion against the traditional guardian spiritual virtues.[8] In other words, the source of evil is random motion among the females, and it involves the female principle, the appetites.

The Platonic remedy for such a deformation is elimination of the family unit and neutralization of the independent female principle. In Aristotle's relatively best *polis* the situation is different and in ways that his overall system would lead us to expect. Aristotle formulated the stable mean between excess of democracy and excess of oligarchy and then added to this formulation an economic analysis of the stabilizing middle class, which he saw as a mean between excess of wealth and excess of poverty. Since innovation is defined as any regression from the means or ideal mixtures, there are any number of different ways that a *polis* may be disrupted, but all are, so to speak, failures of form, failures to reach stable form. A problem of excess is remedied by better channeling or control—not by suppression, but by balancing. Aristotle did not eliminate the family. Rather, he set the household in a position structurally comparable to the irrational part of the psyche and gave the rational male principle mastery over it. In this way, the female could be nutritive in political matters, just as in psychological matters the irrational part of the psyche nourishes the rational. The Platonic statesman, the philosopher-king, is analogous to the Demiurge: he must actively form the matter of his *polis* and neutralize matter's independent (sexual) motion. The Aristotelian statesman is less of an artist and more of a sexual controller; he works not from without or completely above but from within to bring about a harmonious hierarchy of interests and activities. Thus, the key to political practice in the Platonic republic is eugenics, and the keys in the Aristotelian relatively best *polis* are sexual regulation and habituation.

2

In his *Discourses* Machiavelli was only partly Aristotelian in spirit and hardly at all to the letter. He went contrary to Aristotelian tradition by emphasizing warrior-like *virtu* as the foundation for the civic virtue Aristotle had extolled. This stress on military valor was a theoretical innovation, as Machiavelli knew, and it was for the sake of innovation in politics. Machiavelli did not consider a static condition to be necessary for political order in the form of city-state he thought relatively the best, the republic; it could be the *sine qua non,* as it had been in Sparta and was in Venice, but the example of Rome had taught Machiavelli the value of expansion through conquest. He explored the means of maintaining the expanding state while stabilizing the states it had conquered. Formulating maxims of instruction for rulers, he showed how to fit a form of rule on a matter, a people, and how to keep the form in place. Corruption or destabilization was, of course, just as weighty a theme for him as it had been for Plato and Aristotle. But behind the causes his predecessors had outlined (unbalance or factionalization; inequality vis-à-vis the common good) Machiavelli found a root cause: indolence, sloth, effeminacy. Military training for all male citizens was his cure; necessity, the opposite of sloth, prods men to realize or activate their *virtu.*

In his most famous and most influential work, *The Prince,* Machiavelli advocates a particular kind of innovation and describes what it requires of a "new Prince." These are historical circumstances, he argues, when a prince without hereditary privilege or traditional legitimacy can seize on a people, to give them either a first form or a new form. Opportunities for first founding are very rare; reform is more common but very difficult, because even if a city has become disorganized and its people atomized so that the changes of quick new-forming are best, cities still have old ways and customs that must to some degree be respected.

The new prince, like a Platonic Demiurge, takes advantage of a relatively unformed matter, which, although not recalcitrant, has the random motion of tradition in it, and with a bold action he claps a new form (himself) upon it. The metaphors in which Machiavelli presents such action are metaphors of rape: the antique metaphors of form and matter, male and female, are translated into or mingled with the peculiar Machiavellian pair: *virtu* and *Fortuna*.

> I conclude then that Fortune varying and men remaining fixed in their ways, they are successful so long as these ways conform to circumstances, but when they are opposed, then they are unsuccessful. I certainly think that it is better to be impetuous than cautious, for Fortune is a woman, and it is necessary, if you wish to master her, to conquer her by force; and it can be seen that she lets herself be overcome by the bold rather than by those who proceed coldly. And therefore, like a woman, she is always a friend to the young, because they are less cautious, fiercer, and master her with greater audacity.[9]

In Machiavelli's metaphor the two-term Aristotelian image of evolution (matter and form) and the three-term Platonic image of fabrication (matter, form, and Demiurge) are combined. But Machiavelli's product has no cosmic or metaphysical homologue and is not tied to any analysis of the psyche. The historical studies through which Machiavelli wove his metaphor also do not include any comment on the social or political organization of men and women—indeed, women are not mentioned. His only concern is the female goddess Fortuna, whom he metaphorically equates with the matter (the people) she presents to a prince as her gift. The whole society on which the prince tests his *virtu* is female; and the measure of the prince's success is the degree to which the female society, through force or through manipulation of her "desires," can be cured of effeminacy, made male and military.

What Machiavelli envisions in *The Prince* is a small, semifeudal version of the society-wide crises that nineteenth-century thinkers called "revolutionary situations." These were extreme situations either of class conflict or of class breakdown, crises either of legitimacy or of structural disintegration in which no ruler could make claims of legitimacy. Not only the differences in historical material conditions but also the differences in metaphorical modes between Machiavelli and Marx are striking and revealing. Nevertheless, the metaphorical modes used by both writers have one important common element: whole societies are presented as female. As early as 1843, in his correspondence with Ruge, Bakunin, and Feuerbach (published in the *Deutsch-französische Jahrbucher*), Marx had fixed on a metaphor that he repeated throughout his career:

> But the system of profit and commerce, of property and human exploitation leads much quicker than increase of population to a rift inside

contemporary society that the old society is incapable of healing, because it never heals or creates, only exists and enjoys. . . . On our side the old world must be brought right out into the light of day and the new one given a positive form. The longer that events allow thinking humanity time to recollect itself and suffering humanity time to assemble itself the more perfect will be the birth of the product the present carries in its womb.[10]

Marx continued to envision various kinds of alliance between the intellectual "class traitors" of the bourgeoisie and the suffering humanity of the proletariat in the service of a "new form." And he continued to envision the new form as something gestated in the womb of the old society and given birth to by that society. As he writes in the introduction to the 1859 "Critique of Political Economy":

No social formation ever disappears before all the productive forces are developed for which it has room, and new higher relations of production never appear before the material conditions of their existence are matured in the womb of the old society.[11]

Marx's metaphor has many sources.[12] Most obvious in intellectual terms are the traditional Rousseauean and Romantic evocations of "mother nature" and the Hegelian dialectical theory of historical development, with its imagery of new eras, new births. Both of these heritages, either adapted or turned upside down, fitted well with the most widely-propagated symbol of the French Revolution: a woman, sometimes called Marianne, carrying a pike topped with the symbol of the Roman slave rebels, the Phrygian cap.[13] Marx echoes this symbol in his apostrophe to the 1871 Paris Commune: "Working, thinking, fighting, bleeding Paris— almost forgetful, in its incubation of a new society, of the cannibals at its gates—radiant in the enthusiasm of its historic initiative!"[14] Marx's metaphor also accords with his appreciation of the political role women had taken in the European revolutions, particularly in the Commune, and his vision of their equality in the future new society; both the appreciation and the vision had precedents within the French revolutionary tradition, where the term "feminism" was first coined, apparently by Fourier.[15]

But Marx's metaphor also seems to reflect a desire to repudiate the heirs and romantic aggrandizers of the Machiavellian metaphoric type, the Saint-Simonians, whose political sexuality was aggressive, explicit, and ambivalent beyond anything Machiavelli could have imagined. A troop of Saint-Simonians journeyed to Egypt in 1833 (a year they had proclaimed "the year of the mother") in search of a feminine messiah.

Among their many curious projects was one for piercing a canal through the thin "membrane" of the virgin African desert in order to provide the world's peoples with a means to achieve "universal association" in the "nuptial bed" of the Mediterranean Sea.[16] They envisioned a new human type—the androgynous person; a new revolutionary unit—the family; and a new prosperity based on technological innovation. Although their sexual metaphors were more of mystical union than rape, their vision of androgyny was decidedly militaristic. The distinctively nineteenth-century turn in their thought, allowing us to see them in relation to the Marxian metaphor, was an emphasis on the fruit of a mystical union of the sexes, *la palingensie:* They saw revolution as birth and invoked a state of continuous rebirth or permanent revolution.

If we took Marx's metaphor of the pregnant society literally or biologically, we would expect to be informed of the new society's paternity, and we could thus connect the metaphor with the Saint-Simonian fantasies. Marx does sometimes, particularly in his early work, provide the father; he speaks of existing political states as ready to be "impregnated with socialist principles."[17] Socialist principles, carried by socialist intellectuals, also act as father in this passage:

> As philosophy finds in the proletariat its material weapons so the proletariat finds in philosophy its intellectual weapons and as soon as the lightning of thought has struck deep into the virgin soul of the people, the emancipation of the Germans as men will be completed.[18]

But as Marx's emphasis on the proletariat's need to lead itself and be a class "for itself" developed (through polemics with Lasalle and with the Swiss Social Democrats), the fathering role of the intellectuals receded and the logic of violence emerged in the metaphor.

In his earliest work Marx simply invoked the birth of the new society from the womb of the old; by 1848 he saw this birth as a stage (immature life or infancy) requiring temporary measures for its protection. The perils of the new society's infancy were most clearly presented in the "Critique of the Gotha Program," as part of an argument against Lasalle's tendency to compromise the goals of the revolution with bourgeois ideals.

> What we have to deal with here [in Lasalle's program] is a communist society, not as it has *developed* on its own foundations but, on the contrary, just as it *emerges* from capitalist society; which is thus in every respect, economically, morally and intellectually, still stamped with the birth marks of the old society from whose womb it emerges.[19]

Ever since the *Manifesto* of 1848 the metaphor of the infant society in need of protection had entailed (for most countries) the notions of the revolutionary dictatorship of the proletariat and the exercise of force to sweep away the old forms of production. "Between the capitalist and the communist society lies the period of the revolutionary transformation of the one into the other. There corresponds to this also a political transition period in which the state can be nothing but the revolutionary dictatorship of the proletariat."[20] Those whom Marx calls "the sons of modern industry" have to destroy their mother. Thus the violence against the female principle common to the tradition Marx sought to break with recurs in a new way.[21]

3

In very different ways and for very different purposes Machiavelli and Marx both envisioned the innovative overthrow of a metaphorically female society: for Machiavelli she is fickle mistress Fortuna, and for Marx she is laboring mother Capitalism. Plato and Aristotle, by contrast, represented intersocial stability in metaphors of sexual neutralization and sexual regulation. Organic metaphors of one sort or another have been used throughout the tradition to represent "the body politic." But this shift from male-female metaphors for cosmic, intersocial, and interpsychic relations to female metaphors for a secular and, so to speak, a-cosmic society is momentous.[22] Throughout the theoretical tradition political formation has implied control of matter (the female principle), but control has not meant destruction.

Fabrication involves violence. When a given material is violently wrought into a new form the resultant novelty is relative either to a preexistent form imagined by the fabricator (Plato) or to a preexistent form of matter requiring actualization (Aristotle). In the Greek metaphors of fabrication, to which the metaphors of sexual domination run parallel, matter is formed. Marx's innovation is to attribute forming activity to matter itself, to the female principle, and to abandon metaphors of fabrication. In his early "Economic and Philosophical Manuscripts" Marx counters the religious doctrine of fabrication (the doctrine of creation) with an alternative for which he finds a sociopolitical analogue in the image of mother society:

> The idea of the creation of the world received a severe blow from the science of geogeny, the science which describes the formation and coming into being of the earth as a process of self-generation. Spontaneous generation is the only practical refutation of the theory of creation.[23]

But spontaneous generation does not take place in a womb; the old is not presumed as the source and gestator. If revolutionary novelties could exist without constraint from their environment, spontaneous generation would make a much less problematic metaphorical vehicle than "the womb of the old society." As soon as Marx considers the environment surrounding the infant new society, he reverts to metaphors of fabrication and sexual domination to indicate how that new society could survive.

Among Marx's heirs the theorist who argued most consistently for maintaining the image of spontaneity was a woman trained in botany and zoology, Rosa Luxemburg. Her critique of those Marxists who reemphasized the traditional political modalities had two principal elements: she opposed transformation of the Marxian "dictatorship of the proletariat" into the dictatorship of a party elite, which she called "dictatorship on the bourgeois model," and she opposed transformation of the Marxian historical-dialectical method into a method for imposing preconceived systems ("abstract formulas having absolute, general application") on historically specific situations.[24] Luxemburg's commitment to democracy (mass-based action) and to theoretical flexibility (nonfabricatory theorizing) is summarized in the following passage from her pamphlet "The Russian Revolution" (1919), which is a polemic against Lenin's "centralism":

> This socialist system of society should only be, and can only be, an historical product, born out of the school of its own experiences, born in the course of its realization, as a result of the developments of living history, which—just like organic nature, of which in the last analysis it forms a part—has the fine habit of always producing along with any real social need the means to its satisfaction, along with the task simultaneously the solution. However, if such is the case, then it is clear that socialism by its very nature cannot be decreed or introduced by *ukase*. It has as its prerequisite a number of measures of force—against property, etc. The negative, the tearing down can be decreed; the building up, the positive, cannot. . . . Only unobstructed, effervescing life falls into a thousand new forms and improvisations, brings to light creative force, itself corrects all mistaken attempts. . . . The whole mass of the people must take part in it. Otherwise, socialism will be decreed from behind a few official desks by a dozen intellectuals.

Luxemburg did not shy away from the violence inherent in the birth metaphor, but she insisted that the infant society grow without a prescription for further violence.

4

The metaphors of political theorists, like those of any artist, push out the boundaries of traditional conceptions. But, since they push from within, they must always pay for their place with a degree of tradition-boundedness. Marx's thought was bounded by the traditional form/matter and male/female equations even though he gave the elements new roles; and he reverted to the old roles as soon as he considered a new society faced with the old needs for stability and order.

The problem of revolutionary political innovation, which in our era has been nearly compassed by the problem of violence, has been the subject of voluminous and heated debates both within and without the Marxian tradition. Approaching the subject by examining its metaphoric representations can add nothing to the debate concerning the necessity or non-necessity, justifiability or unjustifiability of revolutions or of revolutionary violence. What such an examination can do is show in ideographic terms (so to speak) the traditional limitations of political theory.

If theories of very different sorts, conceived in very different eras, rely on a common metaphor, then focusing on how the metaphor is deployed can both illuminate the differences and set the stage for questioning the commonality. Noting the differences can, furthermore, prevent simplistic approaches to the commonality—can prevent, for example, concepts like "patriarchy" from becoming blunt and unnuanced. If the traditional lexicon is itself to be put in question, the factors that have constituted it must first be surveyed and evaluated.

Such historical inquiry can and should subtend current thought about innovation—particularly as it comes from the women's apartments! What is most obviously learnable is that old visions in which females are the material of fabrications, regulations, or conquests cannot be overcome by reversing their terms. Females as fabricators, regulators, or conquistadors would never get away from the forms of violence time and again imagined as male prerogatives. The shift toward metaphors in which women have a real role—such as Marx's metaphor of capitalist society giving birth to a new socialist society—marks not only a shift toward democratic theorizing but a shift away from simple dichotomies and (hierarchies) like male/female and form/matter. But in Marx's metaphor the female principle is accorded only a very specific and conventionally conceived role (mothering), and males hover in the background waiting to announce not just their paternity and present regulatory capacity but their sonship or future regulatory capacity.

Rosa Luxemburg's vision is, finally, fully democratic and also pluralistic. She metaphorically presents as many flowers of political organization blooming as can bloom. This is Marianne's revolution.

9

The Writing of Biography

Serious contemporary biography seems to me to be besieged at every step with a temptation comparable to the one yielded to at every step by the biographical *paparazzi* of the popular press: the temptation to try to capture the subject as the subject really was, to catch the subject in a moment of truth, to reveal what was hidden even from those close to the subject, even from the subject himself or herself. Here, between these covers, the biographer is tempted to say, is "the essence of a life."

The temptation to be comprehensive or definitive also comes along, of course, but it disappears under its own weight, because there are always unanswerable questions, missing pieces of information, conflicting testimonies, blank periods, and because anyone who has stopped to think at all knows that definitiveness is a myth. Similarly, the temptation to be adulatory in the nineteenth-century Lives-of-the-Great, Carlylean, hero-worship manner—the temptation to write two-volume, after-dinner testimonial speeches—slinks away of its own accord, for we live in the aftermath of a psychoanalytic revolution and know (so we think) that what meets the public eye is never the real story. But the temptation to be—what shall I call it?—a biographical essentialist both remains and takes nourishment from the psychological milieu. And it remains through years of research, through the large spaces of a book-length study. Out of all the things left behind, the papers and documents, the recollections and stories, the biographer expects the subject somehow to appear, like a voice at a seance, and to speak into the pages of the biography his or her heart of hearts.

Like most temptations in the noncriminal domain, this one ought to be faced squarely and understood *before* it is resisted. For to resist immediately, even for good theoretical reasons, a temptation that has its good reasons for arising would be to miss a crucial ingredient in the complex process of writing a biography. Philosophers who pour scorn on the project of *proving* the existence of either things or God, like lovers who ridicule the impulse to *possess* the beloved, make a comparable mistake: they rightly set aside an impossible goal, but they do not acknowledge the importance of the desire for that goal—or the complexity of the desire.

In exploring the biographer's temptation, this lure of essence, I shall note what I take to be its major forms for a biographer whose subject is a thinker and writer and then extend my reflections to the political significance of biography as a mode of historiography.*

It seems to me that there are four—at least—forms of the temptation to capture "the essence of a life." The first stems from a kind of *esprit de système:* you want to find the ruling intellectual universal, the key question, the object of your subject's intellectual quest, and then you want to show the subject's thought and life in their integrality, in their oneness and harmony.

The second form of the temptation also arises from a need for synthesis: you select from amongst the strong traits of character and signs of habitual disposition those that either harmonize beautifully or clash intriguingly in order to present a compelling portrait of the subject's personality. You practice a version of what Virginia Woolf called "The New Biography." The goal here is vividness, lifelikeness. The first form of the essentialist temptation might, if yielded to, result in a portrait of the subject recollected in tranquility; the second, in a cinema "short" or novelistic sketch of the subject doing what the subject essentially did.

The last two forms of the temptation present a whole through a part; rather than being synthetic, they are synecdochical: the subject is essentially some deed or work he or she did or made, or the subject is essentially a representative of some ideal. Pursuing the first of these forms, you select an event or series of events that seems to epitomize the subject's entire life, that seems to be the intersection where all roads in the subject's life come together and reveal their unfoldings, and you make this event or series of events stand for the whole life. This form of the temptation presents itself with a special strength if your subject's life seems to have had a turning point or a crisis after which—or during which—everything changed. The goal here is drama: a play within the play or a *peripeteia* in which a destiny is, finally, manifest. In the last form of the essentialist temptation, the subject is presented as a part standing for a whole, a symbol, a rallying point—a remnant of some past, a sign of the present,

---

*I should note that this discussion is restricted to biographies of people who were not unworthy as people or in the eyes of their biographers. Writing about evil people, like any form of reflection on evil, deserves separate attention, because our modern tradition is conceptually so empty-handed about the whole topic.

or a herald for the future. You capture the subject poised like Liberty leading the people, Justice holding her scales. Biographical portraiture of this sort resembles panoramic painting.

For the sake of order and easy recall, the four forms I have sketched could take the traditional biographical subtitles: Life and Thought, A Life, The Story of a Life, Life and Times. Further elaboration and some illustrations may persuade you that these forms are not figments of my imagination or regrets after the fact of my having written a biography.

Ernst Cassirer's biography of Immanual Kant, called *Kant's Life and Thought,* which appeared for the first time in English translation recently, is a perfect example of the first form. In his introduction Cassirer states his goal with admirable precision:

> the peculiar fascination and the peculiar difficulty of the task . . . consist . . . in discovering and illuminating the *Lebensform,* the form of life, corresponding to [Kant's] form of thinking. . . . In Kant's actual existence . . . thought, in its objective content and in its objective "truth," not only rules life but also receives in return the characteristic stamp of the life to which it imparts its form. Here the peculiar reciprocal relationship prevails in which each of the two moments that influence each other appears simultaneously as determining and determined.

Far from being alarmed by the motto Kant placed above his *Critique of Pure Reason—De nobis ipsis silemus* (about ourselves, we remain silent)—Cassirer accepted the motto as a directive for recasting as a general form all the multitude of little facts about Kant's life so lovingly recorded in earlier biographies. From the many descriptions of Kant's daily routines and affairs, he abstracted what he needed to present "a truly unified whole, not merely . . . the unity of a characteristic type of behavior." Cassirer wanted to capture Kant as he really was: "the total act of judging and reasoning" come alive.

Kant's Life and Thought does justice to the generality, the formality, and the systematic intent of Kant's life and thought, and it satisfies Cassirer's own neo-Kantian need for coherence and integrality. But the cost is very great: the biography lacks both historical consciousness and self-consciousness on the part of the biographer himself. The price seems to be typical for this mode of biography.

If you have never met a "truly unified spiritual whole," it is probably not because your acquaintance is limited. If it is possible at all, oneness of *Lebensform* and thought form is possible only in particular historical moments—moments when there is surface equipoise among conflicting forces and turmoil brewing unheeded in the depths, in the as-yet unmanifest aspirations of emergent historical figures. To approach his subject clearly, Cassirer would have had to take the measure of the distance between the years prior to the French Revolution, when Kant was writing his Critiques, and the years of World War I, when Cassirer was writing *Kant's Life and Thought*. And he would have had to combine his measuring with insight into his own life in the context of World War I, into his own life as an heir of Kant, a neo-Kantian in times profoundly un-Kantian. Cassirer's reticence on both these counts were obviously important to him in philosophical terms—he, too, followed the motto *De nobis ipsis silemus*. But this attitude makes philosophy, which certainly is in one sense *philosophia perennis*, a plant without soil. In our times anyone who writes biographically about a philosopher must take the steps that Cassirer did not take; that is, he or she must explore why it is that in our time life and thought do not cohere very often or for very long—why it is that struggles for integration are not finally successful, even though they can be waged, again and again, heroically.

Nonetheless, Cassirer's ideal is an important corrective of the essentialist biographical temptation in its second manifestation, which can easily result in *Leben* without any *Form* and without any shadow of thought form. Personality portraiture, which emerged historically as *the* biographical mode of the years after World War I, focused on the tumultuous and inchoate wishes that were the special interest of Sigmund Freud. It is not an accident—as the Marxists say—that personality biography burgeoned in the 1920s or that Virginia Woolf praised its founding father, Lytton Strachey, for facing his eminent Victorians as "an equal [who] preserves his freedom and his right to independent judgment." They were not always received, but lessons in the importance of independent judgment and self-development were delivered constantly by that war and its aftermath. Self-analysis was the order of the day and, as Mark Longaker observed in 1934, "the [then] present day reader most often goes to biography because he is interested in himself." Much the same remark could have been made of people who went to biography *writing*.

The precondition of personality portraiture is equality with the subject. But this equality is not a given; it is what the biography writing produces in those who do it well. For, regardless of his or her actual age, the biographer is young in relation to the subject and must begin, in one or more of the possible literal or metaphorical ways, as a child. Thus there is bound to be in the portraying an ingredient, large or small, of what Freud called the "family romance." The ingredient has, it seems, grown larger in the years between Virginia Woolf's manifesto and our own moment. It has recently become fashionable for biographers to present the "family romance" in their prefaces, by offering little analyses of their relations to the subject and the subject's place in their fantasies. The biographer's statement of personal engagement signals that what will follow is an immediate encounter, a biography that will read more like an extended interview than a history book, more like a journalist's notebook than a critical study.

The "family romance" dimension of biography writing is clearest when the biography is a sort of recovery from misinterpretation or obscurity, for this kind of work combines easily with a biographer's own search for identity, a room of his or her own, freedom, and independent judgment. At the present moment, biographies of women are particularly apt to be shaped by quests for definition—this is one of the most interesting ways in which the past now presses upon the present and shapes it. As contemporaries discover the conditions of life for their "mothers," their own sense of how the world is—and often of how it is oppressive—shifts.

More than any other historiographical mode, personality biographies, because they incorporate the "family romance," reflect relations between generations. For public figures about whom interest is constant the period between biographies is often a generation—each generation produces a revision of the previous generation's portrait; for figures about whom interest is not so constant, a new biography often signals that two generations have parted ways or clashed with a particular urgency. Literary figures of the Romantic era, of fin-de-siècle Vienna, the Weimar Republic, or the Bloomsbury Circle, have lent themselves several times recently to generational identity quests, at least in part because these figures were involved in their own generations' definitions. The legacy of Romanticism weighs heavily in biographies where the focus is personality.

Biographies of this sort are predicated on the assumption that (in Leon Edel's words) "a secret myth, as well as a manifest myth [lies] hidden within every creative life." The temptation to capture a personality is phrased as a challenge to decipher a mystery, to read the palimpsest of a text right down to the Ur-text. Thus, for example, Curtis Cate says in the preface to his *George Sand: A Biography:*

> It is clear that 'the Good Lady of Nohant' was anything but a monolithic personality and singularly complex. There is a measure of truth in the acid comment her daughter, Solange, once scribbled, after her [sic] death, on one of George Sand's letters: 'Bien malin celui qui debrouillera ma mere.' (A shrewd one it will be who will unravel my mother.) No wonder her contemporaries were so often baffled by this strange sybil with the huge, devouring black eyes who could be as mute and mysterious as the Sphinx.

Cate's portrait of this complex personality is designed to display Sand as though she were a character in a novel: through episode after episode she acquires all the attributes of a George Sand heroine—and she is thus tamed, prevented from devouring her biographer. Cate even makes George Sand arise again and speak in his preface: she delivers a posthumous diatribe against present-day pornographic "lust and license." Cate can summon George Sand to his service because he is convinced that he has shrewdly possessed her very essence, recapitulated her.

It is more than a little ironic that the main biographical reaction to the temptation to capture a personality—to get inside the subject's self and speak out, to possess the subject's soul authoritatively—has produced not a return to Cassirer-like synthetic vision but a heightening of the personality biography approach. The third form of the essentialist temptation, in which a part of the life stands for the whole, has converted personality portraiture into self-conscious mythologizing.

The main topic of this mode is the subject's achievement of identity; its form might be described as *Bildungsroman* plus psychoanalysis. The moment of identity achievement can come when Freud's three stages—anal, oral, genital—have all been undergone, or when Erik Erikson's seventh and last stage has been reached, or when an "existential crisis" has been met and survived, and so forth. Some form of developmental psychology provides the table of contents for the biography of turning points, the form of biography that had its great days after World War II—after that horrendous and prolonged crisis.

As an example of this type, I offer a passage from Jean-Paul Sartre's biography *Saint-Genet: Comédien et martyr:*

> A voice declares publicly: 'You're a thief.' The child was ten years old. That was how it happened, in that or some other way. In all probability, there were offenses and then punishment, solemn oaths and relapses. It does not matter. The important thing is that Genet lived and has not stopped reliving this period of his life as if it had lasted only an instant.

Sartre presents the moment in which Jean Genet becomes a thief, the moment in which his identity was cast as a mythic project and prepared for future mythologization. The biographer, capturing the life of his subject at an extremity, then tracks the moment to what Malraux called "la pointe extrême de l'oeuvre," the point in the work at which the subject is most essentially himself or herself. The facts do not matter. And the goal is not to unravel a mysterious personality; it is to show one being created in vast geometries of time.

This mode adds to the mode of personality portraiture a heightened self-consciousness about the biographer's role and relation to the subject: that is, the biographer is self-consciously an artificer, a dramatist. The reader is not swept up in the rushing current of a life; rather, the reader is offered an occasion for a catharsis—for release from *mauvaise foi* and bourgeois moral monotony. The truth sought is not literal truth, for no illusion or merger between biographer and subject is allowed; the biographer is not to say omnisciently "he thought" or "she felt," but only (only!) "*This* is the important moment"—the moment when the subject's own concept of self congealed.

Both personality biography and crisis biography have been very challenging to traditionalist historians and literary critics, people who prefer chronicles to interpreters, archivists to artificers. Writers of biographies who consider psychobiography in any form a travesty are particularly vociferous about the danger of letting the unconscious and the irrational loose on the pages of the story of humankind. But, although many people of the "just the facts, please" schools of thought have tried to correct the excesses of personality portraiture and crisis capturing, the most forceful correctives have come from another quarter. We do not any more appreciate biographies in the mode recommended by Carlyle's *On Heroes, Hero-Worship and the Heroic in History*, but we do like their modern analogues: biographies in which the subject is presented as a paradigmatic figure, a man or woman of the hour, the era, or the century—thus, *Walter Lippmann and the American Century*, Ronald Steel's careful chronicle of "the nation's greatest journalist." If the literary critical terminology of deciphering informs personality biography and the developmental psychological terminology of stages informs crisis biography, it is the terminology of philosophies of history and science that inform the mode of Life and Times. The subject is, like a Kuhnian paradigm, a definition of the times and also a boundary at which a revolutionary new time came or will come; or the subject is, like a Marxian superstructure, "in dialectical relation" to his or her times.

In this last mode the status of the subject is of no importance. The subject can be a "larger than life" individual of great achievement or an unknown or even a group constituted historically or gathered by the biographer because of thematic affinities. All that is required is that the subject be or be thought typical, representative. Influenced by the *Annales* school of social history, by Marxism, by structuralism, or by any other theory that distinguishes deep trends and slowly unfolding tendencies from surface phenomena, biographers of this mode try to catch perfect synchronic moments, life moments riding on the surface like buoys over plumb lines that reach to the bottom of the sea. This perspective stands behind a reflection Peter Nettl offered in the preface to his *Rosa Luxemburg:*

It is often held that the importance of a biography can be measured *prima facie* by some notional consensus about the importance of the subject. Reviewers especially equate 'proper' book weight with subject status. This seems to me nonsense—or at least true only at a very crude level of judgment. Every person is interesting if interestingly presented; it is the context that matters.

It is possible—I think it is likely—that the only contemporary individuals whose lives do well in the services of this last biographical mode are those who hated the idea of biography but believed that, in W. H. Auden's words:

> *our* suffering, *our* weaknesses, are of no literary interest whatsoever. They are only interesting in so far as we can see them as typical of the human condition. A suffering, a weakness, which cannot be expressed as an aphorism should not be mentioned.

In other words, only the truly reticent are truly representative; all others are suitable only for propaganda.

I stated earlier that I think these four forms of temptation should be resisted. But it must be obvious by now that I do not think they should be resisted completely. In both its "perfections" and its excesses, each form has something to teach; but in order to learn, a biographer must have a sense of the limits of each.

The Life and Thought mode easily becomes overly general and unrealistic; it stresses form to such an extent that any mere particularity of the subject—much less any foible, low cunning, or silliness—fades to insignificance. No matter what protestations to the contrary the biographer may make, thought dominates over life in this mode. The subject seems to have lived only to think. A sense of limits about this mode seems to me to arise of its own accord if the biographer simply pauses to reflect that those who think, those who truly are thinkers, think in order to live, in order to shape and purify their lives into lives worth living. Albert Camus made a remark in his 1943–1945 *Notebook IV* that contains a warning:

> I took ten years to win what seems to me priceless; a heart without bitterness. And as often happens, once I had gone beyond the bitterness, I incorporated it in one or two books. Thus I shall be forever judged on that bitterness which has ceased to mean anything to me. But that is just. It is the price one must pay.

Personality portraiture and crisis capturing easily become just reflections of the biographer's love or love-hate identification with the subject. A sense of limits about this mode can be learned from psychoanalysis itself: a biographer who remains a child and who wishes to fashion the parental figures according to his or her own desires and aspirations is bound to fail. The growing-up process of biography writing has to leave behind the stage in which character assassination is employed to make parents show their faults or lose their power to dominate. It must pass into the stage where the subject is accepted, just as a family is accepted by an adult. Marcel Proust, whose knowledge of relations between parents and children is exhausting and inexhaustible, offered the maxim for this stage: "After a certain age, the more one becomes oneself, the more obvious one's family traits become." The biographer must outgrow the wish either to *be* or to transform the subject, either to usurp the subject's place or to rebel. The biographer must be willing and able—able because possessed of a secure but not fixed self—to let the traits of the chosen "family," the subject, appear in himself or herself as naturally and inexorably as do the traits of the biological family.

Finally, I think few people would doubt that we all *need* exemplary myths and exemplary lives—the products of biography in the last mode. We need them in our adulthood so that we do not lose, but rather creatively transform, the project of growing up—that is, the project of reacquiring the past, the world into which we were born and in which we do our piece of the road. "Life must be lived forwards," Kierkegaard said, "but can only be understood backwards."

We need examples, yes, but the sense of limits should come with the realization that we do not need—and are even harmed by—examples completely determined by historical model-making and historiographical pedagogy. We need examples who lived in the world and were very much of the world—who were neither beasts nor angels, neither antiheroes nor heroes, but humans. I think Aristotle was wrong—although, as always, for good reasons—when he set poetry and philosophy over against history, saying that the former two are concerned with universals while the latter treats only particulars. Lord Bolingbroke seems to me to have been more correct when he quoted Dionysius of Halicarnassus' saying: "History is philosophy teaching through examples." Biography is, I think, philosophy teaching through stories. But lest this seem programmatic or just dogmatic, I should confess that the life stories that please me please me because they are philosophical.

This last piece of subjectivity brings me to my own practice as a biographer. The subtitle of my biography of Hannah Arendt is not *Life and*

Thought, A Life, The Story of a Life, or *Life and Times;* it is *For Love of the World.* To Arendt the phrase *amor mundi* stood for an attitude opposite to the traditional philosophical perspective of *contemptus mundi.* To me, as I wrote about her, the phrase stood for an attitude toward her life and my readers.

It seems to me that there are two different but related questions that a biographer has to consider before setting out on the project of presenting readers another person's life story. One question is philosophical, the other political.

When biographers use a phrase like "the essence of a life" (which is borrowed from Leon Edel, author of *Henry James*), they assume that there is such an essence and that it is discoverable. The assumption does not have to rest on a rationalist metaphysic; it is as often tied to some form of intuitionism. But whether it is assumed that reason (or scientific intellect) finds the essence or that intuition does the job, the goal is the same: truth. A biography is supposed to be analogous to a truth statement that is adequate to or corresponds to "the essence of a life."

The philosophical problem involved in this assumption is a variant on the one that has been with us throughout the history of philosophy: what is truth? I certainly do not propose to offer a treatise on this question. But I believe that if one does not—as I do not—accept the assumption that there is an "essence of a life," all is not given over to relativism, anarchism, meaninglessness, or any of the other doorways to irrationality that believers in essence fear will open if their answers to the "What is truth?" question are not embraced. In my own practice as a biographer I did without the notion of essence by constructing for myself a schematism of types of statements I thought I could and should make. I borrowed the notion of such a schematism from Karl Jaspers and from a book I wrote about him. It should be immediately apparent that the possibility of stating "the truth" grows more and more remote toward the nether reaches of this schematism.

I first made statements of fact about events in Hannah Arendt's life and about events in the social and political contexts in which she lived. That is, I made a catalogue of events, a chronology, a chronicle, to serve as the organizing framework of my biography. The goal here *was* truth, accuracy, and completeness.

Next, I made statements about Arendt's consciousness as it related to the consciousness of others who shared her world, who observed what she observed, traveled where she traveled, read the books and newspapers she read. The purpose here was to present the truth as Hannah Arendt conceived it and articulated it and shared it with others, by serving as an excerpter of quotations from correspondences, published materials, and documentary sources.

I then proceeded to make statements about Hannah Arendt's culture—
that is, in the broadest sense, about the education of her spirit, her
philosophical and political *Geist*. At this level of my narrative I thought
of myself as producing a meditation on the modalities of the time—on
the interplay of past, present, and future in the psychological, historical,
and philosophical dimensions of one person's life. Beginning in the first
chapter and continuing through to the last, I tried to show how Arendt
lived not just in our times but in time. With this meditation I hoped
to present—not to describe directly or thematically, but to present in
narrative—what I take to be the fundamental chord of her philosophizing: being-in-time, the life of *homo temporalis*.

Finally, I made existential statements about the situations—Karl Jaspers would have called them *Grenzensituationen,* boundary situations—in
which Arendt's life took on its characteristic forms, in which she achieved
not one *Lebensform* but several. I kept in mind Jaspers' philosophical
reflections on what it is to elucidate—not describe, but elucidate—boundary situations like the following (in his words): "that I am always in
situations; that I cannot live without struggling and suffering; that I
cannot avoid guilt; that I must die." On this level of my biography I tried
to develop a theme: it is not possible to know another's existential self,
another's *Existenz;* it is possible only to show the person's forms of communication with companions. In other words, how a person makes and
maintains friendships is *how*—if not *who*—she or he is.

The question that guided me through these levels was very simple—
and very difficult: what kind of biography will build toward the last
level without fixing the relations between the levels, without becoming
architectonic? What kind of biography will preserve my respect for what
will always remain hidden to me?

As for the political question a biographer must, it seems to me, answer,
biographies are many things, many more than I have indicated in this
rough survey. And in each historical era biographies have a different
role to play in the private and public domains of memory. I believe the
biographer's first political responsibility ought to be to think about the
prevailing conditions of memory and to write what is needed for contemporary memorialization. This may, at first, seem like a very limited point
of view, but I believe it is not.

In our time we have had to learn that it is human to remember and
that to be deprived of memory—perhaps even just to remember inade-
quately—is to be dehumanized. One might think, because we are surrounded by more means of memory than have ever been in the world—
because we have libraries, "oral history" archives, films, documentary
exhibits, works of art in all media, even "memory banks"—that we are
protected from forgetfulness. I doubt it. Indeed, all these means seem

simply to lull us into thinking that devices of memory *are* memory. But one must *learn* to remember and thus to judge the past.

On the other hand, the charge "lest we forget" can also be numbing. Many people fear that there have been such horrors in our time, including the horror of living under the threat of an event we call by the abstract name *the unthinkable,* that we must be commanded to remember. Otherwise, it is argued, we will perish by virtue of the past's repeating itself or of a holocaust spread across the planet more definitively than any death camp. But shelves upon shelves of answers to the command "Remember!" can also lull us into thinking that voluminous information about the past constitutes memory.

Memory cannot be contrived and it cannot be commanded. We do not learn by placing ourselves in archives, and we do not learn by being required to receive information about past events. To learn one must actively participate—one cannot just receive.

A biography writer participates by preserving a life story that would, without the act of preservation, be lost, in some measure at least, with the passing of a generation. In my own case the element of storytelling, the handing down orally from one generation to another, was crucial; for me listening to and reproducing the stories I was told were the most challenging tasks of preserving a contemporary's life story. A biography reader participates by interpreting the stories reproduced. My guidance in writing came from a paragraph in Walter Benjamin's essay "The Story-Teller":

> Every morning brings us the news of the globe, and yet we are poor in noteworthy stories. This is because no event any longer comes to us without already being shot through with explanation. In other words, by now almost nothing that happens benefits story-telling; almost everything benefits information. Actually, it is half the art of story-telling to keep the story free from explanation as one reproduces it. The most extraordinary things, marvelous things, are related with the greatest accuracy, but the psychological connection of the events is not forced on the reader. It is left up to him to interpret things the way he understands them, and thus the narrative achieves an amplitude that information lacks.

As I understand it, the message for a biographer implicit here is to leave the search for the interrelations of the levels of a life story—and thus for the meaning of a life—to the reader. The best way to avoid the temptation to capture "the essence of a life" and to keep open the question of its meaning is to trust one's readers; to trust the bonds, the *rapports,* the biographer and the reader have as contemporaries. Such bonds are what Hannah Arendt called "the world."

It seems to me that acts of biographical memorialization must be made from love, which is uncontrivable and uncommandable. And not finally from love of the subject's thought, personality, psychological uniqueness, or typicality—not from any measure of the subject's importance generally or to the biographer as an individual. Acts of biographical memorialization are for the world, from love of the world.

10
Psychoanalysis and Biography

Since World War II many reflections on the nature and method of biography have been published. As a glance at a library card catalogue will reveal, most of these treat biography "as a literary form." But recently it has also been considered as a type of history-writing or even social science and as a type of psychology-writing. These last two characterizations appear together in reflections on what is known as "psychobiography," a subspecies of psychohistory and also a branch of "applied psychoanalysis."

The literature on psychobiography—by historians, psychoanalysts, and general biographical practitioners—is mainly methodological. Commentators focus on how psychological—predominantly psychoanalytic—theory has been and ought to be applied to the data and documents, memories and memorabilia from which a biography can be constructed. This focus is, of course, not detachable from the question of which theory is to be applied. And so it has been the case that methodological discussion of psychobiography has generally followed the course of theoretical discussion of psychoanalysis: the first period of psychobiographical writing, through the 1920s, was dominated by early Freudian theory, while the postwar period has been dominated by various ego psychologies.

Regardless of whether or not they advocate a particular theory, methodological commentators have generally agreed about what kind of psychobiographical practice they find unacceptable. A psychobiographer must not indulge in "wild psychoanalysis"—that is, must not set a simplified theory down on the data and read off the result. When this is done, the result is something as misleading as Binion's announcement at the very beginning of his study of Lou Andreas-Salomé that she had "a craving for her father excited by excretion and attended by darkling visions of re-entering his bowel-womb to repossess his penis."[1] Good practice is, not surprisingly, more difficult to describe, and the number of psychobiographies that any commentator is willing to hold up as exemplary is very small. But most writers do agree that theory or theories should be used flexibly for "listening with the third ear" (in Reik's much-quoted phrase) to biographical materials and then used cautiously in interpretation, with due and frank regard being given to all interpretive difficulties.

Among the interpretive difficulties are those associated with and consequent to the differences between therapeutic practice and biography-writing—difficulties that are obvious but not always obviously taken into account. At the least, there are three areas of difference:

1. The biographical subject is not an analysand: there is no analytic transference to be analyzed and no possibility of confirmation of an analyst's construction; further, the type and quantity of materials to be analyzed are not comparable in the two activities, and there is no free association ordering the biographical materials.
2. The biographer is not functioning as an analyst (even if he or she is one by training), and there is thus only an analogue to "counter-transference."
3. A biography is not a case history: the subject's life must be narrated, not told in theoretical categories, and it must be set in the world, among other people (whose stories must also be narrated), and in relation to intellectual, social, economic, and political institutions and events.

Commentators on psychobiography have developed typologies of psychobiology complementary to these differences. In 1960, for example, Heinz Kohut, noting that most psychobiographies to that date were focused on "creative minds and their creations," distinguished three types according to their aims: biographies supported by psychoanalysis and designed to illuminate the personalities of significant individuals; psychoanalytic pathographies designed primarily to expand psychoanalytic knowledge or to apply existing knowledge; and biographies focused on creativity or disturbances of creativity and designed to explore the development of ego functions involved in creativity.[2] (The line between case study and biography in the last two categories is not always clear.) To these types should be added a fourth: biographies of great figures in history designed to illuminate both a personality and a context, the relation between life history and history.

Methodological reflections of the three kinds I have sketched have helped to bring recent psychobiographical writing to a sophistication not observable in its first enthusiastic period, when bad practice was little more than *biographie de la boudoir* or debunking of exalted reputations and even good practice tended toward what might be called "applied oedipus complex."[3] And the milieu in which psychobiography is practiced has changed. Hardly a recent biography is not unsupported by at least acquaintance with psychoanalysis, and few readers are astonished to find biographical subjects no longer—to use Havelock's characterization—*bien coiffé* and cut off at the chest like Victorian portrait busts. Nonetheless, there is little evidence in the methodological literature that the development of psychobiography since Freud has been important for psychoanalytic theory or that the relation between psychoanalysis and biography can be reciprocal.

In what follows, I am going to take two paths, which will eventually come together. On the methodological level, my questions will be: whether and how psychobiography can take into account the traditional aim of biography-writing—that is, moral pedagogy or the presentation of exemplary lives; and why methodological commentary on psychobiography has ignored the fact that there are so few psychobiographies of women by women and only a few more of women by men. These two tracks will show, I think, how ahistorical methodological reflections on psychobiography have been, but such a demonstration is not my main purpose.

The literature on psychobiography, oriented as it is toward "how to" methodological questions about application of theory, does not touch, it seems to me, the motivational level, the question why do people write biographies? About this question, the literature itself has not been supported by psychoanalysis, illuminating for psychoanalysis or psychoanalytically concerned with creativity—to use Kohut's categories.[4] By focusing my attention on two of the most imaginative modern biographies—Freud's 1910 "pathography" of Leonardo da Vinci and Virginia Woolf's 1928 novel, *Orlando: A Biography*—I shall sketch out a direction for inquiry into this motivational question, not a general answer to it. I have chosen two works that are incomparable in many respects—certainly in their relationship to psychoanalytic theory—for reasons that I shall develop.

1

Works on biography as a literary form, histories of biography-writing, and psychoanalytic retrospectives on the developments leading to psychobiography have all contributed to what might be called the Standard History of Biography. This Standard History acknowledges Greek and Roman founding fathers, sets Christian hagiography out of its bounds, notes the correlation between concern for individuals and new forms of biography and autobiography in the Renaissance, and really begins in earnest with the eighteenth century and the most discussed and praised biography in English, Boswell's *Life of Johnson*. The Standard History then goes on to lament and variously explain the low estate of nineteenth-century mammoth hero-worshipping or minutiae-assembling eulogistic biographies. The twentieth century is presented as the century of both artistic and scientific overcoming. Between them, Freud and Lytton Strachey ushered in the modern biography, and it became a widely shaped hope that the genre would be relatively free of sins of commission, like idealizing falsehoods and suppression of evidence, and sins of omission, like lack of scientificity or objectivity and lack of candor about once forbidden topics. Whether truth-scientific or truth-artistic, the goal is truth.

The Standard History applauds the disappearance of purposes like the one stated by Plutarch, who admitted that he had set out to write his *Lives* for the instruction of others but eventually came to find himself "proceeding and attaching myself [to the writing] for my own; the virtues of these great men serving me as a sort of looking-glass, in which I see how to adjust and adorn my own life."[5] Plutarch's conviction that these great Greeks and Romans should be presented with all their shortcomings of virtue in order that their greatness be all the more instructive was shared by most biography writers of the High Period, the eighteenth century. As Samuel Johnson said: "We must confess the faults of our favorite to gain credit for the praise of his excellences." Mallet's preface to his life of Bacon was typical: "Whoever undertakes to write the life of any person . . . ought to look upon this law as prescribed to him: He is fairly to record the faults as well as the good qualities, the failings as well as the perfections, of the Dead; with this great view: to warn and improve the Living."[6]

For Mallet's law but against the moralism of Mallet's view Lytton Strachey's *Eminent Victorians* took up arms. Strachey held that biography should be for biographical art's sake; all moral "ulterior motives" were to be removed with the purgative "acid and ice" of irony. Since Freud, psychobiographers of any of the three types Heinz Kohut distinguished have also followed Mallet's law—with more emphasis on the theoretical explanation, rather than simple recording of failing and perfections—but rejected his goal of warning and improving the living, including the living biographer. Impartial truth, like biographical art, is supposed to be its own recommendation and is not to serve personal or social moral ends.

The *locus classicus* for the psychobiographical truth-aim is a passage in Freud's essay on Leonardo da Vinci, which the Standard History notes as the strongest rap upon the knuckles ever given to moral didacticism in biography-writing. In the final section of that essay Freud writes:

biographers are fixated on their heroes in a quite special way. In most cases they have chosen their hero as the subject of their studies because—for reasons of their own personal and emotional life—they have felt a special affection for him from the very first. They then devote their energies to a task of idealization, aimed at enrolling the great man among the class of their infantile models—at reviving in him, perhaps, the child's idea of his father. To gratify this wish they obliterate the individual features of their subject's physiognomy; they smooth over the traces of his life's struggles with internal and external resistances, and they tolerate in him no vestige of human weakness or imperfection.[7]

This passage, aimed broadly and nonspecifically at biographers in general, set the terms for modern psychobiographical revisionism; it can be heard, for example, in Jones's biography of Freud as he deals with Freud's "psychoneurotic period" and his relationship with Fleiss by suggesting that hero worship should not obscure Freud's struggle. The passage that follows in Freud's text is, however, seldom quoted: Biographers "present us with what is in fact a cold, strange, ideal figure, instead of a human being to whom we might feel ourselves distantly related." Freud does not say what this "distant relation" is to be—but I shall take the phrase as a clue to the complexity of his study.

Methodological commentators on Freud's essay focus on his critique of biographers' transference to and fixations on their subjects, but, in fact, this critique is only a part of the general theme of the essay, which is the connection between creativity and paternal authority. Although he notes that Leonardo had tried to outdo his father in the elegance of his personal manners and that he had sought a father substitute in one of his patrons, Freud concludes that Leonardo's achievements as a natural scientist depended on his freedom from authority, ultimately paternal authority:

> [Leonardo] dared to utter the bold assertion which contains within itself the justification for all independent research: *'He who appeals to authority when there is a difference of opinion works with his memory rather than with his reason.'* Thus he became the first modern natural scientist.[8]

Freud then goes on to explain psychoanalytically Leonardo's conviction that the study of nature is the source of all truth:

> we see that the 'ancients' and authority simply correspond to his father, and nature once more becomes the tender and kindly mother who had nourished him. In most other human beings—no less to-day than in primaeval times—the need for support from an authority of some sort is so compelling that their world begins to totter if that authority is

threatened. Only Leonardo could dispense with that support; he would not have been able to do so had he not learnt in the first years of his life to do without his father. His later scientific research, with all its boldness and independence, presupposed the existence of infantile sexual researches uninhibited by his father, and was a prolongation of them with the sexual element excluded.[9]

The phrase "with the sexual element excluded" refers the reader back to an earlier discussion of types of sublimation and their relation to infantile sexual researches, children's sexual curiosity. Freud notes that this infant drive undergoes repression along with repression of libido, with three possible results in later life: first, severe inhibition of intellectual activity; second, "compulsive brooding," or the sexualization of intellectual activity; and, finally, the model type, maintenance of successful early sublimation in continued research: "the libido evades the fate of repression by being sublimated from the very beginning into curiosity."[10] Leonardo was a person of the third type, and he paid the price typical of successful sublimation, that is: "Sexual repression, which has made the instinct [or *Trieb*] for research so strong that the addition to it of sublimated libido is still taken into account by the instinct, in that it avoids any concern with sexual themes."[11]

In this discussion Freud by implication raises a question about what factors allow sublimation that does not repress and thus exclude the sexual element, that is, sublimation that could result in independent research of the sort a psychoanalyst or psychobiographer undertakes— research concerned with sexual themes. Even though he notes several times Leonardo's lack of interest in psychology, however, Freud eagerly enrolls Leonardo's cooperation in the project of his study: "Leonardo himself, with his love of truth and his thirst for knowledge, would not have discouraged an attempt to take the trivial peculiarities and riddles in his nature as a starting-point, for discovering what determined his mental and intellectual development. We do homage to him by learning from him."[12] And then as though he had not written his critique of biographers' special affection for their subjects, Freud candidly admits his own affection for Leonardo: "Like others I have succumbed to the attraction of this great and mysterious man, in whose nature one seems to detect powerful instinctual passions which can nevertheless only express themselves in so remarkably subdued a manner."[13]

Freud found in his Leonardo a predecessor and a comrade in research, a fellow searcher after truth, and "succumbed" to his attraction. He also describes the stages and struggles of Leonardo's quest for truth, as well as the inhibitions of his sexual life, his sublimated or "ideal homosexual" affection for young men to whom he could give his own version of the maternal nourishment he had received as an infant. With these remarks, Freud offers his first theoretical elaboration of the concept of narcissism and a gesture toward the reflections on ego and sexual ideals he makes in the 1914 essay "On Narcissism."

In the discussion of Leonardo's sublimations, Freud also gestures toward another concept that is crucial for his later work: Eros, the life instinct. Both of these theoretical elaborations speak to the limits Freud sets around his study of Leonardo: "Instincts [*Triebe*] and their transformations are at the limit of what is discernible by psycho-analysis," he writes. Specifically, "two characteristics of Leonardo . . . are inexplicable by the efforts of psycho-analysis: his quite special tendency towards instinctual repressions, and his extraordinary capacity for sublimating the primitive instincts."[14] The concept of narcissism and the late dual instinct theory, the theory of Eros and the death instinct, were directed at these borders. And a third reverberation of the Leonardo essay, Freud's discussion of the origin of religion in *Totem and Taboo* (1913), with its theory of primal patricide and the formation of a fraternal group, connects the specific study of Leonardo's creativity with a vast vein of cultural speculation. Freud himself said of this direction in his thought that it took him beyond his recognition (gained in self-analysis) of his own hostility toward his father and on toward analysis of his murderous wishes—a direction he did not attribute to Leonardo.

Freud's essay is an example of Kohut's second type of psychobiography: a pathography designed primarily to expand psychoanalytic knowledge or to apply existing knowledge. But Kohut's characterization certainly does not touch on the complex motivations apparent in the essay, and it also obscures how closely related, at the level of motivation, this type of psychobiography is to one designed to illuminate personality and one designed to explore creativity.

Freud had had a long-standing interest in Leonardo. He referred to him in his correspondence with Fliess in conjunction with Fliess's speculations (interestingly enough, not mentioned in the psychopathography) about left-handedness. He noted in other correspondences that his interest was renewed by a patient who had similar character traits without similar genius (presumably, this was the Rat Man, on whose case Freud had based his 1909 study of obsessional neurosis). His decision to write the Leonardo study came as he returned from his journey to America and prepared for the March 1910 Nuremberg conference, that is, at a moment of great confidence in the success of psychoanalysis but also a moment when attacks—personal and theoretical—came from many directions. Freud's expectations for Jung's contributions to "the cause" were still high, but edges of doubt had begun to form because of Jung's tendency to "exclude the sexual element" from psychoanalytic theory.

As a comrade in independent research, Leonardo had the advantage of being quite beyond the fray of discussion and dissension with which Freud was contending: he was a timeless, constant partner. He also served well as an example of how creativity can be rechanneled and renewed and of how inhibitions about bringing work to completion can be addressed with shifts from artistic to scientific work and back—that is, with different processes of sublimation. As a figure both of Freud's imagination and like it, Leonardo gave Freud the opportunity to move beyond the recent summations of psychoanalysis that he had written— to open new paths of research—and to do so in a mode of artistic sublimation. Freud called his Leonardo study "the only truly beautiful thing I have ever written"[15] and felt the need to defend himself in the text against the anticipated charge that he had produced a "psychoanalytic novel."[16] These roles that Leonardo seems to have served are summed up in a letter Freud wrote to Ferenczi six months after he finished the essay. In this letter he both acknowledges that he no longer needed to continue his self-analysis in his earlier manner and makes explicit the concern with his own homosexual cathexis that is implicit generally in the Leonardo study and particularly inferable from the essay's silence over Fliess's special interest, Leonardo's left-handedness:

> You not only noticed, but also understood, that I no longer have any need to uncover my personality completely, and you correctly traced this back to the traumatic reason for it. Since Fliess's case, with the overcoming of which you recently saw me occupied, that need has been extinguished. A part of the homosexual cathexis has been withdrawn and made use of to enlarge my own ego. I have succeeded where the paranoic fails.[17]

The Leonardo study was followed, then, by the case study of Schreber's paranoid psychosis (1911)—a mode of unsuccessful sublimation of sexual curiosity (and homosexual cathexis) that Freud had not listed in the Leonardo essay.

Freud's Leonardo essay is itself an "essay" (in the original sense of the term) of sublimation: it presents the identifications and idealizations of "independent research" but also of withdrawal and redeployment of cathexis for the formation of what Freud called an ego ideal in his 1914 study "On Narcissism." Theoretically, the Leonardo study demonstrates rather than discusses a preliminary answer to Freud's implicit question about sublimation that does not exclude the sexual element: a narcissistic identification or an internalization resulting in an enhancing enlargement of the ego is the opposite of regressive relinquishment of libido and curiosity to authority—originally paternal authority. The corollary to

Freud's critique of Victorian biographers' idealizations based on infantile models—father figures—is his construction of an ego-enhancing idealization that is not a father figure but an androgynous figure. In other words, Freud's practice contains the theoretical implication that nonrepressive sublimation is tied to (perhaps even requires) the formation of an ego ideal incorporating—to adapt Freud's own description of Leonardo—Mother Nature and Father stripped of his inhibiting authority. Such an ideal sanctions redeployment of libido (including homosexual strivings) without repression.

Until World War II Freud's Leonardo study was taken as the touchstone for the theory and practice of psychobiography. Later theorists found it too preoccupied with instinctual drives and childhood events, too little concerned with ego functions, too focused on intrapsychic conflict, and not enough concerned with external conflicts and historical setting. Psychobiographical practice has also moved away from study of creative individuals toward study of (in Erikson's often-cited sexually exclusive phrase) "the great man in history." The scope of psychobiography has enlarged, with case studies giving way to life studies, and its aims have become more strictly scientific and historical. But Freud's criticisms of biographical father-figure idealization have continued to be taken very seriously. His practice, however, his own quite different mode of what might be called androgynizing idealization, has been neither explored nor questioned for its theoretical or its methodological implications.

J. Mack observes; "Whereas before 1955, psychoanalytic biographical interest centered predominantly on artists and writers (those concerned with the inner life and its vicissitudes), since that time, the interest seems to have shifted to the study of figures who have their impact in the public sphere, or, more dramatically stated, upon history itself."[18] Mack notes the theoretical reasons for this shift by citing developments within psychoanalysis, but he claims that the main nontheoretical reason was one of "historical urgency": "We have become increasingly anxious about the men who lead us."[19] This development has taken psychoanalytically informed biography-writing far from biography's traditional aims—self-reflexive adjusting and adorning of the writer's life or pedagogical warning and improving of the living. It has also, ironically, taken (male) biography-writing back to concern with father figures—in a negative key: destruction of bad father figures goes forth without Freud's insights into the ego enhancement permitted by constraining paternal authority in androgynizing idealization. To this generalization, I would like to note a great exception—Erikson's *Gandhi*—a biographical model much less imitated than his *Luther*, which is no exception.

The region of psychoanalytically supported biography-writing where concern with individuals in contexts—life histories in histories—has not been disconnected from concern with the traditional aims of biography-writing or from Freud's concern with ego enhancement is a region for which there is no map—so my turn to it now will result in only a sketch.

2

Biographies of and by women have hardly a place in the Standard History, which simply records that three Englishwomen wrote biographies of their husbands in the late seventeenth century, that during the High Period of the eighteenth century no women attained prominence as biographers, that Mrs. Gaskell published her *Life of Charlotte Brontë* in 1857, and that Virginia Woolf wrote reviews of and manifestos about biography-writing in the 1920s. The rich tradition of minor biographies written from the late-eighteenth century through the decade of the "new biography" announced by Virginia Woolf is ignored—with Woolf's sanction. To date, there exists no history of women's biographies or of women in biographies, and no comment within the literature on psychobiography about studies of women. There has also been almost no comment on the most obvious historical pattern in women's biographical writing: namely, that in periods of feminist activity there have always been upsurges of interest in exemplary women's lives told biographically. This pattern is clearest in biographies of feminist writers—the late nineteenth- and early twentieth-century feminist movements each received biographies of Mary Wollstonecraft, for just one example—but it holds for biographies of women writers in general. Further, and correlatively, there has been until very recently no comment on the most obvious aim of women's biographies: namely, the traditional aim of moral improvement or the creating of looking glasses for the adornment and adjustment of women's lives.

In essays like "Women and Fiction" and *A Room of One's Own* Virgina Woolf helped usher in modern critical concern for women's writing and for the conditions under which women have written. In her essays on biography-writing, in which she analyzed and praised biographies by Lytton Strachey and Harold Nicolson, she contributed to the repudiation of Victorian biographical conventions. In her critical work, however, she brought these two concerns together only to remark that women's biography had not been born. She put its possibility into the future as she contemplated the changes she hoped would come in women's educational, political, and social opportunities:

> Women's gift will be trained and strengthened. The novel will cease to be the dumping ground for personal emotions. It will become, more

than at present, a work of art like any other, and its resources and limitations will be explored.

From this it is a short step to the practice of the sophisticated arts, hitherto so little practiced by women—to the writing of essays and criticism, history and biography.[20]

While she slighted the tradition of female biography—even though she had drawn on it to construct probing portraits of women writers, including Mary Wollstonecraft—Virginia Woolf did, at least, acknowledge that this tradition had always been limited by the very historical conditions that had limited both its subjects and writers. Woolf did eventually contribute a biography that was like any other of the "new biographies" written by her Bloomsbury colleagues, a study of Roger Fry. But the real fruit of her reflections was a novel she wrote in 1928 and called *Orlando: A Biography*. With this book Woolf invented both the subject of her biography and a biographical form in which a character called "the biographer" is in the text not only writing the biography but offering a running commentary on biographical conventions. Her inspiration or model was a "real life" subject, her lover Vita Sackville-West, wife of the biographer Harold Nicolson, whose son Nigel made of Woolf's portrait of his mother the often-quoted remark that it is "the most charming love letter in literature." But Orlando is a biographical novelty: a subject that is an impressionistic history of English literature and biography from 1586 to 1928.

The young Orlando grows up in Elizabethan England as a male, educated, very wealthy, close to the court, and then progresses into adulthood as an ambassador to Constantinople. During his ambassadorship, at the age of thirty, Orlando falls into a trance and on the seventh day of his creative slumber emerges as a woman. After some proto-Romantic adventures among gypsy tribespeople, the female Orlando returns to Queen Anne's England in time to hobnob with the Restoration literary luminaries; that is, she is born again (so to speak) at the moment when women writers emerged onto the English literary scene. Orlando's biographer reflects on what her change of costume and gender means for Orlando's life and letters:

The difference between the sexes is, happily, one of great profundity. Clothes are but a symbol of something hid deep beneath. It was a change in Orlando herself that dictated her choice of a woman's dress and of a woman's sex. And perhaps in this she was only expressing rather more openly than usual—openness indeed was the soul of her nature—something that happens to most people without being thus plainly expressed. For here again, we come to a dilemma. Different though the sexes are, they intermix. In every human being a vacillation from one sex to the other takes place, and often it is only the clothes that keep the male or female likeness, while underneath the sex is the very opposite of what is above.[21]

In the middle of Victoria's reign Orlando, behaving like a Hegelian, succumbs to the damp and chilly "spirit of the age" and marries. Her husband, however, is as androgynous as she and quite undominating, as he spends most of the time of their marriage on a seafaring expedition to Cape Horn. Their son, somehow conceived and gestated, is born in such a magical way that Orlando feels him not at all and is completely undistracted by his presence from her usual pursuits, including her literary project, a poem called "The Oak Tree," begun in her youth and finally finished, published, and awarded a prize as King Edward reigns. Orlando has 360 rooms of her own and a fortune much in excess of the 500 pounds annually that Virginal Woolf had stipulated as the necessary sum for a female writer's independence.

Orlando may be the only female subject of a woman's biography and the only heroine in a modern English novel who transcends—albeit after fantasy fashion—the restrictions that are the thematic foci of women's writing in both genres. *Orlando* is a mock biography, a parody of the styles and conventions of the entire modern Standard History of Biography. The work is also something of a caprice or joke and thus worth taking seriously for what it is: a way to make all too real constraints disappear, to overcome inhibitions—in life and in letters, in family context, and in history. Because Orlando did not exist, it was necessary for Virginia Woolf to invent her/him.

But it is significant, I think, that Woolf's idealizing fantasy is broadly historical—as none of her previous novels had been. Her ideal androgyne could be imagined emerging as a writer only in an idealized moment. This is an exaggerated example of what might be called the female historicity complex. Unlike Freud, who could write of Leonardo as though Leonardo had lived at any time, as though he were timeless, set in a "family romance" not a period, Woolf imagined a biography that recapitulates a sociohistorical development. Orlando, like so many heroes and heroines of nineteenth-century fiction, is presented as parentless. Like children who imagine themselves adopted or express their hostility toward their parents by replacing them with real or imagined ones of more exalted status or accomplishment, the in-the-text biographer gives Orlando neither mother nor father, or, more accurately, presents him as coming from a vaguely conjured male warrior line but without any mother to speak of. Orlando first appears not as a child, but as a youth maternally loved by no less than Queen Elizabeth. He is a creature of his historical setting. And after nearly two centuries of inability to complete her poem *Orlando* the female writer is finally granted, at the end of Victoria's reign, the perfect moment to be the creature of:

> Orlando had so ordered it that she was in an extremely happy position; she needed neither fight her age nor submit to it; she was of it, yet remained herself. Now, therefore, she could write and write she did. She wrote. She wrote. She wrote.[22]

For her biographer (now genderless in the text, not "he" as at the beginning of the book), Orlando is, so to speak, a literary-sexual ideal: a sexual ideal who, when loved, cures by love not just incapacity for love but incapacity for writing. She played this role for Woolf but also for "the biographer," whose biography is saved from "extinction" by Orlando's great literary outburst. The in-the-text biographer does not describe the poem called "The Oak Tree," but simply presents Orlando "thinking and imagining"—that is, neither killing like a warrior male nor loving as women are expected to do ("Love is slipping off one's petticoat and— But we all know what love is"[23])—and then leaves Orlando at her desk to take a rhapsodic two-page-long nature walk while Orlando completes the poem. The form of sublimation signaled here is quite complex: Woolf fashions an ego ideal, the androgynous biographer, whose writing is redeemed by the literary-sexual ideal, the biographical subject Orlando. The redeployment of Woolf's libido (including her homosexual drives) is mediated by the biographer in the text, who is allowed to assume the task of writing that does not exclude the sexual element.

Few women's biographies present so dramatically their writers' constructions of ego and sexual ideals (or lend themselves to questioning how those ideals may relate to homosexual cathexis), but the transposition of a family romance into a historical-contextual romance that is so exaggerated and so amusing in Woolf's fantasy-biography is typical of many women's biographies. In recent biographical writing the transposition takes a quite different and quite serious form. There is a great emphasis on placing subjects in their historical periods and empathically feeling with them their fight or their submission. There is also a strong impulse to rescue women from the standard histories that neglect them, devalue or overlook their achievements as those achievements relate to the possibilities of the times. But such acts of rescue often have the motivation— for the biographers—of self-rescues, and this is what they share with Woolf's work. Thus Bell Chevigny, author of a biography of Margaret Fuller and one of the few recent biographers to have reflected in psychoanalytic terms (hers are borrowed from Melanie Klein) on her writing experience, notes:

Whether our foremothers are famous or their histories neglected, the act of daughters writing about them is likely to be, on some level, an act of retrieval which is experienced as a rescue. When the work is most intensely experienced as rescue, the fantasy of reciprocal reparations is likely to become an underlying impulse in it. That is, in the rescue— the reparative interpretation and re-creation—of a woman who was neglected or misunderstood, we may be seeking indirectly the reparative rescue of ourselves, in the sense of coming to understand and accept ourselves better.[24]

The view here is of daughters rescuing mothers, but the dynamic described seems also to run in the opposite generational direction: the biographer, who re-creates the subject, has an almost parental narcissistic love for her—a love that seeks to redeem her from the historical misunderstandings and distortions in which she has been entangled, as parents may seek to fulfill their own ideals by redeeming a child from sufferings the parents once endured. Although like many contemporary feminists Chevigny emphasizes only relations between women, her use of the word "re-creation" implies that both parents (not just the mother) are joined or rejoined in a projected biography-ideal. But in such an androgynized biographical "position," paternal authority does not inhibit maternal rescue of the daughter-subject or the feeling that the subject is rescuing when rescued.

The delineation of a family romance in historical terms is also apparent in recent biographical writing marked by strong disappointment in "foremothers" and compensatory androgynizing visions. Carolyn Heilbrun's *Reinventing Womanhood* is quite candid on the topic. After telling autobiographically of her disappointment in her own mother, whose lack of autonomy she pitied, and of her admiration for her father, Heilbrun criticizes women's fiction for "failure of imagination"—that is, for failure to supply the kind of autonomous female figures women need as "role models."

With remarkably few exceptions, women writers do not imagine women characters with even the autonomy they themselves achieved. . . . Woman's persistent problem has been to discover for herself an identity not limited by custom or defined by attachment to some man. Remarkably, her search for identity has been less successful within the world of fiction than outside it. [Women writers,] when they wish to create an individual fulfilling more than a symbiotic role, projected the ideal of autonomy onto a male character.[25]

Thus far, there is little disagreement between Heilbrun and Virginia Woolf, but Heilbrun goes further. Lacking suitable role models from the past, real or invented, women ought to adopt, she suggests, male role models—but critically, cautiously, and in a feminist spirit. In a series of biographical vignettes, Heilbrun offers "how not to" examples of male-identified women; these are presented as cautionary tales about the "paranoid style" with respect to feminism of male-identified women, and they carry the message that paternal authority is not to be assimilated with the male models. "Reinventing womanhood" is a project for overcoming the family romance historicized; it is a consciously projected futureward idealization, "toward a new androgyny," for the writer and for succeeding generations to "live up to" and write out in fictions.

The idealizing in women's biographies takes many different forms— many more than I have suggested with the foregoing examples. But these forms have in common a conscious impulse for historical overcoming, or, to put the matter another way, for invention of ideal figures—role models, in social terms, ego ideals in psychodynamic terms—who are historically redemptive by virtue of having been redeemed from patriarchally defined feminine existences. The biographical search is close to fiction both in the sense that it is closely related to similar searches in fiction and in the sense that it involves a type of fictionalization: the conscious impulse in ego-ideal formation creates a character (so to speak) for unconscious projections to inhabit and vivify.

To consider this fictionalization further, it would be illuminating to compare with Freud's Leonardo study a female psychoanalyst's study of a female subject—but there is not one to turn to.[26] The culturist or historicist critique of Freudian psychoanalysis and particularly of Freud's theorizing about female development was largely initiated, as is well known, by women analysts. Freud himself had made it clear that he felt that women analysts would be able to correct his own male theoretical bias and particularly to explore the mother-child, pre-Oedipal relations of both sexes. But it is interesting to note that these critics—Karen Horney and Clara Thompson in the United States, for example—did not write psychobiographically about women of creative accomplishment. Similarly, the wide-ranging attention given by American ego psychologists and British object-relations theorists to the conditions and modalities of artistic creativity has seldom extended to women. One might claim that psychoanalytic theory of female development must be criticized and reformulated—purified of its Victorian or patriarchal or phallocentric biases—before it is applied to women of accomplishment; but this does not explain why psychobiographical study had not been part of such a critical reformulation, as Freud's study of Leonardo was part of the reformulation of his early theory. I think that what is involved here is historical restriction on idealizing: as Heilbrun suggests in her literary context, female ego ideals or referents for the construction of ego ideals are missing for historical reasons—to which the phallocentrism of psycho-analysis has contributed even while its radical critique of civilized discontents has done so much to challenge historical restrictions. Cross-cultural anthropological studies have thus presented themselves to analytic writers as more illuminating than biographical studies, for in societies not so, or not in the same ways, patriarchal as our own, other possibilities for female development can be discovered and inherited theories—with their patriarchal authority—can be more effectively criticized. "Anthropologized" fictions, like those of Monique Wittig in *Les Guérillères,* also go in this direction.

To these kinds of reflections, which are cultural, a specifically psycho-dynamic dimension ought to be added. Freud's explorations of the formation of ego and sexual ideals and the processes of sublimation were confined to males—as his own demonstration in the Leonardo essay was. In his later work on female development Freud claimed that the reproachful hostility a female child feels toward her mother when she discovers her lack of a penis remains with her and may combine in different ways and degrees with reproaches over prohibitions on sexual activity, insufficient feedings, or divisions of attention among siblings.[27] This formulation has been both elaborated and revised along with the concept of the castration complex that is central to it, but the revisionist work has not extended to the relationship between a female child's attitude toward her mother and her modes of idealization or ego-ideal formation (or, in Freud's later theory, superego development). Similarly, Freud's discussions of the ways in which "infantile sexual researches" can be either repressed, converted into sexualized thinking, or—rarely—successfully sublimated into other forms of research or "pursuit of truth" and his later discussion of the relations among these ways of sublimation, narcissism, and ego-ideal formation were developed only for males. He took it for granted that only a woman with a strong "masculinity complex" would make artistic or scientific contributions, but he did not—even given this assumption—ask what modes of sublimation would be involved or consider the capacity of female analysts not to "exclude the sexual element" from their research. Freud's proposition that freedom from or repudiation of paternal authority is the condition of independent research was also made only with regard for male development.

In feminist biographies of women the complexity of a double burden is quite apparent—no matter what specific mode of idealization is involved: paternal authority in its historical manifestations is questioned by the writer—with regard to herself and her subject—in the process of an ego-ideal formation that is problematic precisely because of that paternal authority as it is reflected in the family romance and in social conventions. Virginia Woolf's psychically ingenious double idealization—her projection of an ego-ideal in-the-text biographer who is redeemed, allowed to write, by an androgynous sexual ideal, Orlando—is both a reflection of the double burden and a means of overcoming it. Freud's androgynizing idealization was—could be—simpler, both because it was ahistorical and because he was male.

3

Focusing attention on the motivations of biographers as I have here could be interpreted as a contribution to the denigration of biography—a way of claiming that biography cannot be truthful and objective, cannot be properly historical, a way of claiming that idealizing Victorian biography really triumphed over its critics. I have tried to indicate, however, that there is a great difference between idealization as Freud criticized it in the Victorian biographers and idealization as Freud practiced it in his Leonardo essay. The difference is between repression and sublimation—in Freud's terms. In Virginia Woolf's "biography" the form of the sublimation is also keyed to the personal and historical inhibitions to be overcome, as it is in feminist biographies of the nonfictional, scholarly sort. I have tried to suggest that the sublimation process I have connected with androgynizing idealization is one that allows concern with "the sexual element" in scientific and artistic research by virtue of its critical relation to paternal authority and received ideas. Further, biography that results in the adjustment and adornment of the life—and perhaps also the theory—of the biographer has its own truth. This is not "objective" truth—but, then, what is objective truth?

Even when the methods of modern historical and psychological research are used in them, biographies are portraits of relationships. Virginia Woolf was recognizing this when she placed "the biographer" in the text of her biography—and used this figure in the text both to sabotage biographical conventions and to record and reflect Orlando's life. Freud was recognizing his relationship with Leonardo when he confessed that he had succumbed to "this great and mysterious man" and when he invoked Leonardo's sanction for a study that repudiated the biographical conventions of Freud's own time. Feminist theory and psychoanalytic theory also have in common a more general recognition: namely, that "subjectivity" cannot be eliminated from historical or scientific inquiry—an effort to do this is an effort to conform to another type of idealization, the idealization named "objectivity." Freud's distinction between repression and sublimation ought to be remembered at this methodological level as well. But that is another story.

11

The Education of
Women as Philosophers

It is unfortunate that for reasons of personal and cultural habit when we think about ourselves as askers of questions, thinkers, or, using the generic title, as philosophers, lovers of wisdom, we think of ourselves as selves. That is, we think: *I* am thinking—first person singular, one person solitary, an interiority, a mental factory.

Of course, it is fortunate that we—women—ever do think of ourselves as thinking; and in this light the matter of *how* we do so seems secondary. For there is a great deal in our personal and cultural histories suggesting that thinking is not our province, not our privilege, not even our possibility. So great, indeed, is the weight of prejudice about women's abilities and achievements as thinkers that we often look to the lives of thoughtful women with questions not about how they thought of their thinking but with questions about how they thought at all, how they managed *not* to be as this great weight of prejudice prescribed.

Biographies of women often have about them an air of amazement. They are infused—particularly when they are written by women—with an exclamation: she did it! Institutions for the education of women originate—even when they are circumscribed by visions of educated women as ideal helpmates for educated men—from the imperative form of the same impulse: you can do it! Despite everything and almost everyone outside, here you can do it! In most stories of exemplary women who have managed to do what was not expected of them and of institutions that have tried to make the exception more of a rule, the focus is on sources of support. In every exemplary woman's drama there is a cast—usually a very limited cast—of encouragers, and in every institution's story there are exemplary leaders who encourage a cast of encouragers.

Because women find it no easy matter to think at all, they are more inclined to be aware of (even if not openly acknowledging of) their supporters than men, who, after all, are supposed to be able by nature to set up in the thinking business as solitary entrepreneurs. But for women, I want to argue, the supportive others are always there, and always there *in thinking.*

Thinking, we usually assume, goes on in our heads. It involves a control center that produces thoughts. Thoughts, then, flow forth like a stream unless somehow blocked or distracted. That is, we have perceptions passively or actively received and ideas innate or acquired, which are all by some ruling mental fabricator or organizer fixed for flow into languages of various sorts that allow us to express ourselves. Thoughts are made or crafted or commandeered. Simple.

I want to question this notion, this enthralling picture, of thinking, as a kind of mental organizing of mental material or mental troops. But since I want to question also what this picture means for women, for women who are trying to think, I want to raise my question contextually. So let me continue for a few minutes like a manifesto.

We live as women in a revolutionary era for women: it is a time of nothing less than the first concerted effort by women to question and change definitions of our sex and gender—our femaleness and femininity, our proper place and purpose—that have been proposed, with variations, throughout the history of patriarchies. We live in and with a mass movement that has grown in the post–World War II period from an aspiration to a reality, from a vision particular to a segment of the Western intelligentsia to an achievement known to and contributed to by people all over the world. The feminist movement is truly an Internationale for the first time in history.

It is certainly obvious that, as a movement hoping to secure socioeconomic and political equality for women, the feminist movement is still in its infancy. The changes in women's statuses that it has brought about are everywhere insecurely instituted and under constant threat—in bedrooms, at breakfast tables, in marketplaces, clinics, courts, and political forums—from those who resist change, wish to roll it back, and even sometimes from those who are working for it.

But I think that it is reasonable to claim that, although the movement has miles to go in the matter of rights, it has already made a revolution by adding to the query, what do women want? the question, how and by whom have women's wants been determined? It is one thing, for example, when a psychological study is conducted to try to assess differences between women and men and quite another when the assumptions—the perceptual and conceptual biases—that shape such a study are themselves the object of study.

I do not consider this example to be isolated or academic; the shift it exemplifies is crucial and, I think, novel, even though it is certainly the case that throughout the history of women's struggles for emancipation analysts of the female condition have understood that prejudice predetermines and perpetuates institutions of inequality as much as institutions of inequality reflect and confirm prejudice; that habits of thought organize social relations as much as social relations organize habits of thought. Proclamists of emancipation have also understood that lasting change requires both reform of our ways of ordering our lives in all spheres and intellectual critique. The classics of the feminist movement have won their positions as perennials because their addresses to institutionalized inequality have been combined with studies of prejudice.

But what is new in the postwar era is that the institutions and intellectual disciplines that shape the form and content of education—by which I do not mean simply schooling—are being critically reshaped. Studies of prejudice are no longer reported by voices in the wilderness; they are broadcast in the metropoli of consciousness, in educational settings of all sorts. "The whole pyramid of discrimination," as Juliet Mitchell has written, "rests on solid extra-economic foundation—education."

When intellectual critique is reflexive and self-critical—that is, when it both questions and also questions how its questions have been and are being posed—then intellectual critique is truly philosophical. What is going on now, as the feminist movement's critique reaches into the root systems of prejudice against women, is the education of women as philosophers. But when I say this "as philosophers" I mean not as professional philosophers or even as heirs to traditional philosophical inquiry. What I do mean will take me a little while to say.

1

Within our European tradition philosophizing began in an era of cultural ferment. All around the Mediterranean Sea peoples who had lived in relative isolation encountered each other as traders and soldiers, adventurers and empire-builders. Among the sixth century B.C.E. Hellenes who settled on the Ionian coast, at the edge of an empire (the Persian) being swept with a fervor called Zoroastrianism, there lived thinkers now known collectively as the pre-Socratics. These men began to ask whether the world in all its rich diversity is not really made up of one primal stuff, one regnant power, or one principle. At the same time, among the Israelites (settled uncertainly in their Promised Land), prophets and priests, heirs of Moses, wrote texts declaring that one God created the world and rules over it. For all their differences, in both these traditions the ruler was conceived as the orderer, the world-mind.

Many and diverse are the ways in which the search for a *monos*, a one, transcendent or immanent, has taken place since this foundational era of our history. Each renewal of the search has summoned up the original search reflexively, asking whether and how the monisms of the founders were true. Is the one Anaxagoras' *Nous* (Mind)? Heraclitus' *Logos,* Parmenides' Being? Is it Plato's Good? or Aristotle's telic Unmoved Mover? Is the one God the God of the Jews? or the Christians? or perhaps even the Ahura-Mazda of the Zoroastrians?

In another period of great cultural ferment and contact among peoples—peoples not just of the Mediterranean but of the then circumnavigated globe—there grew up alongside this reflexive questioning that had been the impulse of many renaissances other forms of reflexivity. In the European era known as the Enlightenment people began to question how the *human* mind conducts its philosophical and religious searches. Are all the monisms, so seemingly diverse, mere variations of a single Truth? A Truth for Humanity? Could it be that all the different monisms are themselves manifestations of one universal human Mind?

These were the questions of Enlightenment cosmopolitanism, but there were also questions in the Enlightenment that marked a second new form of reflexivity, quite different from the cosmopolitan one that ushered in mental monism. Is it possible that, rather than being fitted for knowing the single Truth and hindered from such knowledge only by local differences of customs and languages, people's minds are and always have been destined to know only themselves? Do minds know only the walls of their prisons—the walls of diverse, historically determined prisons? Perhaps (so this form of questioning went) human beings are condemned to mind-bound truths and forever precluded from any Truth with a capital "*T.*" These questions were focused on the nature of mental activity, as were the cosmopolitan questions; but they did not reach beyond mental activity to a monistic Mind of Humanity. On the contrary, they opened the way for notions of cultural diversity, mental relativism—the basic ingredients of what might be called the intellectual French Revolution.

This second form of Enlightenment reflexivity is apparent in many kinds of nineteenth-century studies of what we today call "difference": anthropological studies of "primitive" non-European peoples; sociological studies of nonaristocratic peoples of various classes; historical studies of nonvictorious peoples suppressed in the triumph of European civilization; philosophical inquiries into the history of ideas, *Geistesgeschichte,* including suppressed ideas. But it is certainly the case that, before Marx and Freud were heeded, most of these studies contained more or less explicit assumptions about the evolutionary truth of the predominating modes of civilization—that is, they acknowledged the different, but then measured it by the standard of the successful, the ideal mind: given time, evolution will reinstate the Truth.

Feminist writers participated in this great upheaval and expansion of horizon, but often quite ambiguously. The ambiguity of their critiques centered in their attitudes toward reason. From the time of Mary Wollstonecraft until the time of Simone de Beauvoir feminists noted that women do not think as men do—that their minds are not male minds, educated like male minds. Women, it was understood, have been kept in economic, social, and political conditions that deprived them of the rationality of men. Mary Wollstonecraft and Simone de Beauvoir both lamented that women have been kept from rationality and from the transcendent capacities of reason. One of the key aspirations of feminism, to put the matter in other words, was to free women from their circumscribed mental worlds and let them enter into male rationality, participate in it as equals.

To this aspiration postwar feminism has addressed probing questions about whether it is not in effect a reinstatement or reaffirmation of the monistic Enlightenment ideals, one Mind of Man or one evolutionarily ideal mind. Recent feminists have said—to speak baldly—why emulate male rationality? Male rationality, after all, has been supplying reasons—for centuries—for the oppression of women; why emulate it? Male rationality has judged women's mental abilities—as well as their physical abilities—inferior; why emulate it? This questioning is coordinated to an inquiry that Janet Martin summarizes well in her *Reclaiming a Conversation:*

> Since the early 1970s, research has documented the ways in which such intellectual disciplines as history and psychology, literature and the fine arts, sociology and biology are biased according to sex. This work has revealed that on at least three counts the disciplines fall short of the ideal of epistemological equality for women: they exclude women from their subject matter, distort the female according to the male image of her, and deny value to characteristics the society considers feminine.

The phrase "epistemological equality" does not mean equal participation in male rationality; it means equal acknowledgement for male and female minds, lives, and histories.

The first level of critique launched by feminists from Wollstonecraft to de Beauvoir against the prejudice that women cannot think was launched against the prejudice itself. But once this critique had cleared a space and once women in large numbers had begun to speak and act in public on "the woman question," its sequel came. Questions were raised, are being raised, about how thinking or reason is thought about. Do the predominant modes of thinking about thinking exclude or suppress not just groups of people but types of activity that might or might not be specific to those excluded groups? Maybe the definitions of thinking laid down by men, so this critique suggests, exclude what women do. Thus the old feminist question has been re-posed: do men and women think differently? And the answer to it is: yes. Sometimes now the answer is: yes, and furthermore, women's thinking is *better*. But at any rate, the message of this critique is clear: no longer are women or their thinking to be judged by the standards of male rationality.

When I referred earlier to the feminist movement's critique reaching to the roots of prejudice and the consequent education of women as philosophers, I did not mean—as must now be obvious—as philosophers in the monistic tradition. I meant as continuers and radicalizers of the reflexive critical mode that has slowly brought the monistic tradition into question. But before I try to continue the story of what this questioning means for women, I want to consider one further crucial intellectual obstacle that the feminist movement's critique has met and tried to overcome.

If, as I have claimed, the Mind or Reason has been at the center of religious and philosophical monism, how did women's alleged inferiority come to be associated with their anatomy?

There are many ways to approach this question. Let me choose just one—the broadly historical—as an example. Ever since the Enlightenment there have been speculations that the era in which Greek philosophy and the Israelite and Zoroastrian religions were born was an era of transition in the eastern Mediterranean from matriarchal to patriarchal societies, from Earth Goddess religions to religions in which male deities or a male deity dominated. Recently, this speculation has intensified and been supported with archeological evidence and reinterpretations of literary evidence. If this transition did take place, then monistic thought can be seen as male intellectualization triumphant in the sense that, as men placed themselves in rulership over women, they placed the mind in rulership over the body. That is, women became defined by and associated with the body that the mind ruled. Monism, to put the same point differently, involves suppression: for the one to rule, it must rule something other, which is conceived as nonmental—either animally all-body or ethereally extramental, whorish or saintly.

Such a broad historical speculation is not in any strict sense provable, any more than are corollary psychoanalytic speculations about why men began to dominate women and to dominate rationally their own bodies, to regulate their erotic pleasures. The importance of such speculations has been and is that they have helped establish a distinction that is central to feminist critique: the distinction between sex and gender, or between anatomical differences and differences of socialization, education, and political power. Anatomical differences are, so this distinction implies, perennially matters of fact, but, as facts, they are never without valuative interpretation or manipulation; they are never contextless.

The distinction between sex and gender was crucial to Simone de Beauvoir's work. It was she who gave the postwar feminist movement its orienting maxim: "Women are not born, but made." But the issue of anatomical differences has not disappeared from the theoretical scene; indeed, it haunts it. Again and again, either in a sexist mode (like contemporary sociobiology) or in a woman-affirming mode these differences have been brought back as the essential ones and as the sources of mental differences. Women, that is, have been said to have genetic endowments or brain lateralizations productive of mental differences or an essential, timeless "corporeal ground" (in Adrienne Rich's phrase) productive of mental differences. But in the current phase of feminism each and every way that anatomical difference has been evaluated or "genderized" is up for questioning: do the evaluations reflect or transcend the old forms of male/female, mind/body hierarchical dualisms? De Beauvoir's own version of the mind/body dualism has been rigorously criticized, particularly insofar as she thought that, to be free, to be rational, women ought to transcend their reproductive capacity and not have children or insofar as she thought that women who accepted themselves as women, as anatomically female, would desire only other women.

Let me put this development more generally. It has been widely acknowledged that accepting the male/female, mind/body dualisms in a merely reformative spirit—that is, either by reversing the values of the dualisms and elevating female over male and body over mind or by attributing to females the mind power of males at the expense of their bodies—means foreclosing a deep critique of those dualisms.

When I say that the feminist movement's critique has brought about the education—the beginning of the education—of women as philosophers, I mean that, regardless of the terms we use, we all struggle at this philosophical bedrock. Twentieth-century philosophy in its most radical modes has been struggling in a crisis known as "the end of metaphysics." And that means the end of enthrallment by tradition-long metaphysical forms of thought such as the dualistic forms I noted. But what we can see in the last decade is the beginning of a merger of philosophical questioning and feminist questioning. That is, we can see the very beginning of the education of philosophers as feminists.

Now that the pluralistic reflexive critical tendency within the European tradition and the feminist critique have begun to relate to each other explicitly, many developments are possible. Once the framing dualisms of the tradition are grasped as part of the problem and we as critics are aware that our own critiques are historically bound up with, intertwined with, the very foundational thought-forms we wish to criticize, the reconstruction of our history and the envisioning of future possibilities become very rich, complex projects. With what thought-forms are you criticizing inherited thought-forms?—that is the omnipresent question. It could produce a mire of methodologism, and it could produce new feminist factions, but I do not think these are the likely outcomes.

When inherited thought-forms are grasped as enthrallments of the imagination, *all* their ingredients are up for critique. And I think this job will prove too compelling to be reduced to battles over method or to permit rigidification of theoretical and practical experimentation. And, besides, once the European tradition has ceased to enthrall our minds, it and its particularities—the differences of moment within it, the efforts at rebellion or nonconformity it has been laced with—become newly interesting, and so do all of the traditions that it is *not;* in time and space we can hope that the feminist inquiry will become more global, more comparative, more concrete, more subtle. Minds and bodies, not the mind and the body; men and women, not the male and female; masculinities and femininities, not the masculine and the feminine; sexualities and genderizations—the plurals will come forward, and the past will be viewed as a resource, not just as a tragedy. We will see, as Adrienne Rich once wrote, "the damage that was done and the treasures that prevail."

2

It is in this context, or with this hope, that I want to return to the statement with which I began. When we think of ourselves as thinkers, we tend to think of ourselves as selves, I said, as first person singulars, solitaries, interiorities, mental machines.

In our own period of great cultural ferment and contact among diverse peoples—in the period of world wars and since World War II, worldwide shared sense of planetary peril—both the mental monism of the Enlightenment and the mental pluralism of the Enlightenment with its monistic evolutionary bias have been under question. What is at philosophical issue are images of the mind in which one part or function predominates, either structurally or evolutionarily, and (ideally) produces one kind of thought, one kind of truth, one form of rationality.

Within the Western tradition the critical assault on such images has come, I think, not just from philosophy proper but from the practice of psychoanalysis. And these two critiques have gained strength from various forms of sociopolitical critique of what Foucault has called "totalizing discourse" that show the exclusionary import of such images, that show how they exclude non-European modes of thought, classes and races not educated in and for rationalism, and, finally, women whose thinking is derided as feminine, irrational.

Let me focus my attention for a moment on the psychoanalytic critical strand. Even though Freud's metapsychological formulations were indebted to, embedded in, traditional divisions of the mind into hierarchically arranged parts as well as to traditional notions of one mental function maturing over time into natural dominance over others, his key insights all point to a new venue. The mind or psyche has structures, but these are in constant interaction: id, ego, and superego are not separate faculties or compartments; they are definable only in dynamic relation to each other. And unconscious, preconscious, and conscious are not like steps going up, each to be left behind as the next is achieved. Our mental processes are, to speak simply, conversational. We are not solitary when we think; we are full of voices.

These voices are representations of both our drives or instincts and their worldly encounters, from the first ones in our parents' care to the most recent, from the early ones with objects and words to the later ones with ranges of others and with our cultural heritage in all its many forms. These voices represent in us all we have desired and all desires we have desired to have or not to have; they represent all the linkages and severances we have made among our desires and all the interpretations of our desiring with which we order ourselves, setting and resetting, repeating and extending boundaries on the confusing and never entirely lost initial boundarilessness of our natalities. Reason does not rule over instinctual desires in this conception; desires are the reason for reason and reason is the reasoning of desires. Reason without desire is empty, as desire without reason is blind. Even when the two are in tension, in conflict, neither wins.

Freud distinguished between primary unconscious or unarticulated mental processes to which we have very little access and secondary mental processes, conscious processes to which we do have access or of which we are self-conscious. The latter include differentiating, connecting, and categorizing of things, events, and words and also what we generally call thinking. There is obviously a dualistic conception here, but primary and secondary processes are not rigidly distinct or hierarchically related in structural or evolutionary terms. Freud made it quite clear that if conscious secondary organizing processes become severed from the primary processes of the unconscious and the desirous id, they are in danger of running unhealthily empty or being actually ruled by the severed-off processes, just as an adulthood, if it is built too firmly upon repressed childhood instincts, is in danger of running into depression, paralysis, or distortion of thinking. Freud himself valued scientific thinking as the most advanced and valuable form of secondary-process thinking, but he was keenly aware that the conversation of primary and secondary processes in poetry, for example, is responsible for poetry's universality and power, just as he was aware that a clinician listens not to secondary-process mentation but to the complex conversation of processes that is free associational speech.

The value of the idea that our mental life with others and with ourselves is conversational—that it is a constant interconnecting of all sorts of representations of our experience and also potentially an extension of our experience as we hear ourselves and others and reflexively interpret ourselves in and through novel conjunctions or conversational mo-ments—the value of this idea is that, if we take this idea seriously, *live* this idea richly, we cannot become what I have called mental monists. And the corollary to this impossibility is that we cannot become prescrip-tivists of the mental realm.

By these claims I mean several things. First, we cannot assert that any one form or process of mental life is to be cultivated to the exclusion of others or that any one structuring of mental life is absolutely superior. Second, we cannot hope to organize the social world in order to structure the conversation of mental processes, including the conflictual conversa-tions, for our mental life does not reflect directly or reproduce unmediat-edly the social world—it is not in any simple way causally related to the social world.

3

Let me say what these statements imply by returning to the monistic tradition, which, I said, has been questioned within philosophy and by feminist inquiry into the roots of prejudice. Throughout the Western philosophical tradition, since the time of the pre-Socratics, Plato, and Aristotle, we can observe a tendency to establish correlations between images of the mind and ideal images of sociopolitical organization. Plato, for example, asserted that the mind has three parts—reason, spirit, and appetites—and that the ideal *polis* should have three classes—philosoph-er-kings, guardians, and artisans or laborers. Aristotle asserted that the mind matures over time so that reason actualizes its potential to rule over the irrational parts of the mind and that city-state organization, analogously, matures over time so that it grows closer to the ideal of a naturally superior male class ruling over inferior men, youths, and at the bottom of the hierarchy reasonless women and slaves. In the developed Christian tradition the mind is ruled by a divine part—the *lumen natu-rale*—as the creation is ruled by God and as the state should ideally, by divine right, be ruled by kings. Many variations on these notions have existed, some of which seem to come from introjections into the mind of idealized political arrangements, and some of which seem to be projections of analyses of the mind into visions of ideal political arrangements. At any rate, the philosophical *esprit de système* has the effect that images are constructed that protect the hegemony of a part of the mind and also legitimate a mentally superior ruling class or person. Mental monism and legitimations of political domination have mutually supported one another.

With respect to this habit of construction the idea of our minds as conversations poses two challenges. First, it refuses the hierarchical tendency in the habitual constructions by insisting that all mental structures and processes have their importances and that all have their importances relationally but not in relations of, so to speak, unrotating authoritarian rulership. The idea of our minds as conversations is, to use sociopolitical terms, radically democratic, anti-authoritarian; and thus it is no surprise that it should percolate in the philosophical tradition at a moment when radical democracy is an ideal and when forms of authoritarianism have been more cruel than at any other time in history. The image of our minds as conversations is, I think, crucial to progressivism in political theory: it implies that mental and political democracies can be mutually supporting, in accord with the traditional constructing technique but not in accord with the traditional constructions.

But, second, the idea of minds as conversations refuses the homology between mind and sociopolitical organization by insisting that the primary processes of the unconscious do not directly reflect or recapitulate any existing sociopolitical relations and cannot be the basis for envisioning any such sociopolitical relations. Unless you believe that there is such a thing as a collective unconscious, there is no homologue in the sociopolitical sphere for the unconscious and primary processes (though there are certainly processes awaiting an adequate group psychology). And this means that the individual lives and the particularities of individual internal conversations of people will always defy political theoretical constructions, even democratic ones, that are prescriptive.

It seems to me that some contemporary feminist visions are continuations of the long habit of constructing idealized sociopolitical forms as corollaries to images of the mind—and vice versa. For example, among those feminists who advocate for the future some form of matriarchy or some form of lesbian nation as the means for overthrowing or separating from patriarchy, there is an assumption that "natural" female thinking or feminine mental virtues are superior and should dominate over male rationality. Thus emotionality, intuition, maternal, or nurturing thinking or even the "primary narcissism" of mother-daughter (or woman-woman) bonds should rule in mental matriarchy, or mental gynarchy. The tradition of correlating mental images and political images is simply turned upside down.

This kind of upside-down construction has been criticized by other feminists, and their main critical approach has been psychoanalysis because it points to what is left out of such a reversal: the conversation of primary and secondary processes, and, specifically, any appreciation of how the Freudian "discovery" of the unconscious asks us to respect the irreducible differences among us. But the entire habit of construction, I think, also needs philosophical critique, and the education of women as philosophers is the way to such a critique.

Psychoanalytic attention to the conversation of mental process and the general philosophical critique of mental monism that I have been noting as emergent have in common their skepticism toward any form of what Jacqueline Rose calls "utopianism of the psyche." The common caution about such utopianism asks that inversions of traditional habits not replace traditional habits as one ruling group replaces another in a political revolution that does not also involve a cultural revolution, a critique of rulership, a change of attitude toward rulership. But even on the level of cultural revolution this common caution asks that we not assume that social or political changes—for example, changes in the structure of the nuclear family, which is one of the primary loci for the transmission of patriarchy—imply changes in people's psychic structures in any *direct* way. If shared parenting, one of the most frequently advocated social goals, is seen as the way to break up a social syndrome of the "reproduction of mothering" (in Nancy Chodorow's phrase) and to bring about "the autonomy which too much embeddedness in relationship" has kept unavailable to women, then this common caution asks that advocates of shared parenting not neglect processes of the psyche that may very well go on in *any* kind of parenting. It does not seem possible, for example, for there to be child-rearing without unconscious communication between rearer (male or female) and child, a conversation that would not be conflict-free even among angels. This is so (in psychoanalytic terms) both because all children *need* parenting and because we all have in us a plurality of psychic purposes—id purposes, ego purposes, superego purposes—that will conflict to some degree even in the healthiest of us as we outgrow our childhood instinctuality. And it is also so because parents bring their own purposes—often their own narcissistic loves—to the raising of their children. Autonomy is always a struggle—though there is certainly every reason to work toward making it a struggle worth waging.

4

Let me try to indicate what these reflections on "psychopolitical" constructions imply by beginning again in a different key. The simplest way in which mental monism as a prescriptive ideal translates into our everyday life is apparent, I think, in the goal to which we are so often urged to direct ourselves: we are to seek an "identity."

It seems to me that the quest for identity is particularly strong—in our Western societies at least—among women. It is the self-imposed equivalent of what social rites of passages have traditionally been for males: entrance ways into adulthood, into manhood in the sexual sense, into extrafamilial love and work. It marks the need for individuation and autonomy in female terms: the need for definition achieved rather than accepted, chosen rather than enforced, made rather than born. Identity has become for many women the personal translation of emancipation: the political *made* personal, not suffered like a decree or a fate.

Our need for identity is our need not to be dictated to, dominated— not to be, as Simone de Beauvoir expressed it, always the Other, to others or to ourselves. The quest for this identity is in many ways laudable—in sociopolitical terms. But it seems to me that it can also run contrary to— or involve suppression of—our internal conversations and especially the unwelcome conflicts in them and the archaic voices in them that are kept (as D. W. Winnicott once put it) "in a state of uncommunication." To put this matter another way: identity—unity, cohesion—at the price of further repression or denial is an achievement awaiting an explosion. It can be a form of mental monism consciously chosen but nonetheless itself exclusionary.

These remarks about prescriptivism could be understood as implying a critique of feminism's sociopolitical emancipatory goals; but I want to make it as clear as I can that this is not what I intend. What I am trying to suggest is that all of the voices or purposes that are our minds must be heard for us to achieve not *an* identity but a more communicative form of life—the possibility of conversational reconciling, both in ourselves and with others. This, I take it, is the psychotherapeutic hope: making the unconscious or id voices conscious does not mean eliminating them; it means becoming reconciled to them and allowing them many other ends, a plurality that may include the ends of social and political revolution and that certainly will include the goal of thinking in many modalities. As Anna Freud once phrased this hope (in an unpublished letter): "What we are actually trying to do in education and in therapy is to sort out the individual's purposes and to make room for ego (reality) and superego (morality) purposes where the individual had felt hopelessly under the sway of his id (instinctual) purposes."

The education of women as philosophers that I have been describing and invoking is this educational and therapeutic hope phrased as a conversation with a tradition at the moment of its internal crisis: the unsilencing of its suppressed voices and the break-up of its inhibiting monistic formations. From it will come support for thinking in the very processes that thinking has traditionally been said to transcend, or over which thinking has been said to rule.

5

At the beginning of this essay I claimed that, because women find it no easy matter to think at all, given the weight of prejudice against them as thinkers, they are much more aware of (even if not openly acknowledging of) their supporters, those who have encouraged them to do what so much in our tradition holds they cannot or should not do: think. The supportive others, I said, are always there *in our thinking.*

What I meant by this claim is that the exemplary women who have in the past done what was not expected of them have never been entirely absent from our memories or the historical record. Women's history and biography-writing are projects to make this heritage more richly and widely known and to recover the parts of it that have been neglected or distorted—often distorted by the kinds of mental habits I have been discussing. These are projects for redressing injustice and for giving our history a foundation that prevents future injustices. But I also meant that we all have in us voices that are supportive. We all have, for example, the voices of our own initial curiosities about the world and about the so-called facts of life, our first efforts at explaining to ourselves such perplexing matters as the origins of ourselves or the origins of our younger siblings. The education of male and female children as "good" children in narrow and often sexist terms, which it is the business of higher education to question, usually consists of dulling this curiosity with moral or rational strictures, not allowing it to meet freely with the "ego (reality) and superego (morality) purposes" that connect us to ourselves and to others. But the original curiosity remains—even if under the worst circumstance it is tyrannizing because distorted or denied. And it can remain as the primary-process spur to and contribution to all future intellectual activity.

Between prohibitions on childhood questioning and denigrations of women's thinking, there is an obvious link: the assertion of adult power over children and the assertion by individuals or in the general cultural discourse of power over women are both forms of obedience training. This link is, I think, what makes the link between psychoanalysis and philosophy so important for our later lives. But between the exemplary women who inhabit our memories and imaginations and our own curious childhood selves there is also, I think, a link: we turn to exemplary intellectual women with our still-active early desires to know as well as with our later resurgences of this desire in different forms, including those forms we have come to feel are obstructed because we are female.

We internalize exemplary men and women and we need "ego ideals" of both sexes, but it is with women who were marginalized and continued thinking that we associate our own marginalized desires to know.

The culturally transmitted thought-forms and habits of construction I have been examining are the intellectual manifestations of obstacles that have deep roots in our culture and in ourselves. Both restoration of women's voices suppressed in the history of the cultural discourses and restoration of the pluralities of voices in us that have been threatened with monism in our upbringings and in our encounters with the cultural discourses require analysis of those thought-forms and habits of construction. Higher education for women is the outward and visible sign that this analysis is underway, that a cultural revolution is advancing. The inward and spiritual grace of this revolution will take longer—for it is a deeper matter. I have tried to suggest that the education of women as philosophers is the framing of its guiding questions.

12
Anna Freud for Feminists

1

Writing on women and psychoanalysis can focus either on current psychoanalytic theorizing about women or on women as psychoanalytic theoreticians, historically viewed. It is not just a desire to satisfy everybody that prompts me to take both approaches at once.

It seems to me that there are three main reasons why current issues and historical considerations should not be separated in the area of women and psychoanalysis. The first has to do with how many categories of work in this area have been neglected; the second with how lopsided the work that has been done is; and the third with the importance of integrating all the topics that fall under the "women and psychoanalysis" rubric—all the ways of construing the topic—with the larger field of psychoanalysis.

Historical studies of psychoanalytic theories of female sexuality were scarce until quite recently, and those produced since the 1970s have been largely dominated and constricted by disputes about Freud's views. Similarly, aside from individual biographies of women analysts there has been little historical study of the contributions women analysts have made to theorizing about female psychology. These two lacks meet in the fact that there exists no history—adequate or inadequate—of child analysis. No historical attention outside of the psychoanalytic journals has been paid to analysts of children other than those enshrined by such recent feminist writers as Nancy Chodorow, namely, "object relations" theorists (especially Klein and Winnicott) and theorists of individuation and separation (chiefly Mahler).[1]

What historical attention has been given to analysts of adults after Freud and his immediate female followers, among them Ruth Mack Brunswick, Jeanne Lampl-de Groot, Helene Deutsch, and the dissident Karen Horney, has not had among its goals consideration of theories of female psychology in the context of psychoanalytic theory in general.

Particularly, recent psychoanalytic work done under the influence of both the 1960s feminist critique of psychoanalysis and then the 1970s counterwave of feminist revision—from Kate Millet to Juliet Mitchell—has not been historically studied outside of the psychoanalytic journals. No one has assessed whether the hue and cry against Freud the misogynist and psychoanalysis the phallocentric science par excellence has had any effect within psychoanalysis—although it is obvious that it has had a tremendous effect in the culture in which we live and move and have our being. This lack is just beginning to be met with work by female analysts, such as the essays collected in the volume Judith Alpert edited, *Psychoanalysis and Women: Contemporary Reappraisals* (1986).[2]

In both the 1960s feminist critique of psychoanalysis and in more recent revisionist appropriations of psychoanalytic theory there have been two recurrent main, interrelated foci: processes of gender differentiation and processes of individuation or separation, particularly from the mother.[3] A major target of critique is Freud's idea that girls are psychically like boys and "masculinely" attached to their mothers until they become acquainted with—indeed, shocked by—the anatomical differences between the sexes, experience a kind of castration anxiety, and consequently envy of the penis. Gender differentiation, so many arguments go, must involve some story other than one in which a female has to *achieve* femininity. Similarly, Freud's idea that in the process of her shock a girl turns from her mother to her father, switching love objects or moving from a negative to a positive Oedipal configuration, has also come in for criticism. Girls, so many argue, remain more tied to their mothers than Freud thought and than is implied by the Freudian story of girls raging against their mothers for failing to supply them with a penis.

Criticism of Freud's theories has practical corollaries in feminist writings: processes of gender differentiation could be modified if child-rearing practices were modified (so that honor, for example, would be bestowed on the "inferior" clitoris and vagina of the girl); and difficulties in mother/child separation and individuation could be ameliorated by shared parenting, paternal nurturance, and an end to stereotypical mother and father roles. The reformist vision is focused on pre-Oedipal childhood because this has come to seem both the time when damage is crucially done to female self-esteem and the only time when it is truly either preventable or remediable.

Both the theoretical critique of Freud and the practical hopes for equality in upbringing draw on two general claims that Freud was phallocentric or male-biased, given to making his own overestimation of the penis into a program; and that he underestimated the pre-Oedipal period, taking it into account in terms of the stages (oral, anal, phallic) of instinctual-drive life but not in terms of "object relations" or ego development. Many analysts and feminists alike hope that, by focusing on the pre-Oedipal period, the phallocentrism can be addressed—and the story that women start out "masculine" redressed. The consequence of these currents of critique and aspiration is that female psychology has come to be regarded as the province of infant observers and "early analysis" (ages one to three) practitioners. What women want is what the very littlest women want.

Further, this very narrowly focused "female psychology" has been treated by analysts and feminists alike as an isolated topic. In most fields, gender, once it is raised as an issue needing address—connected to practices needing redress—gets isolated as a specialty, usually of interest primarily to women, before it gets integrated ("mainstreamed") into broader inquiries. In the American social sciences the early 1970s was a period of manifestos ("Women in History" or Anthropology or Sociology, etc.), a time of cracking open disciplines. In most disciplines there were versions of the claim Carol Gilligan made for the women she studied as a research psychologist—"in a different voice." Essential differences between men and women, both those existing from birth and those shaped in social settings, were stressed and all work within the disciplines that did not take these differences into account was criticized. Then there followed in the mid-1980s a reaction time in which the sweeping women-essentially-are claims of "Women in X" were reevaluated and made more sophisticated, while the women in the disciplines tried—often with little success—to influence their non-feminist colleagues to take notice of the preceding decade of reformist work. When "essentialism" came to seem like a new version of an old problem—not "anatomy is destiny" but "femininity is destiny"—there was an intellectual crisis similar to the more general political crisis of "second wave" feminism.

There matters stand as of now. But the situation in psychoanalysis has been and is quite different. Since Freud "female psychology" has been seen as an area of special problems, but efforts to connect "female psychology" with "general psychology" have been very slow coming—probably because the originally recognized special problems have never been satisfactorily dealt with. Freud himself made women-essentially-are claims; these were disputed in the 1920s; the dispute still goes on. In coordination with the feminist wave of criticism in the 1970s psychoanalysts wrote many reassessments of Freud's views; but little consensus came from this work, and its followup in the mid-1980s was still largely isolated in books with titles like *Female Psychology: Contemporary Psychoanalytic Views*. An exception to this last generalization is the recent volume by Johanna Tabin, *On The Way To The Self* (1985), which is a very thorough and synthetic psychoanalytic work.[4]

2

With this much very summarily said about why it is important to keep historical and contemporary questions about "woman and psychoanalysis" together, I want to turn now to Anna Freud's work and to the proposition that it should be of interest to feminists. This proposition really does need arguing because Anna Freud's work has never been of any great interest to psychoanalysts focused on female psychology and never of any interest at all to feminists. The matter is compounded by the fact that Anna Freud herself did nothing at all to foster good relations between psychoanalysis and feminism; on the contrary, she viewed feminists as enemies of psychoanalysis, people who rejected it because their goal was to prove that sexual differences were merely the product of social conditioning, merely the reproduction of sexism.[5] That this version of feminism was an extreme one and not necessarily or even usually connected to the charge that psychoanalysis was male-biased was not apparent to Anna Freud.

The most obvious reason for the fact that Anna Freud's work is not cited in either the psychoanalytic or the feminist literatures is that she did not write about female psychology as a separate topic. Not a single one of the essays in her eight-volume *Writings* even has the adjectives "female" or "feminine" attached to any topical noun in its title. She was the only influential female analyst of her Vienna generation, most of whom were her analysands and trainees, who did not devote at least an essay to female psychology.

Biographically, this is a very important silence. It relates, it seems to me, to how little Anna Freud thought of her work as a challenge to the basic elements of her father's theory of female sexuality in any of its major formulations (in 1905, 1919, 1926, or 1931). While his views evolved, her self-understanding also evolved, and the two recorded their revisions in several papers that use material from Anna Freud's analysis. But there was no divergence and thus no need for independent or rebellious formulation on her part. In her fantasy life Anna Freud usually took a masculine role, and she could explain this masculinity to herself quite well in her father's terms: she protected herself against her intense love of him by refusing a feminine role, and she also expressed in her masculinity the penis envy she felt with respect to both him and her brothers. She fit a Freudian female type marked by a "masculinity complex," which in her case was carried to an extreme but not expressed behaviorally in either masculinized manners or homosexuality. The pre-Oedipal period was not crucial to her story as she and her father understood it during her analysis with him (1918–24).[6]

Every analyst is, of course, given special insights and interests and special blindnesses by his or her own constitution and (to use a term of Ernst Kris's) "personal myth." What Anna Freud's story meant for her work was that she came to concern for early infancy and specifically to early mother-child relations more slowly than her contemporaries—particularly Melanie Klein. In 1937, however, with her American friend Dorothy Burlingham she opened a toddlers' nursery in Vienna and set out to study both particular issues—such as how eating problems develop—and general behavior. The importance of good mothering, or the lack of it, was obvious to her, and she kept up her interest in it through five years of directing a residential nursery in wartime England.

Throughout her early child analytic practice and her empirical or observational studies—indeed, throughout her whole working life—Anna Freud refused to focus on the first year or two of life as either *the* determinative period, whether for normality or pathology, or as *the* period for gender differentiation and identity consolidation. As I noted, she insisted on the importance of the Oedipal period. But more than that she insisted on viewing infancy, childhood, latency, prepuberty, and puberty or adolescence as parts of a whole needing to be considered as such. She followed her father in emphasizing the biologically rooted biphasic nature of the instinctual drives—that is, the fact that there are two upsurges of energy well known to every exhausted parent of a preschooler or a teenager (upper and lower age limits at both periods being flexible and also being influenced by societal norms and such living conditions as availability of food and exercise). She viewed puberty as a recapitulation of the infantile sexuality period (and the climacteric as another recapitulation), but she also noted that ego development in latency and during puberty itself can dramatically change a course set down in the first years of life. Theorists who jumped from the pre-Oedipal to the adult, positing a direct, unmediated causal relation of prior to later, seemed to Anna Freud quite misguided.

Correlatively, Anna Freud felt that any "object-relations" theory or ego psychology that ignored Freud's theory of instinctual drives would be distorting. Among the features of Freud's encompassing theory that would be neglected or lost is one of particular importance in the context of a discussion of women and psychoanalysis. Freud had postulated an elementary bisexuality in every person, and Anna Freud emphasized that such constitutional bisexuality is intensified in the pre-Oedipal period by a child's identifications with both male and female parental figures. Both "heterosexual" and "homosexual" attachments are normal for males and females in the course of their Oedipal development. But, given the recapitulation of the infantile sexuality period, Freud had noted that, "a person's final sexual attitude is not decided until after puberty," and Anna Freud agreed with this assessment.[7] As the biphasic nature of the instinctual drives is often neglected or underestimated in analytic—as well as feminist—literature, so is the theory of bisexuality.

Anna Freud had a firm commitment to keeping a balance among all the facets of Freud's theory. She did not single out any one period or elevate any one approach (id-psychology over ego psychology, or vice versa; object relations over instinct theory, or vice versa), nor did she posit any pure, unmixed categories ("feminine" or "masculine"). But this refusal to be reductionist also kept her work from becoming the foundation of any new trend in psychoanalysis or feminism. Similarly, her scientific method dictated both caution about universalizing claims and care about delineating specificities or differences among individuals and among types of development. At her Hampstead Child Therapy Course and Clinic (founded in 1948) Anna Freud cultivated means for collating and synthesizing data from many child analyses and child observational studies—creating what might be called a data collective under the title "The Hampstead Index"—and for testing conclusions with longitudinal projects. The clinic was also famous for innovational research programs, like simultaneous analyses of mother-child pairs (and later father-child pairs) designed to test theories about, for example, the impact of a mother's depression on her child; re-analyses in adolescence of child analytic patients; and analyses in adulthood of children who were orphaned during the war or who survived concentration camps.

In accordance with her conception of psychoanalysis as a mode of therapy for all economic groups, Anna Freud made analysis at her clinic available to children of working-class families, non-English-speaking immigrant families (at first, European Jewish families, later Jamaicans and Pakistanis), single-parent families, families broken up by parental addictions and/or imprisonments. Dorothy Burlingham specialized in analyses of blind children, and the nursery school attached to the clinic always included at least one physically handicapped child in each group of ten to twelve children. The wide spectrum of familial and social backgrounds represented by the clinic's children kept the research from making extrapolations on the basis of work with only upper- or middle-class, nuclear-familied English children.

The work done at the Hampstead Clinic was also coordinated with research projects at various American locations where Anna Freud's Viennese colleagues and students established themselves after their emigrations. Ernst and Marianne Kris supervised projects through the New York Psychoanalytic Institute and then joined Edith Jackson at the Yale University Child Study Center. In Cleveland Anny and Maurits Katan led a Child Study Center after they had worked for years through the Case Western Reserve Medical School. Grete and Eduard Bibring were key figures in the Boston area and exerted a great influence on the

Judge Baker Children's Center. René Spitz in Denver, Edith Buxbaum in Seattle, Anna Maenchen in San Francisco, Marie Briehl and Margarte Ruben in Los Angeles, Helen Ross in Chicago and Pittsburgh, Ishak Ramzy and others at the Menninger Clinic in Topeka—there were many radii in Anna Freud's circle of influence. It is no exaggeration to say that through these people Anna Freud's theory and practice of child analysis was more widely replicated than any other. But that is a different matter than being fashionable or interesting to those—like feminists—with a stake in the results of psychoanalysis.

As Anna Freud accumulated research results at her clinic and from the satellites in America, she reoriented her work. Like her father she had concentrated her attention on psychopathology, specializing in child psychopathology. But she became convinced that, insofar as child psychopathology had been built up as a specialty on the basis of psychiatric categories refined through adult analyses, it was unreliable. She used the Hampstead Index material to argue that child and adult pathologies take very different forms and are not necessarily causally related to each other (for example, an adult obsessional neurotic was not necessarily a child obsessional neurotic; and not every child obsessional neurotic will be an obsessional neurotic as an adult). As she reached this conclusion, Anna Freud undertook two enormous projects of reform.

She created a "Diagnostic Profile" for children to formulate diagnoses and treatment recommendations on the basis of many types of information, including family and school interviews as well as interviews with the children being diagnosed, which were organized according to developmental criteria. Integral to the profile was the second reform project: a formulation of the developmental criteria.[8] These were presented as a series of broad descriptions of stages of normal development—called "the developmental lines." In her developmental lines Anna Freud summarized all the psychoanalytic work that had been done since her father's seminal studies on how children move from their dependent, bonded relations with their mother figures through to independent lives in which their loves are directed outside of their families. She tracked development in many spheres: from being cared for toward bodily independence (in eating, bladder and bowel control, bodily management and hygiene), from egocentricity toward companionship, from autoerotic play toward toys and then work, and so forth.

One of the most exciting features of these developmental lines is that using them diagnostically helped Anna Freud and her staff to describe and treat problems that had no names—at least no names that could be accurately borrowed for the childhood scene from adult psychiatric diagnosis. Discrepancies in development—for example, a child developing normally on one line and abnormally on another—signalled problems, but not problems with symptoms susceptible to psychiatric labelling.

Eventually, Anna Freud formulated a crucial distinction between the infantile neuroses, such as hysteria, obsessional neurosis, and phobias, inferred by her father and other early adult analysts from their adult patients, and what she called "developmental pathologies." Many of the children who came to Anna Freud's clinic and her nursery school with physical handicaps and diseases (such as infantile diabetes), cultural and familial backgrounds of extreme deprivation, histories of sexual abuse or beating, and so forth) could be understood as suffering from "developmental pathologies" and treated accordingly.[9]

3

I have come quite a distance from the topic "women and psychoanalysis." But I have been ranging in order to emphasize how much more there is of interest in child psychoanalysis than the two topics on which feminist attention has been focused: gender differentiation and individuation/separation of female child from mother. As a glance at the popular media in recent months will tell you, "Mothers and Daughters" is a very hot subject, and behind it still stands the perennially warm 'What do women want?' question—that is, a question aimed at unlocking the essence of femininity. I think that Anna Freud's work is a fine corrective to the wheel-spinning that has gone on over these issues in psychoanalysis and in feminist literatures of various sorts. But I also think that her work has a direct contribution to make to the feminist agenda—a contribution other than providing a path back to more general concerns about children and how they develop or fail to develop. So let me turn my attention to the contribution made by Anna Freud's clinic and its research program to the current concerns of "women and psychoanalysis."

Because I cannot assume—for reasons that I have tried to indicate—familiarity with Anna Freud's work outside of psychoanalysis, I would like to offer a text and then comment on it. The passages that follow are from Anna Freud's 1965 book *Normality and Pathology in Childhood,* and they deal with object choice at the various developmental stages:[10]

> Infants, at the beginning of life, choose their objects on the basis of function, not of sex. The mother is cathected with libido because she is the caretaking, need-fulfilling provider, the father as the symbol of power, protectiveness, ownership of the mother, etc. A "mother relationship" is often made to the male parent in cases where he takes over the need-fulfilling role, or a "father relationship" to the female parent in cases where she is the dominant power in the family. In this manner, the normal infant, whether male or female, has object attachments to both male and female figures. Although in the strict sense of the term

the infant is neither heterosexual nor homosexual, he [or she] can also be described as being both.

That the object's functions and not sex decide these relationships is borne out also by the transference in analytic treatment, where the sex of the analyst is no barrier against both mother and father relationships being displaced onto him [or her].

Apart from this object choice of the anaclitic type, however, it is obvious that the pregenital component trends depend for their satisfactions not on the sexual apparatus of the partner but on other qualities and attributes. If these are found in the mother, and if on the strength of them she becomes the child's main love object, then the boy in the oral and anal phases is "heterosexual," the girl "homosexual"; if they are found in the father instead of the mother, the position is reversed. In either case, a choice of object determined by the quality and aim of the dominant drive component is phase-adequate and normal, irrespective of whether the resulting partnership is a heterosexual or a homosexual one.

In contrast to the preceding stages, the sex of the object becomes of great importance in the phallic phase. The phase-adequate overestimation of the penis induces both boys and girls to choose partners who possess the penis, or at least are believed to do so (such as the phallic mother). Whatever course their instinctive trends have taken otherwise, they cannot disengage themselves "from a class of objects defined by a particular determinant" (Freud).

The oedipus complex itself, both in its positive and negative form, is based on the recognition of sex differences, and within its framework the child makes his [or her] object choice in the adult manner on the basis of the partner's sex. The positive oedipus complex with the parent of the opposite sex as preferred love object corresponds as closely to adult heterosexuality as the negative oedipus complex with the tie to the parent of the same sex corresponds to adult homosexuality. So far as both manifestations are normal developmental occurrences, they are inconclusive for later pathology; they merely fulfill legitimate bisexual needs of the child. . . .

When entry into the latency period is made, this particular aspect of the child's libidinal life disappears once more from view. There are, of course, at this time, unmodified remnants of the oedipus complex which determine the attachments, particularly of the neurotic children, who have been unable to solve, and dissolve, their oedipal relations to the parents. But apart from these, there are also phase-adequate aim-inhibited, displaced or sublimated tendencies for which the sexual identity of the partner becomes again a matter of comparative indifference. Evidence of the latter are the latency child's relationships to his [or her] teachers, who are loved, admired, disliked, or rejected not because they are men or women but because they are either helpful, appreciative, inspiring, or harsh, intolerant, anxiety-arousing figures.

The diagnostician's assessments at this period are further confused by the fact that object choice with regard to contemporaries proceeds on lines opposite to those usual in the adult. The boy who looks for exclusively male companionship and avoids and despises girls is not the future homosexual, whatever the similarity in manifest behavior. On the contrary, such clinging to the males and retreat from and contempt for the females can be considered the hallmark of the normal masculine latency boy, i.e., the future heterosexual. At this age the future homosexual tendencies are betrayed, rather, by a preference for play with girls and appreciation and appropriation of their toys. This reversal of behavior is taken for granted in latency girls, who seek boyish company if they are feminine but if they are "tomboys" themselves, i.e., on the basis of their penis envy and masculine wishes, not on the basis of feminine desires for relations with the opposite sex. What appears in overt behavior as homosexual leanings are, in fact, heterosexual ones, and vice versa. What has to be remembered in this connection is that the choice of playmates in the latency period (i.e., object choice among contemporaries) is based on identification with the partner, not on object love proper, that is, on equality with them, which may or may not include equality of sex.

This text goes on, with paragraphs on preadolescence and adolescence that make the same kind of phase-specific comments on the realistic assumption that object choice should never be discussed without an indication of phase. It should be noted that the terminology of negative and positive Oedipus complexes is used, but there is no assumption that the female child before and during the negative phase is like a boy; the assumption is rather that boys and girls are alike in their needs and dependencies. Anna Freud's text then turns to the psychoanalytic literature on homosexual object choice, summarizes it (with much more attention, as in the literature, to male homosexuality than to female homosexuality), and concludes:

That certain childhood elements in given cases have led to a specific homosexual result does not exclude a different or even opposite outcome in other instances. Obviously, what determines the direction of development are not the major infantile events and constellations in themselves but a multitude of accompanying circumstances, the consequences of which are difficult to judge both retrospectively in adult analysis and prognostically in the assessment of children. They include external and internal, qualitative and quantitative factors. Whether a boy's love for his mother is a first step on his road to manhood or whether it will cause him to repress his aggressive masculinity for her sake, depends not only on himself, i.e., on the healthy nature of his phallic strivings, the intensity of his castration fears and wishes, and on the amounts of libido left behind at earlier fixation points. The outcome also depends on the mother's personality, her actions, on the amounts of satisfaction and frustration which she administers to him orally and anally, during feeding and toilet training, on her own wish to keep him dependent on her, on her own pride in his achieving independence of her, and, last but not least, on her acceptance or rejection of pleasure in or intolerance for his phallic advances toward her. . . .

What has to be reckoned with, finally, and what may encourage development in one or the other sexual direction are the purely chance happenings such as accidents, seductions, illnesses, object losses through death, the ease or difficulty of finding a heterosexual object in adolescence, etc. Since such events are unpredictable and may alter the child's life at any date, they upset whatever prognostic calculations may have been made previously.

In both of these passages there are, it seems to me, several important matters of emphasis that need to be noted. First, Anna Freud stresses that the pre-Oedipal mothering figure—be it female or male—is a need-fulfilling figure rather than a sexual object. The emphasis is on needs and accompanying pleasures or pains not on "object relations" per se. Second, the child's recognition of sexual differences, which is not assumed to take place in a single shocking episode, is basic to the Oedipus complex in both female and male children, both of whom esteem the phallus. But just as important for object choice are identifications with the parental figures, female and male, and "the multitude of accompanying circumstances" particular to any individual child's development. Because of this multitude of accompanying circumstances, prognosis about a child's eventual type of object choice is always uncertain. But the further corollary is also clear: the accompanying circumstances are the sort that can so easily produce developmental pathologies, which quite overwhelm the normal processes and configurations of the pre-Oedipal and Oedipal periods. The range and flexibility in these clinical descriptions is crucial. (One might wish, however, that the whole discussion was not in a chapter on "psychopathology," as nothing in it calls for such a designation, and Freud himself had made it clear as early as 1905 that homosexuality should not be considered pathological. He had applauded the replacement of "the pathological approach to the study of inversion" by the anthropological, or by comparative study of sexual practices in different cultures—a replacement that made little impression on psychiatry until the early 1970s and is still a source of dispute in psychoanalysis.)[11]

It was careful attention to developmental lines and stages that allowed the staff at Anna Freud's clinic ten years later to make a major revision in the theory of female development that is embedded in the the passages from the 1965 book that I quoted. And one of the reasons why it is important to keep historical and current issues in the area of "psychoanalysis and women" tied together is that their revision actually echoed proposals made in the 1920s as correctives to Freud's. But in the 1970s they were working in a different context of concern about female sexuality and also working with the resource of the Hampstead Index, with its many cases of female analyses to draw on and compare, so that their report did not suffer as much from a single analyst's limitations of subjectivity or from limitations reflecting the patient population.

Anna Freud's coworkers distinguished two component phases of the girl's phallic stage, one pre-Oedipal and one Oedipal.[12] In the pre-Oedipal phase, called "phallic narcissistic," girls have fantasies of penis possession that serve narcissistic and exhibitionistic ends: they are designed to win love and admiration from others, including parents, but not yet in the context of a triangular Oedipal configuration. The girl must deal not only with the recognition that she has no penis, but with the more general comparision between child and adult genitals, which makes her feel little but which does not necessarily involve any comprehension that genitals are related to differences in sexual or reproductive roles. Most pre-Oedipal theories of how babies are made are still tied to earlier events— theories of oral impregnation, anal babies, urine and feces mixing to make babies, and so forth. Exhibitionism and scoptophilia are ubiquitous and in the services of narcissistic reassurance and pleasure.

As a girl begins to understand the differences in sexual roles, she does not—in distinction from the boy—have immediate visible proof of her future possibility for adult female functioning. Identification with her mother is crucial, as are—a little later— Oedipal wishes toward her father. This makes the mother newly important to the girl, not as a need fulfiller but as an object of identification. The stress here is on identification rather than on a negative Oedipal relationship with the mother (and the work actually suggested that the assumed negative Oedipal relationship was seldom to be found in the analytic material). But the girl identifies with a mother whom she also envies. Thus the mother's own psychology is at this point of particular importance for the girl's development. In summary, the girl

> continues to be dependent on her mother to meet her basic needs, and she wishes too to preserve a positive identificatory relationship with her, and yet she also has to face her ambivalence toward her mother and her envy of her, as well as the pressures of her sexual fantasies toward father. It is therefore hardly surprising that many psychoanalysts, including ourselves, have found it so difficult to disentangle the different wishes, fantasies and affects that make up adult female sexuality."[13]

These descriptions and the conclusion imply that a multitude of factors are at play in this transitional period of any given girl's life: the needs and wishes are many and conflicting, and no one-plot story with a single turning point could possibly compass them or correlate them all to the earlier and later stages of a girl's life in which they originate and come to circulate.

It is not the specific content of Anna Freud's work—important as that is—but the non-reductionist scientific style of it, the range of it, the intricacy and caution of it that, it seems to me, recommend it so highly to feminists who want to learn what psychoanalytic work can reveal about female development—or, one might say more accurately, about females' developments.

Postscript

In her last work, *The Life of the Mind*, Hannah Arendt intimated a train of thought that I find compelling. In the European tradition philosophers of the most diverse convictions have imagined or pictured mental life as organized like a political entity—a *polis*, a *civitas*, a *societas*, a parliament. Without reflecting on it, Arendt made a contribution to this metaphorical tradition—a tradition that offers a suggestive way to ask how the insights of political philosophy and psychology can be brought together theoretically, as a way of inquiring.

Looked at as metaphors, the mental microcosm and the sociopolitical macrocosm (as well as the macrocosm of the cosmos itself) are strikingly tied throughout the European tradition to tripartite structures. The many variations on these habits of European thought could be viewed as simply footnotes to Plato's images of the psyche made up of reason, spirit, and appetites and the ideal political realm of philosophers, guardians, and artisans. But the tripartite structuring continues even into the period when the Platonic modality of a *monos* ruling over a hierarchy was no longer echoed. The foci of Kant's three critiques, pure reason, practical reason, and judgment, like Hannah Arendt's thinking, willing, and judging, are really not in the Platonic mode, both because judgment and judging are novelties as faculties and because no one of the tripartite divisions is the authoritarian seat of rule. Judgment and judging are not low faculties on a tripartite totem pole like Plato's appetites; they are equals in the mental realm and just as politically important as their other thirds.

Why do philosophers in our tradition so often consider the mind or the psyche to be made up of three functions or three parts? The simplest answer is that they really do not; rather, they consider the mind to be made up of two parts that need a mediator or third party in order to meet, or keep their peace, or communicate. Thus, for Hannah Arendt, judging is a mediator between willing, the mental activity resulting in action, and thinking, which is not result-oriented at all and needs translation to be worldly. If thinking inquires about what is right and what wrong, and willing needs this inquiry, judgment provides the translation by asking of any given particular possibility of action "is this right?" The judging function has a similar linking role in Kant's scheme (though the faculties it links are quite different), while the spirit has a defensive role for reason and against the appetites in Plato's more anxious hierarchical scheme.

Quite different homological views of the body politic do come from people who want reason to be suffused through the whole of the mind's life than from those who want reason protected from revolutions instigated by the lower mental classes. As I stressed in the essays above, most philosophers after Plato agreed with him that political innovation or revolution was something to be prevented—often at the price of authoritarianism or what might be called rule by the mentally elite with their internally superior reason. Movements aimed at constitutionally secured sharing of political power or division of function within organizations are a political aspiration only for those whose pluralism begins at home, in their experience of mental life. Similarly, tolerance of political innovation and focus on political novelties are linked to respect for judgment abilities that are not deductive—subsuming particulars under existing universals. Thucydides, as I noted in the essay above on his *History*, admired insight rather than rationality in a philosophical sense (*gnome*, not *nous*), and he praised his exemplary leaders for their ability to expect the unexpected, appreciate the unprecedented. If history is held to repeat itself or the sun is held to have nothing new under it or political life is held to be perfectable, with stability as the ideal and sources of disruption to be eliminated, then no judgment function is needed.

Not surprisingly, those philosphers who like Plato feel that reason has disruptive enemies below often associate them with bodily functions, particularly sexual functions, which do sometimes have what seems like a life of their own. That this association of reason's enemies and bodily functions often encompasses as well the whole domain of feminine life and all females is one of the most notable features of the European tradition. It ceases to be the case as the microcosm/macrocosm homology becomes more dynamically progressive (as with Marx) and more democratically pluralistic (as with Arendt).

Why do philosophers in our tradition commonly consider the mind to be made up of two parts or functions and a mediator of some sort? I do not think that the answer is that we have two parents, two brain hemispheres, two hands, or two anything else. I think it is that we experience our mental processes as interactive, and an interaction requires (at least) two interactors and a place or means or measure of interaction.

Beyond this simple experience, there are very great differences in how the interaction is registered: it may be between equals, between a master and a slave, between siblings from a common source, and so forth, given the character and historical context of the thinker. Comparative study of content or typology-making should intervene here. But, to go on, we also at the most unsophisticated level, experience political life as interactive—and on this level it surely does matter that we have two parents! We register that this person and that one love or hate each other, live in peace or make war; these people and those become divided into this group or class and that other one, loving or hating each other in pluralities, living in peace or making war. Such registrations are elementary even for peoples—like many in India and China—who regard all contraries and contradictions and oppositions as a veil of illusions, which the truly enlightened will understand as nothing.

In *The Life of the Mind,* Hannah Arendt captures the experience of mental life very richly. The most challenging feature of her work is that her interactive mental functions, thinking, willing, and judging, are each presented as intra-active, self-reflexive, interiorly conflictual or dialogic. Decades of thinking about the intricacies of political forms preceded this remarkable portrait of mental life. As I have noted again and again, she implied that the mind is, or at least can be, a multiprocessed (one might say multiparty or polyglot) little republic of conversation. She did not offer an authoritarian image of the mind or one dedicated to war.

The republican image seems to me quite in accord with psychoanalytic metapsychology—it is a political version of the same turn of thought. Sigmund Freud was operating within the tradition when he distinguished unconscious processes from conscious ones and placed between the two a filter, the preconscious. This so-called topographical theory of the mind is hierarchical, like Plato's theory: consciousness is higher, out of the cave, in the light. Freud's revision of the mid-1920s, called the structural theory, is quite a different matter.[1] Id, ego, and superego are very complexly related: id is the source of the other two structures, which structuralize (as it were) from the id; but the primary mental conflict is normally between id and ego, not ego and superego; ego and superego remain always partly unconscious (id-rooted); and so forth. Each of the structures not only exists in interaction with the others but is internally active, intra-active. The model Freud developed was so subtle developmentally and dynamically that he had trouble making a map of it, particularly as he retained the earlier topographical theory as well and also worked with fundamental descriptive distinctions, like that between primary and secondary processes, and "economic" concepts, like pleasure principle and reality principle. People generally—including the many analytic revisionists active at the moment—either find this later production of Freud's hopelessly confusing or in need of clarification. It seems to me a splendid image of a multiprocessed little republic of psychic conversation, and I praised it as such in "The Education of Women as Philosophers" above.

This kind of reading together of Arendt's and Freud's images can easily go a step further. Willing, thinking, and judging are Arendt's names for the functions associated in the Freudian scheme with, respectively, id, ego, and superego. Freud's discussion of the functions of the mind is much more thorough and much more concrete than Arendt's, but hers, as I noted, does keep circling back to such topics as self, emotions, and character, which she had initially ruled out of the bounds of her analysis in *The Life of the Mind*. Had she followed the pull of her own ideas, she would have had to deal with the far side of her boundaries. She would also, I think, have come into the domain of psychopathology— precisely the domain she wanted nothing to do with.

Arendt argued in her most controversial book, *Eichmann in Jerusalem*, that Adolf Eichmann was a man who had simply stopped thinking and judging, who did not ask himself general questions about justice, much less specific ones like "is this right?" Eichmann was not psychopathological; he was thoughtless, banal. But, although she tried very hard in *The Life of the Mind* to say what it is that makes us think in the first place— and claimed that thinking is a "natural need"—she gave no answer to her question about what would make a person stop thinking (although she did imply, as I noted, that in conditions where willing and judging do not or cannot operate thinking withers away).

Arendt's analysis of Eichmann as a thoughtless man seems to me very important and quite right—but I also think that such thoughtlessness is psychopathological and needs to be analyzed as such. Arendt herself noted that Hitler had been adopted by Adolf Eichmann as the source of all directives, the giver of all rules and laws—"the Führer's will is law"— so that Adolf Eichmann needed only to obey, not to think or judge. Freud had many fascinating things to say about phenomena of this sort in his *Group Psychology and the Analysis of the Ego*. But his argument convinces me that a person's surrender of thought to another person as a member of, for example, an army or a church is not a matter that can be understood without concepts of instinctual inhibition and deinhibition.

Freud suggested that group members identify with each other and love only each other because they have all put the group's leader in place of their own superegos; their consciences are projected onto the leader, who then has virtually hypnotic power over them and can release their inhibitions—particularly the inhibitions on their aggression. The group members then do what is pleasing to the leader, the God, the Idea Incarnate, or whatever and act according to the leader's ideals and laws. Anna Freud later described this self-shaping as "identification with the aggressor," and she attributed battles between groups to this defense mechanism.[2] But both the Freuds also stressed that group members who shape themselves in the image of their leaders or their leaders' aggression also thereby disturb all of the mental functions that go along with con- science, like the capacity for self-observation, self-criticism, seeing things from another's point of view (empathy), even humor, which requires interior distantiation or what Hannah Arendt would have called reflexiv- ity in mental functions. People do not just stop thinking; they give up the pleasures of thinking for something they find more pleasureable—a state in which child-like fantasies are enacted with gusto and blessing.

Freud's essay also implies that a member of a hierarchical organization who subserves himself or herself to a leader either has already or develops a hierarchy of psychic functions: ego and id are servants to mental representations of the leader-ideal. Hierarchical rigidity of mental struc- turation, lack of flexibility and reflexivity, fits with political authoritarian- ism. And, in the same way, "democratic" relations in and among mental functions or structures fits with democratic political life. (Here, as earlier, I am using the vague word "fits" because I do not think it is possible to make general causal claims about how the inner and outer worlds influ- ence each other.)

The value of examining images of mind and the body politic in terms of both their similarities and their internal dynamics is that we can get a sense of what conditions are free or freedom-supporting for both our inner and outer lives—a synthetic sense. This sense has always been, I think, part of the sensibility of great historians, and I tried to show it at work in my essay on Thucydides' *History*. Focusing in different ways on such a sense can produce, I think, an alternative to intellectual discourse that is either prescriptively normative (designed, for a recent example, to unclose the American mind) or antinormative, "postmodernist." The type of philosophical discourse that tries to illuminate general conditions for free thought and political life was called by Kant *Kritik*. This discourse, ours in the maturity, perhaps even the decline, of our long tradition, is one that can say of individuals what de Tocqueville said so truly of nations: "Liberty is generally established with difficulty in the midst of storms; it is perfected by civil discord; and its benefits cannot be appreci- ated until it is already old."

Notes

1 Hannah Arendt's Storytelling

1. Hannah Arendt, "Karl Jaspers: Citizen of the World?" in *Men in Dark Times* (New York: Harcourt, Brace & World, 1968), p. 89.
2. Hannah Arendt, "Karl Jaspers: A Laudatio," in *Men in Dark Times*, pp. 71–80.
3. Ibid., p. 74.
4. Hannah Arendt, *Rahel Varnhagen: The Life of a Jewess* (London: East West Library, 1957), p. 16.
5. Hannah Arendt, "Bertolt Brecht: 1898–1965," in *Men in Dark Times*, p. 248.
6. Ibid., p. 242, 249.
7. Ibid., pp. 225–26.
8. Ibid., p. 220.
9. Hannah Arendt, "Martin Heidegger at Eighty," *New York Review of Books*, October 21, 1971, p. 52.
10. Hannah Arendt, "On Humanity in Dark Times: Thoughts about Lessing," in *Men in Dark Times*, p. 10.
11. Ibid.
12. Ibid.
13. Hannah Arendt, "Bertolt Brecht: 1898–1956," p. 228.
14. Hannah Arendt, "Reflections (W. H. Auden)," *The New Yorker*, January 20, 1975, p. 39.
15. Hannah Arendt, "Walter Benjamin: 1892–1940," in *Men in Dark Times*, p. 204.

2 From the Pariah's Point of View

1. Letter to Blumenfeld, March 31, 1959.
2. Letter to McCarthy, October 16, 1973.
3. Adelbert Reif, ed., *Gespräche mit Hannah Arendt* (Munich: Piper & Co., 1976), p. 17.
4. Ibid., p. 20.
5. From an unpublished manuscript (on which Arendt noted "Lecture—Rand School—1948 or 49") in the Library of Congress Arendt Collection.

6. Letter in response to Bruno Bettelheim, *Midstream* (Summer 1962): 87.

7. Hannah Arendt, "We Refugees," *The Menorah Journal* 31 (January 1943): 69–77.

8. Hannah Arendt, "Totalitarianism," *The Meridian* 2, 2 (Fall 1958).

9. Robert Burrowes, "Totalitarianism: The Revised Standard Version," *World Politics*, 21, 2 (January 1969): 272.

10. Arendt, "Totalitarianism," p. 1.

11. Hannah Arendt, *The Human Condition* (Chicago: University of Chicago Press, 1958), p. 205.

12. Hannah Arendt, "Personal Responsibility Under Dictatorship," *The Listener*, August 6, 1964, pp. 187–205.

13. Hannah Arendt, *Eichmann in Jerusalem: A Report on the Banality of Evil* (New York: The Viking Press, 1965), p. 126.

14. Arendt, "Personal Responsibility Under Dictatorship," p. 107.

15. Hannah Arendt, *Eichmann in Jerusalem*, p. 131.

16. Hannah Arendt, *On Revolution* (New York: The Viking Press, 1965), p. 84.

17. Arendt, *The Human Condition*, p. 197.

18. Cited in M.I. Finley's introduction to Thucydides's *History* (New York: Penguin, 1974), p. 30.

19. Arendt, *On Revolution*, p. 49.

20. Ibid., p. 219.

21. Hannah Arendt, "Thoughts on Politics and Revolution," in *Crises of the Republic* (New York: Harcourt Brace Jovanovich, 1972), p. 212.

22. Arendt, *On Revolution*, p. 136.

3 Reading Hannah Arendt's The Life of the Mind

1. Hannah Arendt, *The Human Condition* (Chicago: University of Chicago Press, 1958), p. 5.

2. Hannah Arendt, *The Life of the Mind* (New York: Harcourt Brace Jovanovich 1978), 1:5. (Hereafter, references to *The Life of the Mind* will appear in the text, indicated by volume 1 or 2 and page number.)

3. Hannah Arendt, "Thinking and Moral Considerations," *Social Research* 38 (Fall 1971).

4. Arendt distinguished the thinking faculty from cognition as Kant distinguished *Vernunft* from *Verstand* (1:13); but Arendt's thinking faculty was not, in relation to the Will, legislative. Arendt never specified what her term "meaning" encompasses, but it seems likely that it has more in common with Kant's aesthetic ideas (for which there are no concepts) than with his rational ideas (for which there are no intuitions); I will try to indicate at the end of this essay why this is. At any rate, it would follow from Arendt's distinction that truth is to meaning as concepts are to ideas for Kant. It should be noted that Arendt used the word "faculty" as a translation for *Vermögen* (see her letter of February 19, 1975, to J. Glenn Gray, Arendt Papers, Library of Congress, cited with permission). "Activity" or "power" might have served her better, as she clearly did not intend to invoke faculty psychology. Arendt probably had in mind the Latin orgin of "faculty," *facultas*, which means ability to do a thing; in this sense, "faculty" is the correlative in mental life to *virtu* in political life.

5. The notion that past and future exist as images in the mind, the past as memory and the future as anticipation in the present of the mind's encompassing *(distentio animi)*, is drawn from Augustine, *Confessions,* 11.

6. Arendt did not share Heidegger's concern with the relation of Being and Thought and the identity of the two as proposed by Parmenides. She spoke, rather, of thinking Meaning. But she was aware that the problem that has beset those concerned with Being also besets the search for Meaning: "nobody can think Being without at the same time thinking nothingness, or think Meaning without thinking futility, vanity, meaninglessness" (1:149). The need to reconcile thought with reality, to affirm Being, has traditionally entailed denial of evil; this is so also for Heidegger's identification of "to think" and "to thank." Arendt concerned herself not with the identity of thinking and Being but with the difference *within the thinking ego* that is also an identity: "For nothing can be itself and at the same time for itself but the two-in-one Socrates discovered as the essence of thought. ... And this ego—the I-am-I—experiences difference in identity precisely when it is not related to the things that appear but only related to itself" (1:185, 187). In its self-relation, thinking can concern itself with evil: "A person who does not know that silent intercourse (in which we examine what we say and what we do) will not mind contradicting himself, and this means he will never be either able or willing to account for what he says and does; nor will he mind committing any crime, since he can count on its being forgotten the next moment" (1:191).

7. Cited in Erich Heller, *The Disinterested Mind* (New York: Meridian Books, 1967), p. 215.

8. Hannah Arendt, *Between Past and Future,* (New York: The Viking Press, 1968), p. 225.

9. Ibid., p. 23.

10. All references to *The Critique of Judgment* will be indicated in the text with a section number; the J. H. Bernard translation (New York: Hafner Pub. Co., 1968) will be used.

11. Hannah Arendt, *Eichmann in Jerusalem: A Report on the Banality of Evil* (New York: The Viking Press, 1964), p. 93.

12. Ibid., p. 116.

13. Ibid., p. 136.

14. Ibid., p. 136.

15. Hannah Arendt, "Karl Jaspers: Citizen of the World?" in *Men in Dark Times* (New York: Harcourt, Brace and World, 1968), p. 93.

16. Hannah Arendt, "Karl Jaspers: A Laudatio," in *Men in Dark Times,* p. 77.

17. Arendt, *Between Past and Future,* p. 224.

18. Arendt, *Between Past and Future,* p. 225, on "Immoderate love of the merely beautiful."

19. Arendt, "Citizen of the World?" p. 84.

20. See also the unpublished lecture of 1971 (Arendt Papers, Library of Congress).

21. Arendt, "Laudatio," p. 73.

22. Kant spoke of exemplary products of judgment, normal ideas; he noted that Polycletus' statue Doryphorus, known in antiquity as "the Canon," presented a perfect image of the beautiful human figure. He also spoke of the "ideal of the beautiful," the "visible expression of moral ideas that rule men inwardly" (#17). Kant did not speak of moral examples, because he had moral rules, moral law. For Arendt, it seems, both aesthetic

and moral judging, two modes of the judging faculty, are guided by examples. She did not assume that there is any difference in the process of judging in the two spheres, but, on the other hand, she noted different examples for each—Achilles and St. Francis or Jesus—and did not revert to the Greek notion of *Kalokaiagathon*, the beautiful-and-good.

23. Arendt, *Between Past and Future*, p. 17: "Political philosophy necessarily implies the attitude of the philosopher toward politics; its tradition began with the philospher turning away from politics and then returning to impose his standards on human affairs."

24. Arendt, letter of August 21, 1974, to Fr. Pierre Riches (Arendt Papers, Library of Congress, cited with permission).

4   King Solomon Was Very Wise—So What's His Story?

This lecture was prepared without notes, but interested readers can find the Christian texts (other than the New Testament ones) conveniently collected in Janine M. Idziak, ed., *Divine Command Morality* (New York and Toronto: Mellen Press, 1979); the Montaigne citations in Donald Frame, ed., *Montaigne's Essays* (Palo Alto: Stanford University Press, 1971); and the Kant references in the following editions: *Anthropology from a Pragmatic Point of View*, trans. V. L. Dowdell (Carbondale: Southern Illinois University Press, 1977); *Critique of Judgment*, trans. J. H. Bernard (New York: Hafner, 1968); *On History*, trans. Lewis White Beck et al., (New York: Bobbs-Merrill, 1963), and see also Beck's "Kant and the Right of Revolution" in his *Essays on Kant and Hume* (New Haven: Yale University Press, 1978); *On the Old Saw: That Might Be Right in Theory, But It Won't Work in Practice*, trans. E. B. Ashton (Philadelphia: University of Pennsylvania Press, 1974).

5   Cosmopolitan History

1. See for example Fernand Braudel, "Histoire et sciences socials. La longe durée," *Annales: Economies, Societes, Civilisations* 26 (1958); 725–53.

2. Hannah Arendt, *The Origins of Totalitarianism* (New York: Harcourt, Brace & Co., 1951), p. 436.

3. Martin Heidegger, "Letter on Humanism," in D. Krell, ed., *Basic Writings* (New York: Harper & Row, 1977), p. 220.

4. Martin Heidegger, "Kant's Thesis about Being," *Southwest Journal of Philosophy* 4 (1973).

5. Cited from Albrecht Wellmer, *Critical Theory of Society* (New York: Seabury Press, 1971), p. 137.

6. Hannah Arendt, *The Human Condition* (Chicago: University of Chicago Press, 1958), p. 324.

7. Ibid., p. 185. See p. 298, note 62: "each time the modern age had reason to hope for a new political philosophy, it received a philosophy of history instead."

8. Hannah Arendt, *The Life of the Mind* (New York: Harcourt Brace Jovanovich, 1978), 2: 172–95.

9. Karl Jaspers, *The Origin and Goal of History*, trans. M. Bullock. (London: Routledge & Kegan Paul, 1953), p. xiii.

10. Ibid., p. 3.

11. Ibid., p. 25.

12. Karl Jaspers, *The Great Philosophers*, trans. R. Manheim. (New York: Harcourt, Brace & World, 1957), Vol. 1, p. xi.

13. Ibid., pp. xi & xiv.

14. Martin Heidegger, "The Question Concerning Technology," in D. Krell, ed., *Basic Writings., (New York: Harper & Row, 1977)*, p. 316.

15. Martin Heidegger, *On the Way to Language*, trans. P. D. Hertz (New York: Harper & Row, 1971), pp. 4–5.

16. Hannah Arendt, "Karl Jaspers: Citizen of the World?" in *Men in Dark Times* (New York: Harcourt, Brace & World, 1968), pp. 87–88.

17. Ibid., p. 90.

6   What Are We Doing When We Think?

This lecture was prepared without notes, but interested readers can find the texts mentioned or cited in the following editions (for the Arendt texts, see notes to Chapters 2 and 3): René Descartes, *Discourse on Method*, trans. L. J. Lafleur (New York: Bobbs-Merrill, 1950); Immanuel Kant, *Prolegomena to Any Future Metaphysics*, trans. Lewis White Beck (New York: Bobbs-Merrill, 1950); Martin Heidegger, *Being and Time*, trans. J. Macquarrie and E. Robinson (New York: Harper and Row, 1962); Martin Heidegger, "The End of Philosophy and the Task of Thinking" in *On Time and Being*, trans. Joan Stambaugh (New York: Harper and Row, 1972); Martin Heidegger, *Introduction to Metaphysics*, trans. Ralph Manheim (New York: Anchor Books, 1961).

7   What Thucydides Saw

1. The translations in this essay are mine, although I have tried to keep them close to the easily available Penguin paperback translation by Rex Warner (New York: Penguin, 1974).

2. Marc Cogan, *The Human Thing; The Speeches and Principles of Thucydides' History* (Chicago: University of Chicago, 1981), 194.

3

At 5:62, Thucydides uses an analogous phrase, τὸ ἀνθρώπειον κομπῶδες, the human boasting element; this refers to the kind of storytelling in which men exaggerate the numbers of their own army and understate the numbers in enemy armies—that is, tell themselves what they are pleased to hear..   4

Hannah Arendt, *The Origins of Totalitarianism*, rev. ed. (New York: Meridian Books, 1965), p. 432. Voegelin's review appeared in *The Review of Politics* 15 (1953): 75, followed by Arendt's reply..   5

W. Robert Connor's translation (in *Thucydides* [Princeton: 1984], Princeton University Press, p. 31), "apocalyptic plague," captures well the phrase ἡ λοιμώδης νόσος which literally means "the plague-like sickness." Thucydides elsewhere uses λοιμός and νόσος as synonyms, so this phrase seems pleonastic. But the word λοιμώδης, when used by Hesiod and Homer, had connotations of divine intervention so it is possible that Thucydides used it here to link his account verbally to "the old stories." The word I have translated "violation," βλάψασα, which is usually rendered as "harmful," also has religious connotations. Thucydides' word choices in his passage, in general, seem to imply that he wanted to suggest that the plague was like a divine intervention. (See 3:84, translated below, for the same implication of the verb βλάπτω)..   6

Notes   193

6. For a discussion of this use of *tyche*, see Lowell Edmunds, *Chance and Intelligence in Thucydides* (Cambridge: Harvard University Press, 1975), 192ff., with citations.

7. For a very thorough lexical survey of Thucydides' work in comparison to the tradition, see Pierre Huart, *Le vocabulaire de l'analyse psychologique dans l'oeuvre de Thucydide* (Paris: Klincksieck, 1968) and also Huart's *Gnome chez Thucydide et ses contemporains* (Paris: Klincksieck, 1973).

8   Innovation and Political Imagination

1. Cicero remarks upon the obligation to discuss causes of revolutions and means of preventing them in *De Finibus bonorum et malorum*, 5.4.11. See Thucydides's *History*, 3.82ff; Plato, *The Republic*, 543ff; Aristotle, *Politics* 1301lbl9ff and 1307b25ff. For Aristotle's discussion of the dangers of merely reforming or altering the laws of a city-state, see *Politics*, 1268b20ff.

2. Michel de Montaigne's *Essays*, ed. and trans. by Donald Frame (Stanford: Stanford University Press, 1958), p. 797 (3:12).

3. Ibid., p. 497 (3:17).

4. Karl Marx, "The Eighteenth Brumaire of Louis Bonaparte," part 1, in *The Marx-Engels Reader*, ed. R. C. Tucker (New York: Norton, 1978), p. 595.

5. Plato, *Timaeus*, 693–70b.

6. The parts or functions of the psyche are, of course, more elaborately delineated in *De Anima;* I am following here the discussions in the *Ethics* and *Politics*.

7. Aristotle, *Pol.* 7. 13.8–9.

8. Plato, *Rep.* 546cff.

9. Machiavelli, *The Prince*, 25. Machiavelli makes great play with the Latin root of *virtu*, *vir*, which means man or husband.

10. Karl Marx, "A Correspondence of 1843," in *Early Texts*, ed. and trans. by David McLellan (Oxford: Blackwell, 1971), p. 79.

11. Karl Marx, "Critique of Political Economy," introduction in *Early Texts*.

12. The metaphor is discussed in Melvin Rader, *Marx's Interpretation of History* (Oxford: Oxford University Press, 1979), but neither its sources nor the importance of the female principle are part of Rader's analysis. It is certainly possible to treat Marx's metaphor psychobiographically, but that would not serve the purpose of this chapter.

13. For a study of the female symbolism, see Maurice Agulhon, *Marianne into Battle* (Cambridge: Cambridge University Press, 1980). Michelet evoked the historical precedent for Marianne when he spoke of France as having had "two great redemptions, by the Holy Maid of Orleans and by the Revolution" (in *The People*).

14. Karl Marx, "The Civil War in France," in *The Marx-Engels Reader*, p. 641.

15. See J. H. Billington, *Fire in the Minds of Men: Origins of the Revolutionary Faith* (New York: Basic Books, 1980), p. 644, note 17.

16. Ibid., p. 220.

17. Karl Marx, "Correspondence of 1843," p. 81.

18. Karl Marx, "Critique of Hegel's Philosophy of Right," in *Early Texts*, p. 128.

19. Karl Marx, "Critique of the Gotha Program," in *The Marx-Engels Reader*, p. 529.

20. Ibid., p. 538. In the 1848 *Manifesto* of the Communist Party, Marx spoke of the proletariat "organized as a ruling class" to sweep away "by force the old means of production" and then to abolish its own supremacy as a class when the old divisions of labor were removed.

21. Marx called the English workingmen the "first born sons of modern industry" (see "Speech at the Anniversary of the People's Paper," in *The Marx-Engels Reader*, p. 578). In England and the United States, Marx thought he saw possibilities for the revolution surviving without protective violence (see Engel's preface to the 1886 English-language version of *Capital*).

22. Marx's social theory is not embedded in a cosmic theory (though Engels took steps in the direction of a natural philosophy), but it does, of course, have a psychological dimension: this is the theory of needs. Those proletarians with a "radical need" to eliminate all dehumanizing social conditions will bring about a society with a new system of needs. (See Agnes Heller, *The Theory of Need in Marx* [New York: St. Martin's Press, 1976] pp. 98ff.)

23. Karl Marx, "Economic and Philosophical Manuscripts," in *Early Texts*, p. 155.

24. These quotations and the passage below are from Rosa Luxemburg, *The Russian Revolution and Leninism or Marxism?* (Ann Arbor: University of Michigan Press, 1962), pp. 76, 70, 74.

10 Psychoanalysis and Biography

1. R. Binion, *Frau Lou* (Princeton: Princeton University Press, 1968), p. 6.

2. Heinz Kohut, "Beyond the Bounds of the Basic Rule," *Journal of the American Psychoanalytic Association* 8:567–86.

3. That early psychoanalytic biographies were "case studies" designed primarily to extend generalizations about the Oedipus complex from pathological to normal or exceptional individuals is apparent in H. Nunberg and P. Federn, eds., *The Minutes of the Vienna Psychoanalytic Society*, vol. 1., 1906–1908 (New York: International Universities Press, 1962), particularly meetings 32 and 33, pp. 265ff.

4. An extensive annotated bibliography on the methodological literature has been prepared by William Gilmore, "The Methodology of Psychohistory," *Psychohistory Review* 5:4–33.

5. Plutarch, "Timoleon," *Plutarch's Lives* (New York: Modern Library, n.d.), p. 293.

6. D. Mallet, *The Life of Francis Bacon* (London: A. Millar, 1740), p. vii.

7. Sigmund Freud, *The Standard Edition of the Complete Psychological Works of Sigmund Freud*, 24 vols., trans. J. Strachey et al., (London: Hogarth, 1955–1974), 11:130. (Hereafter cited as *Standard Edition* with volume and page number.)

8. *Standard Edition*, 11: 122.

9. *Standard Edition*, 11: 122.

10. *Standard Edition*, 11: 80.

11. *Standard Edition*, 11: 80.

12. *Standard Edition*, 11: 130.

13. *Standard Edition*, 11: 134.

14. *Standard Edition*, 11: 136.

15. Freud, writing in 1919, *The Letters of Sigmund Freud and Lou Andreas-Salome* (New York: Harcourt, Brace, 1972), p. 90.

16. *Standard Edition*. 11: 134.

17. Cited in Max Schur, *Freud: Living and Dying* (New York: International Universities Press, 1972), p. 256.

18. J. Mack, "Psychoanalysis and Historical Biography," *Journal of the American Psychoanalytic Association*. 19: 151.

19. Ibid., p. 157.

20. Virginia Woolf, "Women and Fiction," *Granite and Rainbow* (New York: Harcourt, Brace, 1958), p. 84.

21. Virginia Woolf, *Orlando* (New York: Harcourt, Brace Jovanovich, 1956), p. 188.

22. Ibid., p. 266.

23. Ibid., p. 269.

24. B. Chevigny, "Daughter's Writing," *Feminist Studies*, 9: 89.

25. C. Heilbrun, *Reinventing Womanhood* (New York: W. W. Norton, 1979), p. 71.

26. For instances of female psychoanalysts concerned with female creativity: H. Deutsch on George Sand in *Psychology of Women* (New York: Grune and Stratton, 1944), 1: 297ff; and P. Greenacre, "Woman as Artist," *Psychoanalytic Quarterly*, 9: 208–26.

27. Standard Edition, 27: 223–46, passim.

12   Anna Freud for Feminists

1. Nancy Chodorow, *The Reproduction of Mothering: Psychoanalysis and the Sociology of Gender* (Berkeley: University of California Press, 1978).

2. In Judith Alpert, ed., *Psychoanalysis and Women: Contemporary Reappraisals* (Hillsdale, N.J.: The Analytic Press, 1986); see especially Zenia Fliegel, "Women's Development in Analytic Theory: Six Decades of Controversy."

3. Freud's major statements on female psychology can be found in *The Complete Psychological Works of Sigmund Freud*, 24 vols., trans. James Strachey. (London: Hogarth, 1955–1974): "Three Essays on the Theory of Sexuality" (7: 125–244); "The Taboo on Virginity" (11:192–208); " 'A Child is Being Beaten' " (17:177–204); "The Psychogensis of a Case of Homosexuality in a Woman," (18:145–72); "The Infantile Genital Organization" (19:141–48); "The Dissolution of the Oedipus Complex" (19: 173–82); "Some Psychical Consequences of the Anatomical Distinction between the Sexes" (19:248–60); "Female Sexuality" (21:223–46); "Femininity" (22:112–35); "An Outline of Psychoanalysis" (23: especially 152–56). These pieces will be collected and introduced in an anthology I am currently preparing: *Freud on Women* (New York: Norton, 1989).

4. Harold Blum, ed., *Female Psychology: Contemporary Psychoanalytic Views* (New York: International Universities Press, 1977). Johanna Tabin, *On The Way to the Self* (New York: Columbia University Press, 1985). Other recent works on the topic include (in chronological order): J. Chasseguet-Smirgel, English trans. *Female Sexuality: New Psychoanalytic Views* Juliet Mitchell, *Psychoanalysis and Feminism* (1974); Jean Strouse, ed., *Women and Analysis* (1974); Jean Baker Miller, *Toward a New Psychology of Women* (1976); Jane Gallop, *The Daughter's Seduction: Feminism and Psychoanalysis* (1982); Mendell, *Early Female Development* (1982); Eichenbaum and Orbach, *Understanding Women:*

A Feminist Psychoanalytic Approach (1983); Bernstein and Warner, *Women Treating Women: Case Material From Women Treated by Female Psychoanalysts* (1984).

5. Anna Freud's objection to feminism can be found in *The Writings of Anna Freud*, 8 vols., (New York: International Universities Press, 1966–1980), 8:235–36.

6. For further biographical discussion, see my *Anna Freud: A Biography* (New York: Summit Books, 1988), chapters 3 & 4.

7. Here Anna Freud is citing Sigmund Freud, *Standard Edition* 7:146 (for the setting of this quotation, see note 10 below).

8. The diagnostic profile and the developmental lines are discussed in *Normality and Pathology in Childhood*, which is volume 5 of *The Writings of Anna Freud*.

9. See "Beyond the Infantile Neurosis," in *The Writings of Anna Freud*, 8:75–81.

10. The passages following are pp. 186–88 and 193–94 of *Normality and Pathology in Childhood* (see note 8).

11. Freud clearly distinguished "the perversions" from the "psychoneuroses" (hysteria, obsessional neurosis, phobias, and so on) and insisted that a homosexual, whose object choice was considered "abnormal" by present sociocultural norms could be completely free of psychopathology. In a 1915 note to his 1905 text "Three Essays on the Theory of Sexuality," he wrote:

> Psychoanalytic research is most decidedly opposed to any attempt at separating off homosexuals from the rest of mankind as a group of special character. By studying sexual excitations other than those that are manifestly displayed, it has found that all human beings are capable of making a homosexual object choice and have in fact made one in their unconscious. Indeed, libidinal attachments to persons of the same sex play no less a part as factors in normal mental life, and a greater part as a motive force for mental illness, than do similar attachments to the opposite sex. On the contrary, psychoanalysis considers that a choice of an object independently of its sex—freedom to range freely over male and female object—as it is found in childhood, in primitive states of society and early periods of history, is the original basis from which, as a result of restriction in one direction or another, both the normal and the inverted types develop. Thus from the point of view of psychoanalysis the exclusive sexual interest felt by men for women is also a problem that needs elucidating and is not a self-evident fact based upon an attraction that is ultimately of a chemical nature. A person's final sexual attitude is not decided until after puberty and is the result of a number of factors, not all of which are yet known; some are of a constitutional nature but others are accidental. (7:145)

12. The research on female sexuality from Hampstead is noted in R. Edgcumbe and M. Burgner, "The Phallic Narcissistic Phase: A Differentiation Between Preoedipal and Oedipal Aspects of Phallic Development," *Psychoanalytic Study of the Child* 30 (1975): 161–80; and R. Edgcumbe, "Some comments on the concepts of the negative oedipal phase in girls," *The Psychoanalytic Study of the Child* 31 (1976): 35–61.

13. Edgcumbe and Burgner, "*The Phallic Narcissistic Phase*," p. 180.

Postscript

1. In a sense, Indian Vedantists imagine an *atman* in each person that is as *Brahman* is in the cosmos, while Chinese Taoists imagine *tao* in a person and in the cosmos. But

this way of speaking presumes that an individual is a discrete part of the cosmos, and no Vedantist or Taoist would use such a part/whole distinction. Similarly, neither would compare an individual and a political entity for the additional reason that a polis or city-state in the Greek sense was not part of their formative historical experience. But, on the other hand, the way in which the oneness of self and cosmos—for example, *atman* and *Brahman*—is imagined has its counterpart in sociopolitical vision: for a Vedantist groups are not aggregates, but unities; there are no discrete selves, no isolated individuals, no individuals considered as essentially "other" or oppositional to each other. Culturally distinct philosophical systems have no specific content of macrocosm/microcosm theories in common, but diverse peoples share a tendency either to link their psychological and sociopolitical understandings either reflectively or unreflectively. Metaphorical fit between psychological and sociopolitical visions does seem to be universal (at least before the kind of intellectual specialization that set "psychology" and "political science" in separate compartments or departments).

Astute discussions of macrocosm/microcosm theories in Eastern traditions can be found throughout Hajime Nakamura's remarkable work *Ways of Thinking of Eastern Peoples: India, China, Tibet, Japan*, rev. ed. (Honolulu: East-West Center, 1964). For a superficial but bibliographically very helpful tour of Western theories, see George Perrigo Conger, *Theories of Macrocosms and Microcosms in the History of Philosophy*, repr. of 1922 original (New York: Russell and Russell, 1967).

2.   The differences between the topographical and structural theories are clearly reflected in the two sociocultural theories into which they were projected: see *Totem and Taboo* (1912) and *Civilization and Its Discontents* (1931).

3.   See Anna Freud, *The Ego and the Mechanisms of Defense* (1936) in *The Writings of Anna Freud* (New York: International Universities Press, 1966), vol. 2.

Acknowledgments

My thanks to the following institutions for inviting my lectures and journals for permission to reprint my essays:

"Hannah Arendt's Storytelling" first appeared in *Social Research,* Spring, 1977.

"From the Pariah's Point of View" was delivered at Wesleyan University's Center for the Humanities in 1977 and published in Melvyn Hill, ed., *Hannah Arendt: The Recovery of the Public World* (St. Martins, 1979).

"Reading Hannah Arendt's *The Life of the Mind*" was published in a slightly longer version in *Political Theory,* May, 1982.

"King Solomon was very wise—So what's his story?" was delivered at Wesleyan University's Center for the Humanities in 1981; the translations in it of Brecht's songs are adapted from Eric Bentley's versions. I dedicate it to the memory of Louis O. Mink, who was my good uncle at Wesleyan.

"Cosmopolitan History" was published in the Jaspers centenary volume of the *Revue Internationale de Philosophie,* 1983.

"What are we doing when we think?" was delivered as the George Rudé Inaugural Lecture in Montreal, 1982, and published in *Maieutics,* 1984.

"What Thucydides Saw," written in 1984, appeared in *History and Theory,* 1986.

"Innovation and Political Imagination" was delivered at the 1980 Little Three Conference (Amherst College) and published in *The Berkshire Review,* 1980.

"The Writing of Biography" was delivered at the Graduate Faculty of the New School for Social Research in 1982 and published in the *Partisan Review,* 1983.

"Psychoanalysis and Biography" was presented to the Kanzer Seminar in Psychiatry and the Humanities at Yale in 1984, and published in *The Psychoanalytic Study of the Child,* 1985.

"The Education of Women as Philosophers" celebrated the Sesque-centennial of Mt. Holyoke College in October, 1985, and was published in *Signs: Journal of Women in Culture and Society,* 1987.

"Anna Freud for Feminists" is based on a talk given to the Princeton University Women's Studies program in December, 1987.

Index of Names